PHOENIX HOLT

ISBN-13:
978-1500877408

PHOENIX HOLT

Gabriella Lepore

Acknowledgements

Special thanks to everyone who joined me online, following and voting on your favourite Phoenix Holt cover, and even making cover art of your own! I'm overwhelmed and humbled by your incredible support. You're amazing, and I hope you enjoy the book!

Thanks, as always, to my family—my parents, for helping in immeasurable ways; Natalie, for a lifetime of adventures; Rhodri, for always keeping bookmarks at his desk!
And to my friends and extended family, thank you for all your support. Kim, Norman, Lorna (you don't, infinity), Shirley Pearly, Carters, Lepores, Nelsons, Xerri, Rachel, Saunders, Chadwicks, Nikki, Janet, Ken, Gareth & Celia.

Thanks to my editor and friend, Elizabeth, who can spot plot holes and spelling mistakes in her sleep!

And last, but definitely not least, huge thanks to my super friend, Ben Alderson, without whose support and unwavering optimism this book would live inside my laptop, doing nothing, and generally being bored. Thanks for saving another book, Be!

For aunties everywhere—the unsung heroes!
And I'm not just saying that because I'm one!

~ Helen, Maureen, Heather, and Elsie ~

Thank you for being aunties.

Chapter One

Pandora's Box

I was the first to notice the fortune teller. Actually, she'd walked past us a few times, trolling the train for a place to sit. Somehow I had a feeling that she would eventually settle upon our cabin.

And I was right.

The cabin door rattled open and the woman poked her head in.

"May I sit here?" she asked in a thick Russian accent.

I glanced at the long empty seat opposite me. I was fairly sure that Sam and Todd wouldn't be too keen on our new companion, but seeing as though they were both snoring quietly in their top-bunk rollout beds, I considered their opinions to be void.

What's the harm? I thought to myself.

"Yes," I said. "Go ahead."

The woman's gold bangles clanged together as she made herself comfortable on the bench opposite me, below where Todd slumbered undisturbed. She placed her crochet bag at her side and folded her hands on the pull-out table that separated us. Shrouded behind a red silk headdress, two ice-blue eyes peered out at me.

I gave her a weak 'hello' smile, then quickly looked away again.

Should I speak to her? I wondered. I didn't want to.

"Your eyes," she said to me, in a husky voice. "They're the colour of old brass."

I blushed. "Oh. Right. Okay." What else was there to say? A stranger in silk robes was comparing my eyes to a rusty old trombone. Only on the train, eh?

"What are you?" she asked, picking me apart with her prying gaze.

Huh?

"Um... I'm a girl," I replied.

Her thin lips crooked upwards into a smile. "I see that. But, what *are* you?"

Okay, second try: "I'm fifteen," I told her. "My name is Sophie Ballester." I hoped that would suffice. I was beginning to regret that detrimental 'hello' smile.

"Ah..." she mulled it over. "You're a Ballester. I am

3

familiar with the name." She scrutinised me for a moment. "You have the face of a Ballester. I can see it now."

I smiled to myself. The woman was clearly nuts.

"Yes," she carried on, mostly to herself. "The brown hair... the yellow eyes..."

I combed my fingers through my hair, self-consciously.

"You're heading to Phoenix Holt?" she pressed.

"Um, yes." I nodded. Okay, I could admit that was a little spooky. How could she have known that? Phoenix Holt wasn't exactly a hot-spot destination. It was just hills and woodland, or so I'd been told. Though perhaps she knew the Ballester name from around those parts. After all, my grandfather's family had grown up in Phoenix Holt. And his sister—my great aunt—still lived there. My stomach knotted at the realisation that I too would be living there.

I gazed out the window. It was dark beyond the pane, and the shadows that whizzed by outside were eclipsed by my own reflection staring back at me. Duplicated in the small window, I looked hollow and drawn. My hair was a mess of curls, and the poor cabin lighting enhanced the sunken shadows beneath my eyes—my 'brass eyes,' as my new acquaintance had oh-so-charmingly pointed out.

4

I looked away from myself. It only reminded me that I hadn't seen a mirror for a few days, which in turn reminded me of why that was the case. The truth was, mirrors hadn't exactly been top priority lately.

I couldn't give a figure on how long 'lately' had been. It had all happened in such a blur that time felt obsolete. One day everything was normal. I lived in the same house where I'd always lived, in Port Dalton, with my grandfather, Wilber, and my brothers, Sam and Todd. My routine was fixed: I woke up, I went to school, I came home, I went to bed. And I liked that. It may have sounded boring to some people, but it was my life and I liked it.

Then one morning, everything changed. I woke up, sure, that stayed the same. Only, on this particular morning, Wilber didn't wake up. And that was that. He was gone.

I grieved for a long time, not even considering that, on top of everything else, I'd have to grieve for my home, also. Perhaps it was naïve of me, but for a while, I truly believed we'd stay in that house. Sam had vowed, there and then, that he would take care of us and keep our little family together. Good old Sam. I had no doubt that he would have stepped up to the plate, but at seventeen years old, social services denied him outright. The problem was, we were orphans who had no known relatives and very few family friends—none of who wanted to take in a fifteen-year-old girl and twin seventeen-year-old boys. So, just as we were beginning to resign ourselves to the devastating idea of being separated, we got the call.

Great Aunt Ness.

Ness was Wilber's sister. His only living relative. The three of us had never met her, mostly because Wilber had never spoken of her, and he'd moved out of Phoenix Holt long before any of us were born. Needless to say, I was surprised to hear her offer. It was Sam who took the call, and he told us that she sounded nice. Although I couldn't help but wonder: if she was so *nice*, then why did my grandfather erase her from his life as though she didn't exist? He wasn't the sort of person to hold a grudge, or act unreasonably, so what could have possibly happened to have caused such a rift between them?

I had horrible visions of a dragon lady trapping us like Cinderellas in the nowhere-land of Phoenix Holt.

"You are very troubled," the sultry voice of the fortune teller broke through my reverie.

I summoned a polite smile.

She extended her hand to me. Her bracelets jangled together in a tuneful sort of way.

Was I meant to take her hand? I didn't. Instead, I

6

went for the *stay still and maybe I'll disappear* tactic.

"Give," she instructed, extending her fingers towards me.

So much for disappearing. Reluctantly, I placed my hand on the pull-out table. The cold surface sent a shiver over my bones.

With a delicate touch, the fortune teller lifted my hand and examined my palm. "There are…" she paused, then started again. "There are many paths for a Ballester to choose from. Many doors to be opened. It is on its way to you. The world is waiting for you to arrive."

Well, Phoenix Holt *is waiting for me to arrive*, I corrected silently.

"The cards," she said abruptly, her accent almost impossible to decipher when she spoke with such excitement. "Where are my cards…" She dropped my hand onto the table and began rummaging through her crochet bag.

"Cards?" I enquired meekly.

"Ah!" she exclaimed, producing a small, hand-carved oak box from her seemingly bottomless bag. She set the box down on the table and flipped the lid open. Wrapped in purple silk was an oblong deck of cards, the top card's surface illustrated by a snake's eye.

I withdrew at the sight.

The fortune teller tossed the silk aside and began shuffling the cards.

I stared down at the now-empty box on the table. It juddered slightly with the uneven movement of the train.

"Three cards," she told me, casting her gaze upon me with unnerving intensity.

"Three cards?" I repeated.

"Past, present, and future."

"I don't know about this. I'm not sure I—"

My protests were cut short by her thrusting the deck into my hands. "Shuffle," she ordered.

I obliged. The smooth cards were dog-eared and bent from a lifetime of use. I let the silken deck slip in and out of my fingers as I shuffled.

"How long do I have to do this for?" I asked.

"You'll know."

"Oh." I paused. "So… does now seem like a good time to stop?"

"Does it?" she shot back.

"Um… does it?"

"Does it?" she returned.

"I think… yes?" I ventured.

"When you are ready," she gestured to the table, "lay down three cards."

I wouldn't exactly say that I was *ready*, but I set out

three cards face down on the table-top.

The fortune teller tapped the first card before turning it over. When I caught sight of the illustration, my heart skipped a beat. It was a black tombstone with a flock of ravens hovering above it.

"Death," she said.

I gulped. Just the card everyone was dying to see. No pun intended.

She noticed my stricken expression and carried on. "Death is symbolic of change. There has been great change in your life. Yes?"

"Yes," I confirmed.

"Of course there has been. The truth never lies." She began muttering to herself in an unfamiliar language. "Now for your present..." She flipped the centre card.

The image was more bearable this time: a woman with flowing blonde hair, releasing a goldfinch into the sky.

"What does it mean?" I asked.

"Destiny," she told me. "Your destiny shall be fulfilled. But not only yours—the destiny of the bird also. Your actions will free another."

I frowned. "So, I have to set a bird free?"

"No, no, no." She wagged her finger at me. "The bird is symbolic." She moved on swiftly, turning over the final card. "Future."

This card was my favourite, though perhaps the strangest of all. The image showed a man drinking from a silver chalice. Behind him stood a beautiful angel, lit by a shaft of bright light.

"Sacrifice," the fortune teller said. "In the end, you will sacrifice yourself to save the one you love."

I stiffened. "Sacrifice myself?" I echoed.

"Yes."

"Do I have to?"

"Yes," she said sharply.

I wrinkled my nose. "I'd rather not."

"No. You must sacrifice," she reproached me. "Sacrifice is good."

The volume of her brisk rebuke evidently woke my sleeping brothers. Or one of them, at least.

"What the…?" Sam garbled with a groggy slur. "Who are *you*?" he demanded. The bunk above me creaked as he rolled over, hanging over the edge to glare at the intruder.

"My name is Pandora," the fortune teller said evenly.

I craned my neck to look up at Sam. His face was contorted in reaction to the sudden influx of artificial light. A few strands of copper-brown hair fell tousled above his eyes—his *brass*-coloured eyes. I watched as he lowered his gaze to the oak box on the table.

"What's in the box, Pandora?" he asked.

"The truth," she replied.

He snorted.

"Maybe you are curious as to what the future holds for you?" she cajoled.

Sam laughed loudly, waking up Todd in the bunk opposite. "Nah," he said. "You can keep all that witchy, mumbo-jumbo junk. I think I'll take my chances with the future."

Todd peered over the edge of his bunk, then rolled back without a word. I hadn't expected Todd to comment. Despite his identical appearance to Sam, Todd wasn't quite as outspoken as his counterpart—or as forthright, for that matter. Todd tended to take a back seat, whereas Sam chose to drive.

"As you wish," said Pandora.

While Sam fidgeted restlessly in his bunk, I couldn't help but think about the cards. I thought of the eternal riddle that was *the future*, and wondered if the future would perhaps turn out to be something that I'd live to regret.

#

The Phoenix Holt train station was just as desolate and forsaken as I'd imagined it to be. There was nothing: no coffee shop, no kiosk, no people. Just one lone platform, sheltered by a worn tin roof and a few weathered trees.

Sam dumped his rucksack on the ground. "This sucks," he groused. "There's not even a road."

I leaned against a tall, black lamppost, gazing out at the interlacing train tracks. It was daylight now, though only just. We'd travelled through the night and I was tired. Tired and therefore rapidly losing the morsel of gusto that'd kept me going up until then.

Todd placed his duffel bag on the pavement. "Maybe there's a bus station," he said quietly.

Sam rolled his eyes. "What, is the bus going to come ploughing down the footpath?" he scoffed. "Don't be dumb, Todd. There's *no road*."

"Then we'll walk," I suggested. "Ness gave you directions, didn't she?" I looked at Sam, vaguely recalling him jotting down notes with the house phone propped to his ear.

Sam mumbled something, then dug through his jeans pockets. He pulled out a small scrap of notebook paper, unfolded it, and plonked himself onto Todd's rucksack to flatten out the creases.

"Sam," Todd bemoaned. "Don't sit on my bag!" He shoved Sam's shoulder with both hands.

"Shh," Sam brushed him off. "I'm trying to concentrate." He stared intently at the notebook paper.

I peered over his shoulder. There was a series of

words scribbled chaotically across the page. Somewhat hesitantly, I took a shot at reading Sam's handwriting. "Head down from the tom stallion—"

"*Train station*," he corrected me brusquely.

"Oh, sorry. Head down from the *train station* towards the lowland. Follow the pole—"

"Path," Sam snapped. "Follow the *path*."

I went on, "Follow the *path* through the woods until we reach the college."

"Not college," Sam huffed in irritation. "*Cottage*. Cottage."

"Sorry, the *cottage*."

Sam crumpled the paper into a ball and stuffed it back into his pocket. "We need to head into the woods."

Todd hovered around the lamppost, his eyes fixed on his bag as it bowed and malformed beneath Sam's weight.

I looked back and forth between them. It was uncanny seeing them together. They were identical down to the very last detail. Everything from the matching strands of reddish-brown hair that swept across their brows, to the straight noses, to the mouths that twitched up at the corner when they smiled. Yes, they were mirror images. But even so, I still struggled to understand why people had such trouble distinguishing between them. I could admit, their features were identical, but their mannerisms were poles apart. Sam was reckless, like a whirlwind of words and movement. Todd, on the other hand, was timid and cautious. My grandfather used to call Sam a loose cannon, and he'd once let slip that he thought Sam was the most difficult of all three of us. I don't think Sam liked that. And honestly, I think it made him worse.

"I've got fragile things in that bag," Todd moaned. "You're going to break them."

Sam let out a strangled groan. "Give it a rest, Todd. I'm sitting on your bag. Get over it."

"My telescope's in there," Todd carped on. "If it's damaged, you're buying me a new one."

Sam laughed blithely. "Yeah, right!" He bounced up and down on the bag for good measure.

Todd cringed. "Wait 'til I tell Wilber about—" His words stopped mid-flow. Of course, we wouldn't be telling Wilber about anything anymore.

That silenced us all.

Sam stood up sharply. "Fine. Just take your stupid bag," he said. He slung his own rucksack over his shoulder and set off into the thick of trees.

Todd rescued his rucksack and clutched it to his chest protectively as he marched after Sam.

I lingered behind, trailing them like a ghost, lost in my own thoughts.

14

We walked on like that for almost an hour. We stuck to formation as we moved downhill through the woodland, following what we hoped was the path. Actually, as far as paths go, this one was rather ambiguous. It wasn't so much of a *path* as a faint hint of trampled-down undergrowth, weaving through the sycamores as it crept down the slope.

I slid out of my jacket and tied it around my waist. It was a mild day for September—not hot, but not cold either. The leaves on the trees were bronzed with the first traces of autumn, and some lay scattered over the ground like crisp red moats circling the broad tree trunks.

A light breeze wound through my hair and brushed against my bare arms. That same breeze lifted a leaf from the ground and sent it tumbling along the path until it was swept beneath Sam's feet.

Sam glanced down, and then kicked the leaf aside. When he looked up again, his focus travelled away from the path.

"Hey," he said, signalling for us to stop, "look at that."

Todd and I followed his gaze. One of the trees had been stripped of its branches and bark, and carved into the shape of a bird. The detail of its long tail feathers was so precise that for a split second I thought it was real. And even after my double take, something about the bird's hollow eyes seemed vividly alive, staring me down with watchful intrigue.

"There's the phoenix of the holt," Sam remarked. He shifted the position of his rucksack before continuing along the path.

"I wonder who carved it," I mused, trotting to keep up with my brothers. "I mean, we're in the middle of nowhere!"

Sam gave me a fleeting smirk. "Who said anything about carving? It's real. The old witch of the forest turned it into a tree as punishment for trying to escape."

Todd chuckled. "And at night it comes to life and—"

"—pecks your face off while you're sleeping!" Sam finished for him.

They both laughed at the idea.

I glanced back at the sculpted phoenix. Its haunted eyes met mine. It didn't unnerve me, though. Somehow, it felt familiar.

I was about to return my attention to the path when something else caught my eye. A person. A boy—just standing amongst the trees, watching us.

My breath caught in my throat.

"Over there!" cried Todd. His voice made me jump out of my skin. I spun around to face him, expecting him to be looking into the trees as I had been, but he was pointing in the opposite direction, through the sycamores to where the ground sloped downwards.

I quickly looked back towards the trees. This time, only the concave eyes of the carved bird looked back at me.

"Wait!" I called to my brothers, my voice going up an octave. "Did either of you see that? There was someone over there!"

Sam and Todd stopped walking and followed my line of vision, then mustered vague laughs.

"I'm serious!" I exclaimed. "There was someone there!"

"Okay, Sophie," said Sam, rolling his eyes. "We believe you." He nodded towards the sloping hill, returning to Todd's point of interest. "It looks like there's a house down there. I can see a chimney."

My lips parted in disbelief as I scanned the woodland in bewilderment. There was no one there. Had there ever been? Yes, I'd definitely seen someone... hadn't I? It was only my first day in Phoenix Holt, surely I wasn't losing my mind already? God, I hoped not.

Ahead of me, Sam jogged down the wooded hill. "Come on," he called over his shoulder. "I think this is it."

All of a sudden, my legs stopped working. I was drowning in nervous energy. Part of me wanted to rush ahead and see my new 'home,' but the other part of me was absolutely terrified by the idea. I didn't want a new home. I didn't want a Great Aunt Ness. And I definitely didn't want to be turned into a tree if I ever tried to make a break for it.

"Sophie," Sam beckoned me. "Come on."

"What's it like?" I asked.

He shrugged. "I don't know. It's a cottage. Come on."

I didn't move. I was aware that I was acting a little farcically, but it was almost as though once I saw it—whatever *it* was—I couldn't *un*see it. I was afraid of giving it the power of being real.

Sam and Todd exchanged a look.

"Sophie," Sam said in an imploring voice. He warily made his way back uphill, as though he feared that if he moved too quickly I'd get startled and bolt. "It's going to be fine," he assured me, lingering at arms length, probably ready to pry me from my spot at any moment.

But I didn't need to be pried. I was going to do this, head held high. So, with a little bit of backbone and a whole lot of denial, I walked on, ready—yes, *ready*—to meet my future.

Chapter Two
Cottage Pie

My first glimpse of our new home turned out to be
surprisingly okay. It was a small, grey stone cottage,
with fleets of ivy creeping their way towards a thatched
roof. Fronting the building was a beautiful garden, rich
with wildflowers and bounded by a quaint picket fence.

As we trudged down the wooded slope, my view of
the cottage became clearer. It was sweet—the sort of
place where I could imagine a garden tea party, or
homemade pies cooling on the window ledge. I inhaled
the fragrant scent of lavender, combined with a faint
trace of chimney smoke. It was nice, in a chocolate-box
kind of way.

Although, I did get the impression that my brothers
weren't quite as impressed as I was. It suddenly dawned
on me just how masculine our old house had been. Don't
get me wrong—I'd loved Port Dalton, but our house

hadn't been the sort of place where you'd expect to find flowers. Well, we'd had one miniature cactus plant, but that was less a decoration and more a missile for Sam and Todd to launch at one another.

I took note of a pink watering can propped up against the picket fence. For the first time in my life, I was in a female domain. Unfortunately for my brothers, so were they.

We reached the fence and Sam hopped straight over, landing boorishly in a flower bed— it seemed that the mutiny had started already. Todd and I strolled through the front gate and onto the neat garden path. A river of tawny pebbles crunched beneath our feet as we honed in on the arched, oak door.

Sam bounded over to join us, colliding into a hanging basket that was obstructing his route. It swayed back and forth, then clunked heavily against his head.

I grasped hold of the swinging basket and steadied it.

"I don't like this," Sam fretted, rubbing at his scalp. "She's booby-trapped the whole place."

"Do you think she's home?" I felt my heart rate quicken. "It seems quiet."

Sam peeked through the spy hole. "Dunno. Shall we let ourselves in?"

"No!" I exclaimed in a hushed voice. "We can't just let ourselves into somebody else's house."

"She invited us," Sam pointed out.

I frowned. "We should knock."

"Okay," he agreed. "Go on, then."

"Not me. You do it."

"I'm not doing it. You do it."

"No," I shrank back. "I don't want to."

We turned to Todd, who loitered on the path with his hands clasped together.

"Todd, knock on the door," Sam ordered.

"Why me?" he protested.

"Because it has to be you," Sam told him.

Despite the senseless logic, Todd surrendered. He stepped forward gingerly, and gave one barely audible tap on the oak door.

No sooner had his knuckles left the door than it flung open.

"Welcome!" The woman in the doorway greeted us with a jubilant smile. "Welcome, welcome, welcome," she cooed, holding out her hand for us to shake.

We all stared at it.

"I'm Ness," she introduced herself. She was shorter than all of us—probably no taller than five feet, with a rounded frame and a jolly grin. She wore a canary-yellow dress, and its hem skimmed her fuzzy slippers and slouched stockings. Her hair was like a bonnet of curls which, for the most part, were a faded brown hue.

I guessed her to be in her early seventies, though she hustled us indoors with the dynamism of a much younger woman.

"Welcome," she gushed again.

Like stunned rabbits, we stood in the hallway. Now, any good escapee would tell you to *know your exits*. In this instance, I only had one, and it was behind me. The front door—the only way in and the only way out. To my left was an arched doorway leading into a cosy little den. To my right was a pine-clad country kitchen. And directly in front of me was a narrow wooden staircase.

"Wonderful to meet you," Ness sang, kissing our cheeks.

Sam recoiled in horror.

"Thank you for letting us stay—" I began.

"No, don't thank me," she interrupted, speaking in solemn earnest. "You belong here."

"Oh. Okay, then," I responded with the *smile and nod* technique.

Sam wiped his contaminated cheek. "Good to meet you."

"Oh, you, too. You, too! Now, let me see…" Ness debated, thoughtfully. "Which is Sam, and which is Todd?"

"I'm Todd," said Sam.

I glared at him.

His mouth twitched upwards at the corner.

Ness turned to Todd. "Then you must be Sam."

"No. I'm Todd," he corrected her.

She blinked at them through ochre owl-like eyes.

Sam grinned. "I'm Sophie."

"No, *I'm* Sophie," I said.

Ness took it in her stride. She mimed a good-natured fist shake at Sam.

"Well, it's lovely to meet you all," she said. "Whoever you are!"

Sam flashed her a charming smile, like butter wouldn't melt in his mouth. "I'm Sam," he admitted.

Ness's eyes flickered between the two boys. "My, oh my. There's no telling you two apart, is there?" She stared at Todd for a long, quiet moment. "Ah, yes. I understand. I can tell that you'll be the one to watch." She laughed genially, despite her odd forecast.

Todd shifted in discomfort.

She's got that wrong, I thought. Was her comment meant in jest? It hadn't seemed to be. But it was Sam who had switched the identities. Surely Sam was the one to watch, wasn't he?

"And you," Ness was addressing me now, "you have Wilber's curly hair." She tugged gently on one of my loose tendrils, then lightly pinched my cheek. "And you all have his eyes."

24

For a moment, her expression grew wistful. I imagine ours did as well.

"Anyway," Ness moved on swiftly, "who's for a cup of tea?" She didn't wait for a response. Instead, she herded us through the archway into the den. "And how about some breakfast? I'll bet you're famished."

I should have been hungry. After all, I hadn't eaten anything since boarding the train the previous day. But my stomach felt too jam-packed with nerves to hanker after food.

In any case, Ness bustled off to the kitchen, leaving us alone in the den.

Once she was gone, I let out a breath. I suddenly realised that my polite smile had been fixed in place from the moment we'd walked through the door. And since its genesis, it had become less of a smile and more a deranged baring of my teeth.

I looked around the room, wondering how long it would take to truly adjust to it being *home*. The den was compact, with a burgundy rug and a red and purple patchwork sofa. Two rocking chairs stood at either side of an enormous log-burning fireplace.

Our little trio made a beeline for the sofa. It was smaller than it had looked, however, so we had to relinquish the luxury of breathing.

Compressed between Sam and the arm of the sofa, I

inspected my surroundings. The walls were traditional grey stone, and the ceiling was oak beamed. A flood of warm orange sunlight crept through the window and settled on the rug. I noticed some framed photographs glinting on the windowsill and made a mental note to take a closer look at them later. Finally, my gaze fell upon the fireplace, a feature that I found to be strangely fascinating. It was like nothing I'd ever seen before. For one thing, it was huge and marvellously authentic in its brickwork. But more interestingly, on the chimney wall, several inches above the dormant firewood, was an elaborate sketch of a bird—one that was similar to the bird we'd seen sculpted in the woodland. It was like a hieroglyphic, telling a story that I was desperate to read.

The more I studied it, the more captivated I became by it. The bird was striking; it was spectacular in every way. Its bowed wings spanned the width of the chimney, and its penetrative eyes bore into me, paralysing me with their enigmatic stare. I envisioned the logs ablaze, their amber flames leaping higher as they danced around the bird, setting its eyes aglow with sizzling red embers.

I was so engrossed in the fantasy that I scarcely noticed when Ness reappeared.

"It's a lovely fireplace, isn't it?" She set down a tray of tea and buttered toast.

I nodded in agreement. "Is the bird a phoenix?"

"Oh, yes, it is."

"Kind of a theme around here," Sam noted. "What is it, the town mascot or something?" He pounced upon the plate of toast and devoured an entire slice in practically one mouthful, showering crumbs over the rug.

"Yes, I suppose you could say that," Ness chuckled. She took a seat in one of the rocking chairs. "More like the town protector, though. This *is* Phoenix Holt, after all. Your grandfather did tell you the stories, didn't he?"

I furrowed my brow. "No. What stories?"

Ness's snowy eyebrows shot up. "He didn't tell you about Phoenix Holt?"

I shook my head.

Ness deflated. "Oh," she murmured despondently. "Well, I can tell you all about it." She brightened a little. "I'm sure you've heard of the phoenix before? The mythical bird that was rumoured to consume itself in fire, only to rise from the ashes, renewed? Heavens," she said, dreamily, "it's a magnificent creature, unsurpassed in its splendour."

I watched her speak, her ochre eyes glistening with enthusiasm.

"Legend has it," she relayed, "that a phoenix once made its home here, in this very holt. It watched over the land and protected the people who lived here. Then, when the inevitable time came for it to depart from this world, the glorious bird burst into flames, never to be seen again. However, as the story goes, it did leave behind one reminder: a trail of silver ashes running like a stream through the woodland. The ashes sunk into the earth and sprouted a rare flower that only exists here in the holt."

"Is that true?" I asked. "About the flower, I mean?"

"Absolutely. You'll come across it soon, I'm sure. You can't miss it, really. It has bright red petals that are shaped like feathers. We call it *phoenix tail*."

Sam yawned. "Birds and flowers," he muttered under his breath. Then, a little louder, he said, "So, what else is there to do around here? Or is flower spotting as good as it gets?"

I cringed at his insolence, but Ness didn't seem bothered. She chortled and said, "I'm sure we can find lots of fun things for you to do. Although, I must say, flower spotting is *my* favourite activity. But I suppose it would have to be; I am an apothecary, after all. I use the flowers that I gather from the holt to aid me with my herbal remedies."

Sam narrowed his eyes. "You're an apothecary? On the phone you said you were a head teacher."

"Oh, I am. Head teacher during the week, apothecary

on the weekends. I lead a double life," she chuckled merrily. "I'm just like that Superman fellow."

"Clark Kent, more like," Sam teased.

Ness looked confused. "Who's Clark Kent?"

Sam let out a weary sigh. "Never mind."

I steered the conversation back on track. "Which school do you work at?"

"Averett Academy," she told us. "It's a small boarding school a mile or so away. It's the school you'll be attending."

"Boarding school?" Todd echoed. "So we'll be *living* there?"

"No, no. But there are no other schools around here. Don't worry, the Academy's not exclusive to live-in students." She smiled warmly at us.

"When do we start?" I asked, hardly thrilled by the imminent doom.

"Well, let's see. Today is Monday... How about you start tomorrow? I'm sure you'd like to get a routine going right away."

Oh, hooray, I thought. Even for a self-confessed advocate of routine, this spelled dismal.

"I hate to abandon you on your first day here," Ness went on, "but I'm afraid I'll still have to go in to the Academy today. Will you be okay by yourselves?"

We nodded.

"Wonderful!" She clapped her hands together. "I should be home by around four o'clock. Get yourselves settled in. There's not much space here, but I've arranged two bedrooms upstairs. Are you boys happy to share?"

"As long as I get the best bed," Sam joked. He swiped a piece of toast from Todd's hand and stuffed it into his own mouth.

Todd blushed.

"Plenty more bread in the pantry," Ness assured us. "Is there anything else you'd like to ask me before I leave?"

Todd cleared his throat nervously. "I'd like to ask something," he said, his tenor soft as it always was when he spoke to strangers.

"By all means." Ness waited patiently as he fumbled to find his voice.

"Why have you never contacted us before?" he blurted out at last.

I sat up a little straighter. Good question.

Ness sighed. "Wilber left Phoenix Holt nearly forty years ago," she explained. "After that, I'm afraid we lost touch. He put this life behind him and moved on with his new life in Port Dalton with your dear grandmother—rest her soul—and little Larry."

My breath caught.

30

Beside me, Sam choked on a mouthful of toast. "Larry? You mean, our dad?"

Ness gave us a sympathetic smile. "Of course. Your dad. I was so sorry to hear of your loss. I understand that you were all very young."

Sorry for our loss. It was a phrase I'd heard far too often. It seemed the standard protocol for whenever our parents were mentioned. Which, incidentally, was not often. Sam and Todd had been three years old at the time, with me barely in my first year. After it happened, we went to live with Wilber, who had already lost his wife and seemed to find the topic of his son far too painful to discuss.

"Did you know Larry?" Sam pressed. "What was he like?"

"I only met him as a baby," Ness told us regretfully. "When Wilber moved to Port Dalton, we lost contact. Wilber didn't want his wife and child to be a part of this world. Sad, but that's how life goes sometimes. Anyway," she rose to her feet, "I'm sorry I can't give you more information."

I wanted to push the subject further, but she was ready to take her leave.

"I'll be on my way now," she said. "If you need me, the school's telephone number is on the fridge."

Her abrupt exit didn't allow for any more questions.

But I couldn't help wondering about one more thing: What *world* did Wilber so desperately not want his family to be a part of?

#

 By midday we were officially bored. We'd already explored every facet of the cottage—a feat that had taken us no more than ninety seconds to complete. There were the two rooms downstairs—the den and the kitchen—both of which we'd already seen. Logically our next point of search was the unknown territory upstairs.

We quickly discovered that the narrow wooden staircase led to pretty much the same layout as the ground floor: a tunnel-like corridor with a few pokey rooms at either end. On the left side, we stumbled upon what was clearly Ness's bedroom, decorated in light, floral patterns. Next door to that was a bathroom, painted peach and cluttered with house plants.

On the right side we found Sam and Todd's bedroom. The blue and black striped wallpaper was peeling in the corners, and was faded where the window's sunlight had bleached it. In the centre of the room were two fold-out beds, a metal clothes rack, and not much else.

My bedroom proved to be slightly more enigmatic,

insofar as we couldn't find the darn thing. In fact, the hunt alone occupied sixty of those ninety seconds of search time. Perhaps the reason why the room was so hard to find was because the door wasn't a conventional door; it was a curtain. A weighty, red velvet curtain that, until pulled back, had appeared to be concealing just another window. To our collective shock, we discovered that the curtain actually veiled a small, circular area—a space that seemed more like a structural accident than a legitimate bedroom.

Of course, my first thought was, *Why me?* But as I dumped my rucksack on the floor and gazed around at the makeshift furniture—mostly upturned boxes with sheets draped over them—I began to feel almost moved. There were tea lights and fresh white roses lined up along the window ledge, pink chiffon drapes tied open with purple ribbon, and a soft pink throw blanketing the tiny bed.

Ness had built me a girl's room.

I'd never had a girl's room before.

We set to work unpacking our bags. Again, it was a task that didn't take much longer than a couple of minutes. It baffled me to think that all my worldly belongings could fit into one rucksack—although travelling light had proven to be to my advantage, considering the size of my new bedroom.

Once my clothes had been safely tucked into boxes, I joined my brothers in the den. It was around eleven o'clock when we made the harrowing discovery that Ness didn't own a television. It was around ten past eleven when we began to pine for television, and at around eleven-fifteen we decided to substitute television for sight seeing.

By eleven-twenty, the torrential rain began.

Betrayed by the weather, we were forced to abort our plan and make the best of being cottage inmates.

Todd and I found a tattered backgammon board. Since neither of us knew the rules to backgammon, we settled for a poorly structured game of monopoly on a backgammon board. We sat in the den, pretending to have fun, while the wild raindrops hammered against the roof and echoed inside the chimney.

Sam paced in and out of the room, desperately seeking entertainment. Preferably entertainment that didn't involve sitting still.

He stormed into the den. "Argh!" he bellowed. "I can't take this anymore! I'm going to... Argh!"

"Sit down," I suggested. "Join our game."

"I'm not playing board games," he hissed, outraged by the idea.

I scowled at him. "Go away, then."

I felt mildly guilty when he actually did go away.

However, moments later, he called to us from the hallway.

"I've got a better game," he declared.

Todd and I looked up from backgammonopoly.

Sam stood in the passage between the den and the kitchen, holding a broom in one hand and an orange in the other.

"Cottage Cricket," he announced.

The name alone set off major alarm bells in my head.

Sam tossed the orange to Todd. "You bowl," he instructed. Then, looking at me, he said, "You field." From where he stood, there was a straight run to the den.

"You're going to bat?" With a dubious expression, I eyed the broom in his hand. "*That*'s your bat?"

He shrugged. "It'll do. It's better than a mop."

"And the orange is the ball?" I guessed. "Won't it explode when you hit it?"

Sam's eyebrows knotted together in irritation. "No. Of course not."

All of my senses told me to stop the game, but instead I said, "If it lands in the fireplace, you're out."

So we took our positions: Sam lined up to bat, Todd clutching the orange, and me not really doing anything.

The game began.

Todd pitched the orange to Sam. Sam swung the

35

broom.

I heard the thump, followed by a blur of colour whizzing past my eyes like a blazing bullet. The orange hit the stone wall of the den and ruptured open. Pulp and peel splattered over the wall.

We all gathered around the remnants and stared at the rug as segments of fleshy orange seeped into its multi-coloured fibres.

Sam rubbed his jaw. "Huh."

"Ew." I crinkled my nose.

Todd wiped a splash of rogue orange juice from his cheek. "Who'd have thought that that would happen," he mused.

I resisted the urge to remind him that *I* had thought it.

"I've got an idea," said Sam. "Let's use a sponge! I bet she keeps one in the bathroom."

Wow, I noted silently. *Sam suggesting we clean?*

"Good thinking," I said encouragingly. "And I'm sure she's got some stain remover, too."

"No, no," Sam laughed and cuffed my shoulder, "not to clean up with. We could use the sponge as a ball! I'll go find one."

"No, Sam!" I yelled. "Clean this up first!"

He was already gone. His footsteps boomed like surround-sound as he thudded up the old wooden steps.

Then, abruptly, they came to a stop.

"Sam?" I called.

Silence.

I shared a look with Todd.

"Sam?" I tried again.

After a long pause, his voice returned to me. "Get up here."

"Which one of us?" I shouted back.

"Both!"

"What do you want?"

"I want you to come here!"

Todd was the first to go. I followed after him, emerging into the upstairs hallway to see Sam stooped down on all fours.

I stared blankly at him. "Problem?"

He muttered something, his eyes fixed on the wall, his head bowed away from us.

Todd and I peered down at the wall-mounted air vent that appeared to have Sam entranced.

"Look," Sam murmured.

"Yes," I said. "It's a vent."

"I wonder where it goes," he muttered to himself.

The rectangular grid on the wall looked like any other air vent, except it was perhaps a little bigger than what I was used to.

"I think it leads outside," said Todd.

"But it doesn't," Sam insisted. "Listen to the wind outside." He gestured to the roof overhead where the gale bore down on the cottage. "It's wild out there, right? Now listen to the vent duct. Nothing. This doesn't lead outside."

I folded my arms. "So? Who cares?"

"Well," he went on, "if it doesn't lead outside, then where does it lead?"

Todd shrugged. "It's just an air vent. They don't really lead anywhere."

"We'll see about that." Sam yanked on the metal grid until it came apart from the wall.

I watched him, wondering what he was planning on doing. Surely he wasn't going to crawl into the—

Oh, wait. That was *exactly* what he was planning on doing.

"Sam!" I grabbed hold of his ankle before he could vanish into the duct.

He kicked his leg free. "Follow me!" he shouted, his voice tinny inside the metal confines.

"Sam, get back here!" I cried. "You'll probably end up in a sewer or something!"

Todd let out a nervous yelp before climbing into the duct after Sam.

"Todd, not you, too!" I exclaimed. "You're better than this!"

His trainers disappeared into the tunnel.

Great, I thought. *Now what am I supposed to do? Go with them?* I took a moment to contemplate the alternative— stay in the hallway alone.

With a weary sigh, I shrank to my hands and knees and crawled into the vent. I heard the clang of metal ahead of me.

"Todd?" I called. "Sam?"

Sam's voice floated back to me, "See? You can always count on me to find something fun to do."

"Fun?" I grumbled. "I wouldn't exactly call this *fun.*"

"I didn't hear you coming up with any better ideas," Sam shot back.

"Backgammonopoly!" I reminded him curtly.

Considering the fact that the cottage was so tiny, the vent passageway felt never-ending. The light of the hallway had faded into the distance, taking with it our sight. We shuffled on in complete and utter darkness, which only added to our so-called fun.

I was on the verge of suggesting we turn back when I collided into Todd.

"Why did you stop?" I asked, untangling myself from his feet.

"Sam stopped," he told me.

"It's a dead end," Sam reported back, his voice closer now. "Wait a minute... maybe not. It might be some sort of hatch."

There was a rattling sound while Sam scuffled with the blockage, followed by a bright light lancing through the tunnel.

"No way," Sam murmured.

"What?" I tried to peer around Todd to get a better view.

To my astonishment, Sam and Todd climbed out of the duct.

We must have arrived somewhere else in the house, I deduced.

I had been right about that, but what I hadn't anticipated was *where* in the house that would be.

A hidden room.

I scrambled to my feet and stood with my brothers, in awe of our find.

The room was circular and dome shaped, like a turret. Along the walls were neat shelves stocked with labelled glass jars. It reminded me of an old-fashioned sweet shop, only in this case, the jars were full of herbs and plants instead of sweets. In the centre of the room was an oil lamp burner, and above it stood a black clay pot on four legs and a tube-like chimney running straight up through the ceiling.

In awe, I wandered over to the shelves and began reading the labelled jars.

Canada snake root, carnation, damiana, dill seed...

"This must be where Ness does her apothecary work," I guessed.

Sam grimaced. "What a nut-case. Is this for real? The woman has a whole room just for her flowers."

"It's her job." I reasoned. "She's an apothecary. She's bound to need a... whatever this is."

"Weird," Sam went on as though he hadn't heard me.

Beside the huge clay pot was a wooden music stand, and propped on it was a leather-bound book. Todd picked up the volume and began flipping through the pages. The paper was stiff and yellowed with age.

"What's the book about?" I asked him.

"An ode to flowers," Sam quipped.

Todd turned the page. "It's recipes, I think." His shoulders tensed.

"What's wrong?" I asked.

Todd stared down at the worn paper. "I don't know..."

Sam bounded over to him and eased the book out of his grasp. He began flipping through the pages himself, reading aloud mockingly.

"Divine Healing..." He turned to the next page. "Drawing an Essence..." He turned the page. "To Break a..." To my surprise, he paused on that section and scanned the text. As he studied the transcript, his face

41

crumpled into a look of confusion.

"What does it say?" I joined Sam and Todd at the burner.

All of a sudden, Todd snatched the book from Sam. "Let's just go," he said, dumping the book back on its stand.

Sam looked at him strangely but said nothing.

I furrowed my brow. "What's wrong?" I asked again.

Sam drew in a deep breath. "Nothing," he said at last. "This is too weird. Let's do something else." Without waiting for a response, he sauntered across the room and ducked into the vent.

Todd promptly clambered into the passageway behind him. I glanced at Todd's vanishing feet, but before I followed, I lifted the old book.

As I touched the smooth leather binding, my fingers began to tingle. It was as though the book was alive, warming my skin. Merging with my skin, almost.

I hastily returned it to the stand.

And then I noticed it: the brown leather cover had been engraved with gold lettering.

Potions, Hexes, and Spells, it read.

My mouth went dry. *A spell book?*

Suddenly it dawned on me, Great Aunt Ness was a witch.

Chapter Three

Stuck in the Middle With You

By the next morning, my head was jumbled with questions. Questions that I wasn't entirely sure I wanted the answers to. I tried to rationalise with myself. After all, Ness *had* told us that she was an apothecary. It made sense that she had a private work room. And as for the spell book... well, each to his own, and all that.

As for my brothers, we didn't speak about what we'd found. In fact, we kept unnaturally quiet for the rest of that day, avoiding the topic with each other and certainly not confronting Ness on the matter. At one point, however, Sam did ask Ness in which drawer the spoons were kept, then hastily clarified his meaning by spelling out the word 'which.'

On that first night, I went to bed at the overly polite time of eight o'clock and awoke at sunrise. I shivered under my blanket for an hour or so before I dared to get up. I'd now learnt two things about Phoenix Holt—it was in the middle of nowhere and it was cold in the mornings.

Fortunately, I'd been so preoccupied with fretting about my new life that I'd scarcely had any time to fret about my new school. Until, that is, it came time to get dressed. Averett Academy students didn't wear uniforms, which, as backwards as it may have sounded, came as a disappointment to me. In short, uniforms eliminated choice. Without them, there was simply too much choice. Smart or casual? Daring or safe? Plain or patterned? After a lengthy deliberation and tornado-esque destruction of the few items I had in my bedroom, I settled upon jeans and a purple top—casual with a splash of colour.

I rushed downstairs ten minutes later than I'd planned, and *twenty* minutes later than Ness had planned. Sam, Todd, and Ness lingered at the door, waiting semi-patiently. I secretly envied how effortlessly stylish Sam looked. He wore jeans and a black T-shirt, and his auburn hair was tousled with that just-rolled-out-of-bed look—a look only attainable from the literal act of *just rolling out of bed*. Todd, on the other hand, was far more preened. His hair was combed to the side and he wore a smart shirt-and-trousers combo.

We set off for school on foot. Phoenix Holt wasn't particularly car-friendly, so I figured I'd have to get used to walking. Either that or become a hermit—a lifestyle choice that I wasn't entirely ruling out.

We trudged through the woodland. There was no path to distinguish the route, so it felt like an aimless trek. A *long*, aimless trek. But Ness led the way, unwaveringly confident in her intrinsic navigation system.

"We're not far now," she told us, trundling along her invisible path.

I chewed anxiously on my thumbnail. Three new kids in a small town boarding school? We'd be straight under the high school microscope, ready to be scrutinised, dissected, and condemned.

"What's Averett Academy like?" I asked. "Do you think we'll blend in?"

"Oh, you'll be fine," Ness assured me. "Everyone will be looking forward to meeting you."

Oh, great. Just what I *didn't* want to hear.

"I won't stand out though, will I?" I persisted.

"No," Ness replied. "Not at all."

45

Sam propped his arm on my shoulder as we walked. "Why *wouldn't* you want to stand out? It's a new school. You need to leave your mark before you turn into just another face in the crowd."

"I like being a face in the crowd," I said.

"Ha! You wouldn't be saying that if you had an impostor permanently wearing your face. Walking around, stealing your good looks and patenting them as his own..." He threw Todd a quick scowl. "Of course, I'm much more handsome than he is."

"No, you're exactly the Same. You're clones," I teased them. "A science experiment gone wrong."

"Gone *right*, I think you mean. Anyway, we can't look *that* much alike; *I* never have any trouble telling us apart. Besides," Sam carried on, "you should get used to the fact that you're never going to blend in. You're a Ballester."

Ness, who had been walking a few paces ahead of us, turned around. "So you *do* know about the Ballester name!" she exclaimed, her full cheeks rosy with excitement.

The three of us exchanged puzzled frowns.

"Only that it's my own name," Sam answered slowly.

"Yes, that's right," Ness mused. "Yes, it's your name." She chuckled and tottered on ahead.

I stared after her in bewilderment.

"Now *she*," Sam whispered, "is of a different breed altogether. Loonbags. There's one in every family."

I shushed him.

We caught up with Ness at the end of the woodland, where the trees opened into a small meadow scattered with silvery gravestones. At the end of the meadow was an old stone mausoleum. I was too far away to get a good look at it, but I could distantly make out the shape of two hunched gargoyles crouching on the rooftop.

A trodden-down footpath ran alongside the graveyard. We picked up the trail, skirting the meadow in single file. As we walked, I watched the morning sun twinkle on the granite headstones.

"This path takes us straight to the Academy," Ness told us.

Sam eyed the winding track. "Can I go on ahead, then?"

"Of course," Ness replied. "But wait for me outside the school entrance."

Having been previously constricted by the group, Sam relished the opportunity to break free. He slung his backpack over his shoulder and bolted. Todd set off in pursuit, leaving me alone with Ness.

Super.

It was less than a minute before the uncomfortable small talk began.

Ness went first. "So," so started awkwardly, "what do you think of Phoenix Holt?"

"It's lovely," I managed.

"Very different from Port Dalton, I'm sure."

I nodded.

"Are you homesick?"

"No," I lied.

"Sophie, deary," Ness coaxed gently, "it's okay if you are."

I said nothing.

"If I'd had to leave my home, I'd be feeling homesick, too," Ness reflected. "Especially after losing your grandfather so suddenly—"

"I'm fine," I insisted, a little more defensively than I would have liked.

"Okay, dear," Ness placated me. "But if you ever need to talk, I'm always here."

I made a sort of 'mm-hmm' noise.

"I know I'm not your Grandpa, but I'm an awfully good listener."

I couldn't help but warm slightly to her sentiment, though I still didn't respond.

Ness carried on, "Anyway, I'm going to do my best. I can promise you that much, at least."

I looked down at the pebbled ground.

"Though, I should warn you," Ness joked, nudging

my elbow, "I'm not sure I'll make a very good parent. I didn't get the chance to be a mother."

I looked up and smiled at her. "Well, I didn't get the chance to be a daughter, either, so maybe we'll make a good pair."

To my surprise, she took my hand and squeezed it. "I think you might be right." Her pale yellow eyes searched for my reaction. "Do you think you'll be happy here, living in Phoenix Holt?"

I knew I would regret the bluntness of my answer later, but in the spirit of sincerity I let the truth slip.

"I don't think so," I replied.

#

We arrived at Averett Academy a few minutes before the first bell. Sam and Todd were sitting on a stone wall, their legs swinging in unison. Behind the wall was an old, gothic manor house, nestled at the foot of a hill. I did a double-take. Surely that manor wasn't the school?

"Is that the boarding house?" I asked Ness.

"Upstairs is," she clarified. "Downstairs is the school."

"Intimate," Sam remarked wryly. He dropped down from the wall and eyed the building, with its dull brickwork and tall lead-framed windows.

I began to notice the other students loitering around the yard.

My heart began to race with anticipation.

I spotted a group of formally dressed boys heading in through the main entrance. They walked silently, with expressionless faces.

Summoning the bravery to peek further afield, I caught sight of a second gathering of boys; again they were in smart attire with a vacant air about them.

Ness came to a stop several metres from the manor.

"Sam and Todd," she said, "you'll be in the upper group. Sophie, you'll be in the middle group."

I stared perplexedly at her.

"There are three groups," she elaborated. "And I believe there are around sixty in total."

"Sixty classes?" I frowned. The school definitely didn't look big enough for sixty classes.

"No, dear." Ness shook her head. "Three classes. Sixty altogether."

"Sixty per class?" My eyebrows shot up.

"No, dear," she said again. "Sixty in the whole school."

My jaw dropped. "Sixty *people*?"

"Give or take."

"And three classes?" Sam recounted.

"Yes. The upper group, the middle group, and the

lower group. Each group is determined by age. We average around twenty per class."

I gawped. "Twenty per class?"

"Give or take."

I let out a nervous breath. "How old are the kids in the middle group?" *My* group.

"Between fourteen and seventeen. Give or take."

"So how come Sam and Todd aren't in the middle group? They're seventeen."

"I decided the boys would benefit most from being placed with Mr. Hardy. At any rate, they'll be turning eighteen soon enough."

Yeah, in eleven months, I thought ruefully.

"Which reminds me," Ness continued, "you two boys can go on ahead. Over sixteens don't need a mentor. Unless you want one, that is. Do you?"

Sam snorted. "Uh, a big fat *no* to the mentor, thanks."

"I don't want a mentor either," I protested.

"Oh, I'm afraid it's compulsory, dear," Ness informed me. "Every student under sixteen needs a mentor."

"Why?" I spluttered.

Sam fidgeted restlessly. "Todd and I don't need to be here for this. We're going to take off now."

"No!" I gasped. "Don't go without me!"

"Why not?" Sam huffed. "We're not in the same class. Besides, you have to bond with your mentor," he said with a grin.

"You can't leave me," I pleaded with Sam. "I don't know anyone." I grabbed hold of his T-shirt in a last desperate attempt to bind myself to him.

He peeled my fingers away, one at a time. "Off, off, off," he instructed. Then he turned his attention to Ness, deliberately looking over my head so as to avoid my beseeching eyes. "Which way to our class?"

"You're with Mr. Hardy," Ness reminded him. "Through the main doors, third room on the left."

In light of my failing pleas, I threw in a splash of emotional blackmail. "I'll never forgive you if you go without me," I avowed to Sam.

"Okay," he said. "'Bye."

My heart sank as the boys jogged towards the manor.

Ness chuckled. "Don't worry. I'm sure it won't be as bad as you're imagining."

I sighed. "Why do I have to have a mentor?" I asked again as we headed for the school. "I really don't want one."

"It's nice for the younger students to have someone they can turn to if they need anything."

"I thought I had you for that."

Ness grinned. "Yes, you do. But it's important for you to have a peer also. Someone you can approach if you don't feel like talking to an old fuddy-duddy like me." She heaved open the oak manor door by its iron handle and ushered me inside.

The foyer was poorly lit, with a slate floor and chestnut-coloured wood panelling on the walls. There was a wide stairwell in front of me and a corridor to either side. Ness guided me to the right.

As we set off down the corridor, I noticed that the décor was much the same as in the foyer area: slate floor, wood walls, and the occasional muted lamp fixed to the panels.

Ness and I walked in silence, with only the click of our footsteps to be heard. A few paces ahead of us, two boys slipped through another oak door into what I assumed was a classroom. They seemed to be around eleven or twelve, so I guessed they'd be in the lower group.

Lots of boys here, I noted absentmindedly. *I haven't seen many girls yet. In fact, I haven't seen* any *girls yet*.

I cleared my throat. "Ness, where's the girls block?"

"Hmm? Oh. What's that now?"

"I haven't seen any girls around."

"What about me?" She flounced her long skirt blithely.

I smelled tactical dodging. "Do they study in a separate wing?"

"No. No separate wing."

"Oh, Ness," I wailed. "Please don't tell me this is an all-boys school."

"Boys, girls," she generalised. "We're all human, aren't we?"

"They're boys!"

"Now, Sophie, let's not be small minded."

"You told me I wouldn't stand out!"

"And I'm sure you won't."

"But I'm a different *gender*—"

"Here we are," Ness cut me off. "Welcome to my office." She opened a dense wooden door to reveal a neat room with a mahogany desk and cherry red walls. "Make yourself comfortable."

Ness seated herself behind the desk and began rifling through a stack of papers. I slumped into a leather chair opposite, gazing out at the hills and woodland beyond the window, wishing I could be out there instead.

"What do we have here…" Ness muttered to herself, slipping on a pair of bifocal glasses. As she scanned her paperwork, her wire-rimmed glasses crept down the bridge of her nose, trapping strands of wispy, silvery-brown hair around her ears. "Ah, yes. These are your enrolment papers. Sophie Ballester. Previous school: Port Dalton Comprehensive, et cetera, et cetera." She slid the papers across the desk. "Sign here, would you, dear?"

I scrawled my name on the dotted line.

"Excellent." Ness tucked the sheets into a file folder. "Now," she murmured, "who did I have in place to be your mentor? I'm sure I wrote someone into your notes..." She licked her thumb and began leafing through another stack of papers. "Ah-ha! Yes. Excuse me one moment."

I sat rigid, gripping the arms of my chair while Ness pressed a buzzer on the intercom.

And elderly woman's voice crackled through the system. "That you, Ness?"

"Hello, Mabel," Ness replied, speaking slowly and clearly. "Mabel, the secretary," she mouthed to me. "She's deaf as a post, poor lamb. Makes a wonderful peach cobbler, though."

"You there, Ness, lovey?" Mabel's voice came again.

"Yes, I'm here, Mabel. How's the arthritis today?" She caught my eye, lowering her voice to address me again. "She's got terrible arthritis, god love her."

"You know me, Ness. I don't like to complain," Mabel responded.

I'd swear I saw Ness roll her eyes.

"Shall I put the kettle on?" Mabel asked.

Ness clasped her hands together. "Wonderful! A cup

of tea would be marvellous. Now, Mabel," she spoke seriously, "before you start on the tea, could you ask one of the boys to send in Jaxon from middle group?"

There was a pause on the other end. "Jaxon?" Mabel said at last. "You're looking for Jaxon, are you?"

"Yes. I want him to mentor a new student."

Another pause. "Jaxon?" She sounded incredulous.

"Yes, please."

"Right. I'll have him sent to your office," Mabel replied. "Then I'll see you for elevenses, shall I? I've got some lovely fresh scones."

"Delightful, Mabel. Bye, now."

And Mabel was gone.

"Who's Jaxon?" I asked.

"Jaxon will be your mentor," Ness told me. "You're both in middle group," she explained. "He'll take you to your classroom and show you the ropes. If you need anything, just ask him."

I had no intention of asking anyone anything, but I nodded all the same.

A few minutes later, there was a knock on the door.

"Come in," Ness called.

I twisted in my seat to see the arrival. The handle turned and the door creaked open. A boy of around seventeen stepped into the office.

My eyes widened in surprise. It was *him*. It was the

boy I'd seen in the woods when we'd been searching for the cottage. Only this time, my sighting of him wasn't quite so fleeting.

He had sandy blonde hair and opaque grey eyes. Much like his fellow students, he was smartly dressed, wearing a shirt and trousers, though somehow he looked scruffy. However, my prime focus was drawn to his face, where a broad, sunken scar ran from his temple diagonally to his jaw, marking everything in its path.

He flinched when he noticed me staring.

Ness rose from her chair. "Jaxon, this is Sophie. I want you to mentor her."

Jaxon pursed his lips, frowning at the idea.

"If he doesn't want to…" I stammered.

His smoky eyes flickered uneasily around the room. His fists clenched.

"Off you go then, you two," Ness beamed, oblivious to the tension—or disregarding it, anyway. "Sophie, Jaxon will take good care of you."

"I don't think he wants to—" I began.

"Goodbye, dear," Ness interrupted me. "I'll see you at lunchtime."

I was mortified. Couldn't Ness see that this boy had no desire whatsoever to mentor me? I could hardly blame him. I wouldn't have wanted to mentor him, either.

I stole a glance in his direction.

He caught my gaze and offered me a strained smile, but said nothing.

"Oh, and Sophie," Ness added as I rose stiffly from my seat, "remember what we talked about: open mind."

Open mind? I fumed. *Yeah, right. I'd like to tell her what my open mind thinks right now.*

As I crossed the room, Jaxon stepped away from the doorway, allowing me to pass through. And that was that. I was back in the corridor, this time with a new companion.

We walked rigidly through the dimly lit hallway. Neither of us spoke.

I listened to the beat of our footsteps as they hit the slate floor. The rhythm fell in sync with my heartbeat, pounding and echoing in my ears like the slow thud of a hammer.

We stopped abruptly outside a door and Jaxon gripped the handle.

Our classroom, I assumed.

I stared down at his grazed knuckles that enveloped the brass door handle. I wanted to say something to him, but I wasn't sure what exactly that something was. I decided to not overthink it and opted to let my mouth decide for me.

"Your hand is cut," I said. *Hmm.* Maybe I

*under*thought it.

Jaxon hesitated, frowned, then laughed quietly before opening the classroom door.

Chapter Four
The Missing Sin

I learned a lot about middle group in a very short span of time. My teacher's name was Mr. Garrett. He was fast talking, wildly animated, and more than a little eccentric. He wore a midnight-blue velvet suit and mad-professor glasses. His head sprouted two tufts of snow-white hair that looked like the possible result of an electric shock.

When I crossed the threshold into the classroom I was greeted with stunned silence. The other students stared at me as though I were some sort of alien aberration. Of course, being female, that was exactly what I was.

The room itself was shadowy, lit only by weak lamplight. A dozen or so boys were seated at long tables in rows, all facing Mr. Garrett and his blackboard.

Jaxon took his seat in the front row. His notebook and pencil were already laid out on the desk—his pencil quite clearly chewed to within an inch of its life. I froze in the doorway, utterly shell-shocked, until he nodded impatiently towards the empty place beside him.

I hurried across the room to my seat on the end of a long work bench. The sound of my chair scraping the floor sliced through the pin-drop silence.

After the astonishment of my arrival had worn off, Mr. Garret gave me a fervent welcome, followed by a brief recap. I quickly discovered that the class had been studying myths and legends. Once I was sufficiently caught up, the teacher dived straight back into the lesson.

"Who can tell me the difference between a Divellion and a Daemon?"

He scribbled the two words onto the blackboard in chicken-scratch scrawl.

Give me maths, science, literature, I'm fine. But this? This was definitely not my expertise.

Somewhere behind me, a boy cleared his throat. "A Daemon is a malevolent creature born into dark power," he answered in a low, bass tone. "A Divellion is a malevolent being that *thirsts* for power."

I traced the voice to the back of the classroom. The boy's appearance made him seem much older than sixteen or seventeen. He was brawny, with matted black hair and dark circles beneath his eyes.

"Correct!" Mr. Garret waved a piece of chalk at the rest of the class. "Reuben is absolutely correct. A Daemon is a source of dark power. A Divellion is a power hunter, thriving off the power it steals. So, which is the more dangerous—the Daemon who sources the power, or the Divellion who craves it?" He waited for a show of hands. "Lewis," he gestured to another boy in one of the seats behind me.

"The Daemon is the more powerful," Lewis responded coolly. "It's the source. There's nothing more powerful than the source."

Mr. Garret peered over the rims of his glasses. "Anyone care to challenge Lewis's theory?"

Reuben raised his hand again. "The Divellion is the more powerful."

"Why?" Mr. Garret pressed.

"Because the Daemon may source the power, but the Divellion hungers for it. What could be more dominant than the primal urge of hunger?" He raised an eyebrow. "The Daemon is content with what it has, but the Divellion is insatiable, always seeking more."

Inspired, Mr. Garret scribbled the word 'insatiable' onto the blackboard. "Precisely," he breathed. "Magnificent, Reuben."

Magnificent? Okay, so now I knew who Mr. Garret's star pupil was. Although Reuben's subject of knowledge seemed to be a rather questionable one.

So much for getting a good education, I thought to myself. *This is pointless.* I glanced at the wall-clock, wondering when the real curriculum would begin.

Beside me, I noticed Jaxon doodling in his notebook. I watched him out of the corner of my eye. He had rolled up the sleeves of his shirt, exposing taut muscles in his forearm from gripping his pencil. With his head tilted in concentration, strands of sandy blonde hair brushed across the beginnings of his scar.

How in the world did he end up with a scar that bad? I wondered. I peered closer. The marking crossed his entire face!

Suddenly, Jaxon looked up. His charcoal eyes flickered to mine.

My cheeks flushed, and I hastily returned my attention to Mr. Garret.

"Who can tell me how a Divellion attacks?" the teacher was saying.

I sighed. *Seriously? Is he still on this?*

A new voice spoke up. "They bite, and the venom from their fangs will draw the power essence out of the victim."

"Very good, Cameron," Mr. Garret praised. "The

Divellion's hunting technique is akin to that of a snake. First, they must catch a scent. Once a trail is picked up, the predators will stalk their victims until they have identified the weakest member of the group. When the opportunity arises, the Divellion strikes, feeding from the chosen until the heart stops beating. Upon the kill, the essence of the victim will transfer into the Divellion, and the ritual is complete. Sophie Ballester?"

Oh my god, that's my name. Why is he calling my name?

"Yes, sir?" I replied meekly.

"How does one go about vanquishing a Divellion?"

"I... I don't know," I stuttered. "Bug spray?"

There were a few sniggers around the classroom and I felt myself turn bright red.

Mr. Garret gave the culprits a stern glare. "Anyone else want to tackle this one?"

Of course, Reuben the Magnificent stepped in. "There are two certain ways to vanquish a Divellion: one is with a potion, and the other is decapitation."

"Tremendous, Reuben! However, as very few have the ability to create a potion powerful enough to take down the corporeal form, I would advise that you aim for the latter." He chuckled blithely.

Okay, I thought to myself, *it's official. This is, without a doubt, the most bizarre lesson I've ever been made to sit through*.

And it didn't end there. There was a further two hours of 'Divellion talk' before the blissful sound of the lunch bell forced Mr. Garret to call time. Alas, it wasn't quite over for me yet, because he asked me to stay behind after class.

I watched enviously as the other students filed out to lunch—Jaxon included. Once the classroom had emptied, I made my way to the teacher's desk.

"Sophie Ballester," Mr. Garret uttered my name approvingly. "Delighted to meet you."

He grasped my hand and shook it roughly.

"How are you enjoying life in Phoenix Holt?" he asked.

"I like it," I replied, on autopilot.

"It must be such a thrill for you to return to the place of your heritage," Mr. Garret gushed.

I summoned a smile. "Uh huh," I agreed vaguely.

"I remember your grandfather. A good man, he was."

My eyebrows rose. "You knew Wilber?"

"Yes, yes, although he was several years my senior, so it was more a case of knowing him through reputation. But Ness has always been a very dear friend to me, and she spoke so very highly of him. Oh, she missed her brother terribly after he left. I'm sure he missed her, too."

Did he? I wondered. I was still trying to get my head around the fact that my grandfather had even *had* a sister, let alone a sister he missed.

Mr. Garret carried on, oblivious to my hesitant expression. "Anyhow," he said, his tone jovial, "what did you think of the lesson?"

"Great," I lied. "Very informative."

"And you understood everything?"

"Yes. I think so." *Apart from the point of it*, I added silently.

"Splendid! My goal was to make the subject relevant to you, as well as the boys. How did I do?"

"Um… good. I mean, great," I revised. "Very… relevant."

"Excellent, excellent. Any questions?"

"Nope."

"Wonderful! Well, I'm sure I've detained you long enough. Though, I must say, I am glad that we've had the chance to chat."

"Me, too," I replied, trying not to frown in confusion.

Mr. Garret smiled broadly. "Until the clock strikes one, young Ballester."

Um, what? Did that mean I was free to go?

I edged backwards, retreating to my desk. My teacher didn't try to stop me, so I presumed I'd guessed right.

I hastily gathered my notebook and pen and slipped them into my shoulder bag. Just as I was about to leave, I noticed a balled up piece of paper on the desktop.

Jaxon's sketch, I realised at once.

Quickly checking that Mr. Garret's attention was elsewhere, I retrieved the ball of paper and flattened it out.

I gasped, taken aback. The artwork was incredible. It was as lifelike as a photograph, and yet it'd been drawn freehand with the blunt nub of a pencil.

The sketch was of a pier. But not just any pier—a pier that was eerily familiar to me. Everything from the wood-planked flooring and rusted structure to the sheets of frothing water licking at the sides. I knew it all.

It was Port Dalton.

I'd sat on that pier a thousand times. More, even. And Jaxon had drawn it down to the very last detail. Every dent, paint chip, and imperfection—it was all there.

But the idea that Jaxon had been to Port Dalton seemed implausible. I mean, it would have been a pretty random coincidence if he had.

I'm seeing what I want to see, I decided, accounting the likeness to the nostalgia of my homesick brain.

I set the drawing back down on the desk and headed for the exit.

The corridor was empty, which proved to be both a blessing and a curse. A blessing because I wasn't particularly in the mood to socialise, and a curse because the cold, dark corridor was a little too 'horror movie in the making' for my liking. I could see it perfectly: *Murder in the Maintenance Closet*, or *The Revenge of the Hallway Hacker*.

When I finally made it outside and into the refuge of daylight, I found myself facing yet another horror. A very real one, this time.

At first I wasn't sure what was happening. All I saw was a raucous group of boys forming a large circle and cheering like a pack of rabid hyenas.

Fight, I figured.

I decided to give them a wide berth, scanning the green for a secluded spot to hide away and eat my packed lunch, but the fracas was harder to side-step than I'd hoped.

My heart skipped a beat when I saw Sam tumbling through the onlookers, his T-shirt tangled and his lips blood smeared.

Sam regained his balance and charged at his challenger.

"Stop!" I yelled, pushing my way into the scuffle.

I couldn't see much beyond the mass of huddled bodies, and I was jostled and shoved from every directions. Apparently everyone wanted a front-row seat.

"Sam!" I called, catching a glimpse of two pairs of legs scuffling on the ground. "Sam!" I tried again.

"Now's not a good time!" he yelled back.

I edged forward, squashing myself between two beefcake boys. My view was marginally better, but I still couldn't see Sam. Although I did manage to spot Todd. He was hovering on the outskirts, hopping from left to right in a flap.

The circling boys goaded and chanted—cheers that I was willing to bet were not for Sam.

I cringed.

With a final effort, I forced my way through the crowd, ready to clobber the enemy with my shoulder bag.

But, in what was perhaps a stroke of good fortune, a whistle blew, causing the bloodthirsty spectators to scatter like crows at the sound of a gunshot.

"Ballester!" a male voice hollered. "Thompson! My office!"

Sam's brawny opponent scowled and straightened out his collar. "Mr. Hardy," he appealed in a ragged voice, "he was asking for it."

Mr. Hardy, a giant beast of a man with a thick neck and strong jaw, squared up to the Thompson boy. "*You* should have known better."

I glanced helplessly at Sam. He staggered to his feet, blood dripping from his mouth and nose. He shot me a guiltless look.

"And as for you, Ballester," Mr. Hardy turned on Sam now, "you may think you're untouchable—"

Before he could dish out the rest of his onslaught, Ness appeared on the scene.

"Oh, good grief!" she shrieked, evidently catching sight of Sam's not-so-pretty face. "What on earth has been going on out here?"

Sam stared at his feet.

Ness exhaled loudly. "Thank you, Mr. Hardy. If you could take young Thompson inside, I'll deal with Sam."

Without another word, Mr. Hardy marched back towards the school, his victim in tow.

"Oh, Sam." Ness shook her head solemnly. "Fighting? On your first day? What were you thinking?"

"He started it!" Sam exclaimed.

Always a top-notch defence, I thought, rolling my eyes.

Ness placed her hands on her hips. "Well? Let's hear it, then. How exactly did he start it?"

"He was in my way," Sam justified weakly. "And he wouldn't move." He didn't seem to want to meet Ness's eyes.

"So you decided to pick a fight with him?" she demanded.

"He wouldn't move," Sam repeated. "Would he, Todd?"

Todd's flustered face was pillar-box red. "No, he wouldn't."

"That is no excuse," Ness scolded. Her eyelashes swept downward. "I am very disappointed in you, Sam."

His expression hardened. "You think I care?"

I frowned. "Sam..."

"What?" he exclaimed, holding up his palms. "I'm always the bad guy, aren't I? You might as well say it. Wilber did."

Now it was my turn to look to the ground.

Ness sighed, and when she spoke again her voice was softer. "I don't think you're the bad guy, dear," she told him. "In fact, I know you're not. But if you fight in my school again, I'll make you come flower spotting with me every day for a month. Got that?" She offered him a hint of a smile.

"A month?" Sam's mouth twitched. "Jeeze, it's not like I killed the guy."

"Well, don't say I didn't warn you," Ness cautioned. "Now that you know the consequences, maybe you'll use your head next time."

Doubt it, I thought to myself.

"Right," Ness moved on. "I'm taking you two boys home. You can think about your actions and start fresh tomorrow. Sophie dear, I'll come back for you at four o'clock. Okay?"

I nodded my head numbly.

As Todd and Ness turned to leave, Sam caught my eye.

"You shouldn't have done that," I mouthed to him.

He shrugged.

"You face is bleeding," I mouthed again.

Another shrug.

"Wilber didn't think you were a bad guy," I added.

He smiled vaguely, then set off in pursuit of Ness.

"You're not the bad guy," I said aloud. Though I knew he didn't hear me.

#

My afternoon lesson was just as boring and pointless as the morning session. Back in the same room, I listened to Mr. Garret drone on about local myths. I tuned in and out. Mostly, my attention was elsewhere. Again, I sat beside Jaxon in the front row. Again, he sketched. And again, I watched him.

Towards the end of the lesson, Mr. Garret began handing out worksheets. After passing them around, he planted himself at his desk, where he began reading a dog-eared mystery novel.

I frowned. I hadn't anticipated being tested today. I was beginning to regret not having paid attention.

So, with very little optimism, I stared hopelessly at my worksheet. Next to me, Jaxon pushed his to one side and continued to draw in his notebook.

"Aren't you going to do the work?" I whispered.

He glanced up at me, startled by the sound of my voice. Almost as though he'd completely forgotten I was there.

"The worksheet." I pointed to his discarded paper. "You need to do it." *Oh, no. Why did I say that?* I could have kicked myself for being such a dork. *It's okay,* I consoled myself. *I can fix this. All I have to do is say something better. Something cooler.* "Um…" I said. My shoulders sagged. *Yeah, that was* much *cooler.*

Jaxon's brow furrowed.

"I mean, whatever," I went on, attempting to sound blasé. "I wouldn't want you to get into trouble with Mr. Garret, that's all…" *Warning to self. Babbling about to commence in five, four, three, two…* "But, don't do it if you don't want to. Who cares? It's not a big deal or anything. I mean, it's your choice. Freedom of speech and all that …" *Oh no, I wish I didn't have freedom of speech right now.*

Jaxon glanced at my worksheet, then at his own, then back up at me. His eyes smouldered like liquid iron.

To my dismay, my ramblings weren't over. "I think your drawings are probably much more worthwhile than the worksheet, anyway. Um, not that I've ever seen your drawings or anything..." *Stop talking, stop talking, stop talking!*

Jaxon cocked his head to the side. He stared at me for a long moment, possibly trying to figure out why I was so weird. Then, to my surprise, he reached for his worksheet and began reading the questions.

I let out a breath.

I focused on my own paper, sweeping my hair to the side and hiding my blushing face behind a wavy brunette curtain.

Question One: List the seven deadly sins.

Okay, I could do that.

Gluttony, Lust, Envy, Anger, Greed, Sloth...

That was six. One more to go.

I tapped my pencil on the desk. What was that final sin?

In my peripheral, I could see Jaxon writing sinuously across his worksheet, already at the bottom of the page. Perhaps sensing my gaze, his eyes drifted up to mine.

I managed an awkward smile. "Stuck on the sins," I explained in a hushed voice.

Jaxon reached out and slid my worksheet across the desktop toward him. He skimmed over what I'd written, then with a flurry of his pencil, he added to my answer and passed the paper back.

Pride.

"Thanks," I said, turning an even deeper shade of red. "I was drawing a blank on that one."

He smiled in his usual ambiguous way before returning to his own work.

I exhaled again.

Question Two: Which of the sins will a Divellion prey on?

Not this Divellion rubbish again, I thought tetchily. I felt like writing my answer as, *I don't know and I don't care.* But instead I took a shot at *Gluttony*, founded on the logic that it was my first answer in Question One.

To my astonishment, the worksheet was swooped out from under my nose.

Across the table, Jaxon held it prisoner. He scanned my answer, then drew a line through it and replaced it with something else—presumably the correct answer. Satisfied, he slipped the worksheet back to me.

Envy, it read.

"Thanks," I whispered.

He shrugged, and kind of smiled again. I noticed a small dimple form at the corner of his mouth, and for a moment, something about him was almost playful. But then, whatever it was, was gone.

We carried on in silence. The rest of the questions were somewhat existential, and I got the impression that there was no wrong answer. In fact, questions four, five, and six all began with the words, 'In your opinion…'.

At a quarter to three, Mr. Garret turned down the page of his book and placed it in the top drawer of his desk. "Good job today, everybody," he said, abruptly rising from his seat. "I think we'll finish early. Class dismissed! Oh, and worksheets to me as you leave," he added as an afterthought.

There was a sudden rush of scraping chairs and murmuring voices. The boys marched out, dropping their papers onto the teacher's desk as they went.

Jaxon and I stayed seated.

"Thank you for today," I said. "You know, for this mentoring thing, and for helping me with the work…" I glanced at my completed paper.

Jaxon looked at me briefly, then turned his attention to the wall in front of us.

"I'm sure I'll see you around tomorrow," I added.

He continued to stare ahead, his expression deadpan.

Point taken.

"Okay, bye," I said. I leapt up from my seat, tripping over myself to get away. Anything to avoid the embarrassment of being ignored—again.

Chapter Five
Said in Silence

Class finished shortly before three o'clock, but Ness wasn't meeting me until four. Biding my time, I loitered around the schoolyard for ten minutes or so, walking the perimeter of the stone-walled enclosure. I watched my fellow students scatter, going their separate ways. Some retired to the boarding quarters upstairs, while others set off into the woodland or hills.

Gradually, the passers by became fewer, until only I remained.

The afternoon had brought a chill to the air, and the cool September breeze sent a shiver over my skin. I considered waiting indoors, but I was beginning to feel like an intruder, overstaying my welcome in somebody else's home. I came to the conclusion that my best option would be to start walking. I knew it wouldn't be easy to navigate my way through the maze of woodland, but the path to the graveyard was a clear route, and I figured I'd bump into Ness somewhere along the way. In fact, I imagined she'd probably thank me for saving her a huge chunk of the journey.

So, with that in mind, I began my trek.

I had been right about one thing—following the path was easy. And, as it happened, the solitude of the walk provided me with some much needed alone time. A chance to reflect on my day. Or my day and a half, as the case was.

First of all, there was Ness. I liked her. Well, I didn't *dis*like her, anyway. Although I had to admit, her hidden room had sparked a few misgivings on my part. The book we found suggested she studied the occult; did that make her a witch? And if so, was I okay with that? I wasn't sure yet.

Then there was Phoenix Holt.

I sighed at the thought.

It would certainly take some getting used to. No doubt about it, this place was completely cut off from the rest of the world. And an all-boys boarding school? That was far from ideal. I was already starting to pine for my girlfriends back in Port Dalton. Phone reception was a no go in Phoenix Holt, but I made a mental note to ask Ness about internet connection ASAP. If I couldn't text or call, I could at least email.

I turned a corner, emerging into the gently sloping graveyard. It seemed that I'd come to the end of the footpath, and yet there was still no sign of Ness.

I scanned the meadow. Sprawling sun-kissed grass was dotted with flowers and polished headstones, and some distance away stood the old mausoleum.

But this time, that wasn't all there was.

There was a boy, standing before a grave, reading the words etched onto the tombstone.

I stopped in my tracks. "Jaxon," I murmured.

He glanced up at the mention of his name. When he caught sight of me, his shoulders tensed.

"S-sorry," I stammered. "I didn't mean to interrupt..." I trailed off.

He stared at me, his eyes as haunting and as pale as the mist that skimmed the grass. Dark blonde hair swept over his brow, and under the sun's dipping light, his scar looked even deeper, like a jagged tear dividing his face in two.

My breath caught in my throat. The sight of him had frightened me.

Looking away, my focus fell upon the headstone beside him. "Are you okay?" I asked. I recognised a wistful melancholy, an emotion that I'd identified in myself when I'd stood at Wilber's graveside just days earlier.

Jaxon didn't reply. He glowered, and then turned his back on me.

For a moment I was stunned by his abrupt action. I was hurt by it, actually. Quite clearly he wanted me to leave.

So I did.

I set off into the trees, with a stride that quickly turned into a run. And before I knew it, I was racing into the woodland, stumbling along the rutted ground. I couldn't stop myself. I kept going until I could physically run no more.

My legs buckled and gave way beneath me, sending me skidding onto my hands and knees in the earth.

And that was where I stayed, huddled amongst the foliage, my lungs burning and my breath rattling in my throat.

"What are you doing?" I muttered to myself as my eyes began to pool. "Running away?"

I looked up to the grey sky above. Trees caged me in from all angles, suffocating me. Where did I think I was going? I was trapped in Phoenix Holt with no friends, no freedom, and no hope.

And to make matters worse, now I was lost, too.

Great.

Why didn't I wait at the school? I berated myself.

Stupid hindsight.

"Someone help me," I cried, desolately.

#

It was a long time before help came. And it happened quite out of the blue.

I hadn't moved from where I'd fallen in what felt like hours. I'd cemented myself to the spot in defeat. My palms were grazed and dotted with blood, and my knees stung beneath their denim shield.

By the time dusk set in, I'd more or less given up hope of ever getting back the cottage.

But all that changed when someone tapped me on the shoulder.

I hadn't heard anyone approach, so the sudden company took me by surprise. My heart leapt into my throat. Clutching my chest, I scrambled to my feet.

Jaxon.

Without a word, he took my hand in his and brushed the dirt from my palm. Then he lifted the hem of his shirt and began blotting my grazed skin.

"Thank you," I said, guardedly.

He let my hand slip from his, then turned and made for the trees. Pausing briefly, he glanced over his shoulder at me, as though he were waiting for me to follow.

I did follow. I trailed behind him, lacing in and out of the sycamores. It was dark, but I could see him beneath the moonlight as we crunched through the undergrowth.

"You don't say much, do you?" I remarked after a very long spell of silence.

He glanced over his shoulder at me and frowned. His pace slowed ever so slightly and I fell into stride with him.

"*Can* you speak?" I ventured.

Jaxon let out a silky laugh. He shot me a quick grin, bringing the hollow dimple to his cheek.

"Ah," I smiled. "Was that a 'yes'?"

He didn't respond.

"A 'no'?" I guessed again.

Nothing. But he kept smiling.

"You're very strange, Jaxon," I chided. "And, if I'm honest, you're not a particularly good mentor."

He pursed his lips and gave a good-natured shrug.

While I was busy trying to decipher him, a raised tree root caught me off guard. I tripped and stumbled forward.

In the same beat, Jaxon's hand was on the back of my top, between my shoulder blades. The next thing I knew, my feet were off the ground, just by a few inches, but it was enough to make me lose my breath. Then, without even so much as a backwards glance, Jaxon propped me back upright and carried on walking as though nothing out of the ordinary had happened.

I stood frozen to the spot. It took me several seconds to gather myself, and not because the stumble had shaken me, because of *him*. With the most effortless of movements, he had caught my fall with one hand and lifted me clean off the ground as though I weighed nothing more than a feather.

"You're strong," I called to him, staggered.

He kept walking. And we didn't mention it again.

After a long and arduous trek, we came to a stop on a wooded hill; the cottage was nestled at the foot of the incline.

We'd made it.

I let out a sigh of relief and turned to face Jaxon. The light evening breeze swept strands of barley-coloured hair across his forehead.

"Well," I concluded, "thanks, I guess."

He tilted his head to the side, watching me as though I were the strangest thing he'd ever come across.

"I shouldn't have called you a bad mentor," I added. "You're kind of okay."

His lips twitched into a reluctant smile.

"I'll see you at school," I told him.

He bowed his head.

I took that as my cue to leave and set off downhill towards the cottage.

Jaxon waited on the slope.

Once I'd made it to the picket fence, I glanced back at him.

There he stood, in exactly the same spot I'd left him, somehow looking both rugged and regal in his stance.

I gave him a little wave.

He inhaled slowly. Then, after a moment of hesitation, Jaxon spoke.

"Hello," he said.

And he strolled away.

#

Safely reunited with the cottage, I trundled through the front door, smiling to myself.

"What took you so long?" Sam demanded, intercepting me before I'd even had chance to close the front door.

The sound of his voice startled me. "Huh?"

He simplified, "You? Doing?"

"School," I replied, though I knew that wasn't the answer he'd been looking for.

Sam huffed. "They were worried about you," he

grumbled. "Now, come on." He seized my wrist and hauled me up the wooden stairs.

"Let go!" I protested.

"You're never going to believe this," he griped. "He's outdone himself this time."

"Who's outdone himself?" I asked, squirming to free my wrist.

Sam towed me to the top of the staircase before relaxing his grip. "Do you realise that your brother is a sly, devious, two-faced weasel—"

"Don't be so hard on yourself," I said kindly. "You're not *that* bad."

"Not me!" Sam snapped. "*Him*. Todd. You wanna know what your so-called brother is doing right now? While *we're* all out looking for you?"

I wrinkled my nose. "You're not out looking for me. You're here."

Growing impatient, Sam stamped his foot on the hardwood floor. "Yes, but *he* doesn't know that. *He* thinks I'm out combing the woods for my poor little sister. And the second my back is turned… Bam!"

"Bam?" I asked.

"Bam. He's off sneaking around like the sly sneak that he is."

"Todd?"

"He's in the apothell-cary room!" Sam waved his

86

hands around wildly. "Can you believe that?"

I gasped. "Todd's in Ness's apothecary room?"

"Yes!"

My hands flew to my mouth in shock. "Why?" I looked down at the metal air vent glinting on the wall in the upper hallway. I, for one, had no intention of going back there. Quite frankly, it had given me the creeps.

"Because he's obsessed with it!" Sam accused. "He keeps finding ways to slip it into conversation. Asking questions about that old book, checking to see if I think there's any truth to it. I mean, a spell book! Come *on*!"

I clasped my hands together nervously.

"So I decided to test him," Sam went on. "I told him I was going into the woods to search for you, and as soon as my back was turned..."

"Bam?" I guessed.

"Bam!"

"Wait a second," I said, frowning. "Ness is out looking for me?"

"She went to get you from school, but they told her you'd already left. She came back to the cottage, and when you weren't here, she went to look for you."

I sucked in my breath. "Oh, no. Is she mad at me?"

"No, she's... I don't know... worried or something. Anyway, forget that. We've got more important—"

"She's worried? Should I go after her? Which

direction did she head?"

"I don't know," Sam moaned. "The outside direction. Who cares? She'll come back eventually. Anyway, I told her not to bother."

I furrowed my brow.

"I knew you were fine," he explained with an aloof wave of his hand. "So, what are we going to do about Todd?"

"You didn't *know* I was fine," I argued. "I was lost!"

"You weren't *that* lost."

I raised my eyebrows. "I didn't realise there were levels of lost. I thought all lost was lost."

"You weren't lost," he said, rolling his eyes. "I knew you were out there." He gestured vaguely to the hallway wall. "Now, can we please talk about something other than *you* for a second?" He nodded meaningfully to the air vent.

"Are you thinking what I'm thinking?" he said seriously.

"Probably not."

"We catch him in the act!" Sam declared.

I stifled a yawn. "Do we have to? It's been a long day. I really don't want to crawl through the duct again."

Sam folded his arms. "Sophie."

I sighed. "Is it really that big of a deal? If he wants to go in there, can't we just let him?"

"That's not the point!" Sam exclaimed. "He went behind our backs. As his brother and sister, it's our job—nay, our *duty*!—to bust him."

I sighed again. Honestly, I didn't particularly care about busting Todd. And I definitely didn't want to go back to the apothecary room. Just the thought of it made me uncomfortable. Granted, I didn't know much about witchcraft—mostly because I preferred to steer clear of it—but I didn't want to accidentally hex myself or something.

Sam crouched down and rattled the vent until the grid came apart from the wall. "Follow me, Soph!" he instructed as he clambered into the duct.

In seconds he had disappeared into nothing more than a distant clunk of metal echoing throughout the passage.

Gingerly, I crawled into the tunnel after him.

I can't say I was pleased to be tackling the air vent again. Somehow, this time around, it felt even darker, and even more claustrophobic, than it had before.

After what felt like an eternity, a bright shaft of light poured into the tunnel.

"Caught you in the act!" I heard Sam remark as he tumbled out of the air vent into the apothecary room.

"I- I-," Todd stammered. "This isn't how it looks—"

"Shame on you, Todd," Sam shook his head

disapprovingly.

I crawled out of the tunnel, emerging into the dome-shaped room once more. Everything was as I'd remembered it—wall to wall jars, a huge black pot on stilts, and an overpowering scent of burnt lavender. Then I noticed that the hefty, leather-bound book was lying open on the music stand with Todd standing before it.

"Todd!" I gasped. "Have you been doing..." I lowered my voice, "spells?"

"Have you?" Sam interrogated.

"No! I was just... I'm just looking at it," he justified weakly.

Sam scowled. "Without your brother around to get in the way. Is that it?"

I gave him a peculiar look. He was taking this a little too personally.

"No," Todd protested. "It's not like that. I was curious, that's all."

"We're all curious," Sam shot back. "But *we*," he pointed between himself and me, "would never go behind your back. We'd never lie to you."

"Okay, okay," Todd appeased him, stepping away from the book. "Maybe you're right. Maybe I should have told you. I didn't think you'd care this much."

Sam stared at the floor for a moment. When he

looked up, he stuffed his hands into his jeans pockets and strolled into the middle of the room.

"So, what's this?" he said, rapping his knuckles against the black pot. "Is this the cauldron?"

My stomach flip-flopped. It *was* a cauldron!

"I don't know, Sam," Todd groaned. "Can we just leave? I don't want to be here anymore."

"No, Todd," Sam retorted in a passive-aggressive tone. "You're the one who's *curious*," he mimicked. "So, let's check this place out. Satisfy your curiosity." He glanced at the open book. "Is this the spell you were going to do? Hear You Me," he read aloud.

"No," Todd mumbled. "I wasn't going to do it. I was reading it, that's all."

Sam stared down at the scripture. "This says the spell allows you to hear the innermost thoughts of others." He glanced at us.

I grimaced. "You've got to be kidding me? You don't actually want to do a spell, do you?"

Sam ignored me and carried on scanning the yellowed page. "The effects only last a few minutes. It opens the mind and gives insight into the unsaid."

I laughed out loud. "Don't be ridiculous."

"Anise Hyssop," Sam muttered. He strolled to the wall of shelves and located the jars labelled 'A'.

"You're not seriously going to do this, are you?" I

asked in disbelief as Sam popped open one of the 'A' jars.

He ambled back to the cauldron and dropped a handful of dried plant into the pot. Then, returning to the book, he read again, "Powdered bay leaves..." He made off towards the shelves again, this time heading for 'B'.

"Sam, don't play around with this stuff," Todd implored.

"Why not?" Sam replied, preoccupied as he scooped out a handful of bay leaves from a glass jar. "*You* were going to."

Todd threw up his hands. "I wasn't! Please, can't we leave?"

I edged forward until I was close enough to peer down into the cauldron. A mound of dried herbs was nestled at the bottom.

Anxiously, I fiddled with a thread on my top. "It's not really going to work though, is it?"

Sam shrugged. "Only one way to find out." He glanced at Todd, then back at me. "Anyone joining me?"

We both looked to our feet.

"Just me, then," Sam answered for us.

"Don't do this," Todd tried again.

He carried on. "Sprinkle of sage, bethel root..."

The more ingredients that filled the pot, the faster

my heart pounded. By the time the recipe was complete, my pulse was racing.

"Okay," Sam murmured, "time to light this sucker." He took a box of matches from beside the burner and ignited the wick. A wild blue flame shot upwards, spreading across the bottom of the cauldron like a ripple of water.

I shrank back. "What happens now?"

Sam deliberated for a moment. "Well, the potion brews, and then I'm going to drink it."

Drink it? The idea made me queasy.

"Oh, yeah," Sam added, as he reviewed the open page, "and I guess I'll have to say some words, too."

Todd swallowed. "It's an incantation."

Inside the cauldron, the flowers had already turned to pulp and were dissolving into a murky grey liquid.

Sam drew a pencil from his jeans pocket and used it to stir the mixture. "Double double toil and trouble, fire burn and cauldron..."

The three of us stared down at the concoction. It wasn't bubbling, exactly.

"Simmer!" Sam finished, then mimicked a wicked cackle.

It amazed me to see him acting so relaxed. I was terrified. I didn't want Sam to drink the potion. And worse, I was gripped by a horrible instinct that this would be the start of something much bigger. Like the tempting of a fate that I *really* didn't want.

It seemed I wasn't the only one feeling uneasy.

"Sam," Todd wheezed. "*Don't* do this."

Sam laughed lightly. "Quit worrying. You're like an old woman sometimes, Toddy-boo."

Todd's mouth pressed into a tight line. "I don't feel comfortable with this—"

"Give me a break!" Sam exclaimed, letting the pencil clatter into the pot. "You said you were curious, right? So stop being such a baby! It's herbs. It's not going to kill me."

I bit my lip.

Sam rolled his eyes. "Now, would one of you hand me one of those syringe-looking things?" He gestured to the shelves.

Neither of us moved.

"Fine," Sam huffed. "I'll do it myself."

He collected a long glass pipette tube with a bulbous end from the shelf and brought it back to the pot.

I listened as a rush of air wheezed through the tube while Sam absentmindedly squeezed the top. Above the cauldron, clouds of black vapours drifted up into the chimney pipe.

My hands began to tremble.

Sam dipped his pipette into the pot and drew the

liquid into the glass confines. He raised it to eyelevel, inspecting the grey contents that sloshed around inside.

"Delicious," he remarked wryly. Then, hovering the pipette above his mouth, he winked at us. "Cheers," he said, before releasing a drop of the brew onto his tongue.

Standing as motionless as a statue, I stared at him.

Sam winced, then quickly read aloud from the open page, "I am heart, I am head, let me hear the words unsaid."

We all fell silent.

For a minute or two, Sam looked sort of trance-like. His eyes were unfocused and he appeared to be deep in thought. All of a sudden, he turned and stared at us. *Through* us, even.

"How do you feel?" Todd asked.

Sam didn't respond.

"Can you hear our thoughts?" I whispered. Now there was a question I never thought I'd have to ask.

Sam laughed strangely.

"Say something," I pleaded. "You're scaring me."

Sam grinned. "What's thermonuclear?" he asked Todd.

Todd's eyebrows shot up; he was evidently surprised. "It's nuclear fusion. We studied it in astrology club."

"Geek!" He turned to me next. "Who's Jaxon?"

I felt the blood rush to my face. "Nobody," I replied quickly.

Oh my god, stop thinking, I pleaded to myself. *Stop!*

All of a sudden, Sam's expression hardened. He looked Todd square in the eyes. "*What*?" he asked, coldly.

Todd stiffened. "I didn't say anything."

Although Sam registered the response, he seemed to be listening to something further. Something beyond my ears.

"Todd," he murmured, his face ashen. "How could you have known that?"

Todd took a step backwards. "I didn't say anything. I didn't..."

There was a long, tense silence before either of them spoke again.

"No," Sam mumbled at last. "No, you're right. You didn't say anything." He massaged his temples, composing himself. "I was just messing with you."

I blinked in shock. What had just happened?

"We should go," said Sam in a low voice. "Ness might be home by now."

I grabbed hold of his arm. "What happened?"

He broke free and sidestepped past me. "Nothing. I told you, I was just messing with you."

Chapter Six
Targets

The rest of the evening passed by uneventfully. Ness returned to the cottage, fraught but relieved to find me there, and none the wiser to our little trip to the apothecary room.

As for Sam, he isolated himself, keeping conversations brief and heading to bed early. He claimed to have a headache, but I couldn't help but wonder what exactly defined the term 'headache' in this case. Was it the standard 'take a pain killer and you'll be fine' sort of thing? Or more the 'hearing people's thoughts and can't shut them off' diagnosis?

It certainly begged the question: had the spell worked?

I tried not to let my imagination get too carried away. Sure, he'd known about Jaxon, but he could have come across him at school. Spells and potions seemed implausible to me. They defied everything that I believed to be fact. Although I wasn't so sure I could trust *fact* anymore. I mean, the hidden room alone defied logic. Try as I might, I couldn't find any evidence of it from anywhere else inside the cottage. And from the outside, the room simply did not exist. And if, for argument's sake, the spell *had* worked, why would Sam deny it? My brother was a lot of things, but coy was not one of them.

No. None of this made sense.

But in spite of my scrambled brain, by the next morning my thoughts had wandered to a much more pressing enigma.

Jaxon.

I couldn't wait to see him, and this time I was dressed and ready for school in record time—wearing jeans and a white lace top. I plated my hair and added a dab of lip gloss. My nervous excitement had provided me with a handy seven a.m. energy boost.

Sam, on the other hand, was distinctly lacking in energy. He was withdrawn and heavy with lassitude, wandering around in a state that was extremely out of character for him.

"Is everything alright, Sam?" Ness asked him as we made our way to the Academy.

"I'm fine," Sam replied. "Everything's fine."

"Are you sure? Because if you're worried about anything. School, the other boys—"

He cut Ness off midstream, "I'm not."

Perhaps wisely, she dropped the subject and surrendered to idle chitchat with Todd instead. I tuned in and out of their conversation as they discussed star formations and planetary alignment.

As Ness and Todd passed through the school's stone-walled enclosure, I gripped the sleeve of Sam's jacket.

"What's wrong with you?" I asked, steering him off the path and onto the lawn.

He shook his arm free. "Nothing. What's wrong with you?"

"Nothing. Why are you acting weird?"

"I'm not. Why are *you* acting weird?"

I rolled my eyes. "*I'm* not," I hissed. "*You* are!"

He glanced over at Todd and Ness, who were ambling towards the main entrance, deep in conversation.

"Sam," I implored, searching his eyes. "Is there anything you want to tell me?"

"Yes," he said solemnly.

I braced myself.

"You're short," he said.

"What?" I frowned.

"You're too short," he carried on. "I thought you'd grow. But now, I'm not so sure… I think that's as big as you're going to get."

I glared at him.

"Don't worry," he said as he patted me on the head. "I'll bet there's surgery you can have for that. I'll help you raise the money." He ducked past me and jogged back towards the path.

I rushed after him, struggling to catch up as he ploughed through a small cluster of boys.

"Sam!" I yelled.

He ignored me.

I watched helplessly as he disappeared through the double doors, kicking aside a scattering of autumn leaves as he went.

I knew I'd lost him.

Resigned, I made my way inside. There was no sign of Sam. There was no sign of anyone, actually. All alone, and apparently undersized, I crept along the dark corridor towards my classroom. The layout was beginning to feel familiar to me now. Or at least I knew where my classroom was, which was good enough.

I reached the door and stopped in my tracks. My palms were suddenly clammy.

Don't be so stupid, I scolded myself. *He's just a boy—*

"What's wrong with it?" a smooth voice whispered

into my ear.

Startled, I jumped out of my skin. I spun around to trace the voice.

Jaxon smiled obscurely at me.

"I didn't realise you were standing there," I spluttered. And then I hastily added, "So, you're talking now?"

"Yes," he said. "I'm talking to you."

His voice was kind of beautiful. It was husky, yet silky at the same time.

"What's wrong with it?" he asked again.

My stomach gave a flutter. "What's wrong with what?" I answered in an inferior squeak.

"The door," said Jaxon, smiling carefully.

"Nothing's wrong with the door," I replied. I glanced at it. "I was just about to...um...go through it."

"You have to open it first," Jaxon said in a wry murmur. "Like this." He reached past me and clasped the brass handle.

I snuck a peek at him as he leaned around me. He wore an untucked shirt and a loosely knotted tie. His eyes smouldered grey and his sandy-coloured hair looked windswept. And he smelled incredible.

"See?" he teased. "You open it, and then you can go through it. That's how doors work."

"I know," I mumbled, flustered. "I am a frequent

user."

His eyes glinted playfully and he stepped aside, allowing me to cross through the doorway.

Inside the classroom, most of the other boys were already seated. I noticed Reuben the Magnificent and his clan occupying the entire back row. There were a few surly looking boys in the middle row, but the front row was entirely empty. I was willing to bet that its vacancy had something to do with the alien girl that now inhabited it.

"You don't have to sit next to me," I said quietly to Jaxon as he moved to the same seats we'd had the previous day. "I don't mind if you want to sit with your friends."

He took his seat and dropped his notebook onto the spacious desktop.

"I'm being a good mentor," he whispered with a grin.

I sat down beside him in the front row. "Have you done this mentoring thing before?" I asked while we waited for Mr. Garret to show up.

Jaxon shook his head.

"Who was yours?" I prompted.

"I didn't have one."

"You didn't have a mentor? Ness told me it was compulsory."

Jaxon stared at his hands, knotting his fingers

together on the mahogany desk. "I don't know…" He pursed his lips. "Maybe I did. I came here two years ago… Hardy was my mentor, I think. I can't remember much about back then."

Wait, I knew that name. "Mr. Hardy?" I repeated. "The teacher in the upper group?" I was referring to the thickset man who had intervened in Sam's fight the day before.

Jaxon nodded. "Mr. Hardy."

"My brothers are in his class. He was your mentor?"

"I don't know. I think so." Jaxon scratched his head. "What is it that a mentor does, exactly?"

I held up my palms. "I think they're supposed to show you around and give advice."

Jaxon laughed. "Do you want me to give you advice, Sophie?"

I smiled. I liked the way he said my name.

"Okay," I replied. "It is in your job description, after all."

He returned the smile. "My advice to you is…" He thought about it for a moment. "Always look both ways before crossing a road."

"There are no roads in Phoenix Holt," I pointed out. "Have you got anything more relevant?"

I'd been joking, of course, but suddenly Jaxon wasn't smiling anymore.

He cleared his throat. "You want real advice?" he said. "Watch out for us."

"Us?" I repeated.

His gaze flickered around the room at our fellow students.

I frowned. "Why?"

"We're not like you," he answered roughly.

I stiffened. What was that supposed to mean?

With that, the classroom door swung open and Mr. Garret bounded in.

"Good morning!" he boomed. "I trust you are all well and rested and ready to embark upon a new day of learning."

There was a murmured response from around the room.

"Excellent!" Mr. Garret declared, stroking the leaves of the potted plant that he kept on his desk. "Then let us begin. Pencils at the ready!"

I shook off the unsettling impact of Jaxon's tone and picked up my pencil, preparing for another day of inane curriculum.

"Now," Mr. Garret said, wide-eyed behind his spectacles, "first order of business: throw your pencils at the pin-board, because we're going outdoors!"

The class, with the exception of myself and perhaps my serene mentor, erupted into cheers and whoops of delight. And if my horror of a unisex P.E. lesson wasn't traumatic enough, a barrage of javelin-like pencils shot over my head, massacring the pin-board that hung from the wall.

I ducked, covering my head with both hands.

The boys hooted in baritones as the pencils speared towards the pin-board. Several even penetrated the target, jutting out like darts on a bull's eye.

I heard Jaxon laugh along with the rest of the class.

"Sophie Ballester?" Mr. Garret called. "Jaxon? Don't you want to throw your pencils today?"

What kind of teacher is he? I wondered in bewilderment. *No, I do not want to throw my pencil, lunatic man.*

But no sooner had I thought it than someone else's pencil whizzed past my eyes, so fast that it was hardly visible.

Jaxon's pencil.

It hit the pin-board and pierced the surface with such force that the entire wall panel trembled.

I sucked in my breath while my classmates burst into applause.

"Jaxon takes it again," a boy in the row behind me cheered.

Then came a voice I recognised. "It was an easy shot. Anyone could have made that if they'd been sitting in

105

the front."

Hmm, I thought to myself. *Seems like Reuben wants to be the only magnificent one around here.*

"Sophie Ballester," Mr. Garret sang out, jolting my attention back to the front of the class.

Does he have to use my full name every time? I groaned inwardly. *It's not like there are any other Sophies here.*

"Yes, sir?" I replied.

"Would you like to throw your pencil? All in good fun."

Not really, I thought, all too aware that I didn't exactly have a prize pitching arm. But I gave it my best and tossed my little pencil at the pin-board.

To my mortification, it didn't fly like the others' had. Instead, it went straight up and straight down, landing on my desk more or less where it had started.

I must say, I enjoyed the three seconds of silence before the laughter exploded. Figuring that I couldn't be any more humiliated than I already was, I rose to my feet, pencil in hand and head held high. I marched to the pin-board and stabbed the lead tip into the target.

I turned to Mr. Garret.

"Shall we go outside now?" I said, my chin tilted upwards.

"Uh. Yes," he agreed, readjusting his glasses. "Right

you are. Lead the way, Sophie Ballester!"

#

I stood outside the main entrance. The air was mild, but a light breeze rippled through my hair. I swept the strands away from my face and gazed out at the autumnal trees. The woodland seemed endless, as though no world existed beyond it. Perhaps it didn't.

Behind me, the manor door opened and Mr. Garret trundled through, followed by the middle group.

I smiled vaguely at my teacher.

He smiled back. "Right-o, boys... and girl," he added. "Follow me." He began pacing along the outskirts of the manor.

I quickly realised that we were heading to the back of the building—a territory where I'd not yet dared to venture.

The stone wall encircling the school stretched much farther that I'd imagined, looping around an acre of grassy space at the back. Beyond the wall, lush green hills soared to the sky, their peaks dusted with a sprinkling of snow.

Jaxon appeared at my side. "You like it out here," he noted.

I laughed under my breath. "Yes."

"Welcome to our first training exercise of the term," Mr. Garret announced, standing before the group. "This morning we will be practising aim, technique, and skill. In other words, *modus operandi.*"

A redheaded boy raised his hand.

"Yes, Lewis?" said Mr. Garret.

"What are our weapons?" the boy asked.

Weapons? I frowned.

Mr. Garret's gaze drifted towards the school building. "You're about to find out," he replied. "Hello there, Mabel!" he called, cupping his hands around his mouth for extra leverage.

I turned to see a doddery-looking lady with blue-rinse hair, a pink shawl, and a string of plastic pearls tottering towards us with a wheelbarrow.

"Hello, lovey!" Mabel yelled back to Mr. Garret.

I immediately recognised her voice from Ness's intercom. And, although I had envisioned Mabel to be a, shall we say, *mature* woman, I was surprised to see just how mature she actually was.

I watched her slowly manoeuvre the cumbersome wheelbarrow towards us. The rusted structure screeched with every step.

"Should we help her?" I whispered to Jaxon.

He gawped at me as though I were totally insane. "No!" He shook his head vehemently. "Mabel doesn't like it when we help." He paused. "Unless she asks."

"Pride?" I guessed.

Jaxon smiled. "The missing sin."

Mabel tipped the wheelbarrow's contents onto the lawn and dusted off her hands. "Archery today, is it, Mr. Garret?"

I stared down at the heap of wooden archer's bows on the grass.

"Indeed it is," Mr. Garret confirmed. "How are you keeping, Mabel?"

"You know me, Mr. Garret," she said sombrely. "I never grumble. No time for it."

Mr. Garret nodded his head in earnest. "Ah, well—"

"Although," Mabel cut him off, her lined face deflating, "I've had terrible trouble with the old toes, lately. *Terrible* trouble."

Toe trouble? I mused.

There was a chorus of sympathy noises from the boys. I got the feeling they'd had plenty of practice.

"Oh, dear me," Mr. Garret uttered compassionately. "You shouldn't have carried that wheelbarrow. One of my boys could have done that—"

"No," Mabel raised her palm, denying him flatly. "You know my motto, Mr. Garret. If I'm fit enough to come into work, then I'm fit enough to operate heavy machinery." She lowered her hand. "Any rate, that being said, I won't be coming back for the bows. I'll be going in for my morning coffee now, and I'll be putting my feet up for the rest of the day. The youngsters can bring the equipment back to my office after they've finished." She beamed, exposing a blinding set of false teeth. "And how are my lovely boys?" She looked fondly amongst the group. "What strapping young lads you are."

I glanced at my classmates. Actually, Mabel was right. They were strapping young lads. All of them. It hadn't been so obvious when we'd been seated in class, but now, standing at full height, I could see that all of the boys were stronger and broader than any group of teenagers I'd ever known.

Maybe it's a product of growing up in Phoenix Holt, I decided. *Chopping down trees, eating hearty meals. None of that low-fat, non-fat, non-dairy, frappe latte mochaccino business of city life.*

"And who is this?" Mabel's focus landed on me. She blinked as though she couldn't quite believe her eyes. "This isn't...? Is this Wilber's girl?"

I recoiled from the spotlight. "Yes," I said meekly. "I'm Sophie."

"Well, Sophie, come over here and let me take a look at you."

I groaned internally as I stepped forward.

"Oh, my, you're a Ballester all right," Mabel gushed.

"Isn't she, Mr. Garret?"

"Yes, she is," he agreed.

Mabel took hold of my hands and planted a kiss on my cheek. I heard a few sniggers from the boys behind me.

"How are these boys behaving?" Mabel asked me. "Are they being kind to you?"

"Yes," I said. "They're nice." Well, what else could I have said? The boys in question were all within earshot.

All of a sudden, Mabel released my hands and glowered at the other students.

"You'd *better* be nice," she snarled, far more aggressively than I'd imagined possible from such a frail-looking woman. "Or you'll have *me* to answer to."

Some of them flinched at her tone.

Her scowl instantly dissolved into a smile. "Okay," Mabel chirped, her sweet alter-ego dominant again. "That'll be all, then." Leaving us in a stunned silence, she toddled off towards the school.

Mr. Garret called out to her again, "Mabel, don't you want your wheelbarrow—"

She raised her hand to silence him. "I can't hear you anymore, Mr. Garret. I'm stone deaf, remember." And with that, she was gone.

Huh. So that's Mabel, I mused.

Mr. Garret cleared his throat. "Right. Shall we begin?

111

Gentleman...and lady...choose your weapons!"

I was almost knocked down in the charge. By the time I'd regained my composure, only one bow remained on the grass.

I guess this one's mine, then, I thought, bending down to claim it. It was heavier than I'd expected, and crafted from smooth, solid wood with a taut string stretching from the top to the bottom. Attached to the bow was a red velvet holster swathing three slim arrows.

"Take your positions!" Mr. Garret hollered.

Without missing a beat, the boys formed a neat line, standing shoulder-width apart and facing the far boundary wall.

Jaxon took his place at the end of line and signalled for me to join him.

"Ready?" Mr. Garret bellowed.

No! I thought, taking the spot beside Jaxon.

It quickly became clear that I was the only one *not* ready. With impeccably timed accuracy, all of the boys straightened their shoulders and lifted their bows.

"What are we meant to be doing?" I whispered to Jaxon.

He glanced at me. "Lift your bow," he said.

I copied his position: bow raised and body straight.

"You see the trees," he went on.

In front of the boundary wall was a procession of tall

oaks. They faced us like an opposing army.

"Aim!" Mr. Garret shouted.

I heard the swoosh of arrows being drawn and bowstrings being eased back.

"Aim for the tree on the end," Jaxon instructed me. "The one opposite you."

I snuck a peek at him. His bow was held high, the string drawn back and the arrow in place. I noticed his eyes squinting in concentration; the muscles in his arm tautened as he held his aim.

Ineptly, I reached for one of my own arrows. The slender dart was tipped with a razor-sharp point and had two red feathers affixed to the other end. I fumbled to lock it into place, and did my best to draw the string back—although what had seemed like a simple act was actually infuriatingly tricky. The tight structure of the bow made any leeway near impossible. And yet, beside me, Jaxon held the pose with remarkable ease.

"Fire!" Mr. Garret commanded.

Before I could even blink, a round of arrows sped across the clearing—just like the pencils in the classroom, only this time on a much grander scale. Almost all of the arrows had speared the tree trunks and were boldly jutting out from the split bark.

I released my bowstring and watched as my arrow soared through the air. It curved to the left and landed in the grass some distance from my target oak.

I may have missed the target, but I couldn't have been more pleased with myself. I'd shot an archer's bow!

Call me Hood... Robin Hood.

"I did it!" I exclaimed.

Jaxon looked to my tree, searching for my arrow. "Did you?" he frowned.

"Yes! It's over there. Look!" I shook my bow in the direction of a patch of grass midway between us and the trees.

"Oh, yes," Jaxon reflected. "I see it. Well done."

I beamed with pride.

"Lewis!" Mr. Garret called. "Steady your arm. You almost missed the target. Even the most minor of mistakes could cost you your life."

So dramatic, I chuckled to myself. *Only P.E. teachers think P.E. is life or death.*

"Reuben," Mr. Garret continued, walking up and down the line like an army general, "good work, my boy. Very precise."

Figures, I thought. *Reuben the Magnificent strikes again.*

Mr. Garret reached the end of the line. "Jaxon," he said. "Very good. *Very* good indeed."

My focus travelled to Jaxon's tree. It was identical to

mine, except his had a slender arrow piercing the centre of the trunk.

I spun around to celebrate, but the look on Jaxon's face made me think twice. His expression was detached. Stony, even. He didn't respond to Mr. Garret's comment, and he stood rigid when the teacher gave him an approving pat on the shoulder.

Why isn't he happy? I wondered.

"And Sophie Ballester," Mr. Garret moved on to me. "Uh... let's see... what can I say? Hmm... well... good try."

"Thank you, sir," I accepted, humbly.

"Okay," Mr. Garret raised his voice again. "Positions!"

Next to me, Jaxon sprang back into his shooting stance.

"Ready!" Mr. Garret called. "Aim!"

I raised my bow and fixed another arrow into place, exuding a little more confidence this time around.

"Fire!"

I released the string and my arrow shot through the clearing. Again it swerved to the left, landing almost exactly where the first missile lay.

"I did it again!" I cheered.

Jaxon tucked his bow under his arm and ran his hand along his jaw. "Well done," he congratulated me. "It's very rare to hit the same wrong target twice in a row." He wrinkled his nose. "Were you aiming for that spot?"

"Nope," I told him, decidedly smug. "I wasn't even trying."

"Very impressive," he mused.

"I know. Who says two wrongs don't make a right? Hey, perhaps if I turn at a ninety degree angle next time, I might hit the tree."

Jaxon gave me a slanted smile. "Well, in light of the fact that *I'm* standing at that ninety degree angle, I'd rather you didn't."

I smiled back. "So, how did you do?" I asked, shading my eyes to scan the clearing. I found his tree beside mine, but there was only one arrow in the trunk. The arrow from his first shot.

"I did okay," he replied, casually.

"What did you hit?" I asked.

"My target."

"The tree?"

"Yes."

I squinted against the morning sunlight. "I can only see one arrow."

"Uh, yes."

"So, where's the other one?" I pressed.

"It's there," he offered vaguely. "On the target." He seemed hesitant, as though he were uncomfortable with the conversation.

116

My eyes widened as I realised what had happened. "Your second arrow split through your first arrow?" As I stared at his tree again, I could see it clearly. His second arrow was projecting out from the trunk, with two strips of the first arrow curving away on either side.

"That is…" I was lost for words.

Mr. Garret, on the other hand, was not.

"Good job, Jaxon!" he whooped. "Tremendous shot."

I felt a prickly tension in the air. I was willing to bet that some of the other boys weren't quite as pleased for Jaxon as their teacher was.

"Again," Mr. Garret commanded. "Positions!"

I raised my bow.

"Ready!… Aim!…"

I stole a glimpse at Jaxon. The breeze tousled his hair, but other than that he was flawlessly motionless. Well, apart from his eyes, that is. They were alive with intensity.

"Fire!"

Jaxon's muscles flexed as he drew the bowstring back. And then the arrow was gone. It exploded across the clearing in nothing more than a blur. Again it hit the target, spearing through the existing arrow and splitting yet another dart clean in two.

I was amazed, completely in awe of him. I took my own shot, uninterested in its result, unable to pull my eyes away from Jaxon.

"You're… *incredible* at this," I told him, dropping my bow to my side.

"Look!" he said brightly. "You hit your target again."

I followed his gaze. All three of my arrows lay on the grass beside one another.

I smiled distractedly. "Hat trick. I wonder if Mr. Garret will recognise my unique skill," I joked.

Jaxon shrugged. "It's hard to miss, really. After all, you are the only one who seems to have that particular skill."

"And you're the only one who seems to have *that* particular skill," I said, gesturing towards his tree.

"No," he replied, looking down to the ground.

I had an inkling that that was as far as the subject would go.

After a brief inspection, Mr. Garret went through his customary praises, then instructed us to collect our arrows.

"Jaxon," he said, "you'll need two new arrows. Go to Mabel's office; she'll have a supply." As Jaxon turned to leave, Mr. Garret called to him again. "On second thought, you'd better get more than two. Get yourself a handful."

Out of the corner of my eye I saw Reuben scowl.

As Jaxon jogged across the lawn, I couldn't help but

admire him. He was, in every sense of the word, extraordinary. He was the most puzzling person I'd ever encountered. And yet, despite his elusiveness, I felt completely in tune with him. I was in rapture, desperate to find out more, yet utterly content with whatever it was that he chose to share with me.

I watched until Jaxon had disappeared from sight. And just as I was about to return my attention to Mr. Garret, a new figure emerged.

Mr. Hardy.

The stocky upper group teacher was followed by a gang of boys, all carrying archer's bows. I spotted Sam and Todd at once, though from a distance I struggled to distinguish between them. Until, that is, one of them shoved roughly past another boy.

Sam, I deduced.

I waved at them, grateful to see familiar faces.

Mr. Garret greeted the newcomers with a smile, but his body language became markedly tense.

Mr. Hardy approached us. "I'm sorry. I wasn't aware that you'd be using this space," he explained courteously. "We can come back later."

I could tell that Mr. Garret wanted to say 'yes,' but instead he went with, "No, no. Plenty of room for all of us. Middle group, shuffle along," he ordered. "Two per tree, from now on."

As requested, we made room for the other class.

I didn't get a chance to speak to my brothers, because Mr. Garret hastily pulled our focus back to the lesson. Though when I did manage the occasional glimpse at the upper group, I quickly discovered that Mr. Hardy was nothing like my own teacher. He was sterner and broader. *Not at all approachable*, I thought.

For a while, I listened as Mr. Garret fielded questions and imparted his knowledge. But my attention went elsewhere at the sound of a commotion.

"Is that your best shot, Ballester?" a boy from the upper group jeered.

I glanced over to see Todd hanging his head in shame while a couple of thickset boys sneered at him.

I felt a pang of sorrow. I couldn't bear to watch Todd being teased like that.

And apparently I wasn't the only one. Sam swung around to face the boys.

Oh, no. Now the only thing I felt was fear.

Slinging my bow over my shoulder, I slunk off to diffuse the situation before it escalated. But I was too late.

"Do you want to see *my* best shot?" Sam challenged, twanging his bowstring.

A robust boy snorted. "You don't belong here," he hissed. I recognised him from the scuffle the previous day. Thompson, his teacher had called him.

"You didn't answer my question," Sam retorted. "I asked you, *do you want to see my best shot*?" He spoke slowly and calmly, but there was a wild fury in his eyes.

"Go on," Thompson sneered. "I dare you."

Oh, no. Don't dare him! My heart leapt into my throat. "Sam, no!"

Again I was too late. Sam swiped an arrow from his holster and fired it at Thompson.

I froze. In the fraction of a second between the release of the arrow and the impact, a whirlwind of questions tore through my mind: Would there be a lot of blood? Would Thompson die? Would Sam go to jail? How often could I visit him? How would I ever survive without him?

And then, something happened beyond belief.

Thompson caught the arrow.

Caught it. In midair! As though it were nothing more than a tennis ball.

He tossed it aside and lifted his own bow, aiming it at Sam.

"No!" I screamed. Before I knew what I was doing, I had aimed *my* bow at Thompson.

Great, I thought. *Now I'll be the one going to jail.*

Muffled behind the hum of delirium, I heard the distinctive swish of bowstrings being drawn back. Not

Thompson's, Sam's, or even Todd's, but every other bowstring in the clearing. And they were all aimed at me.

Sam threw his weapon to the ground and raised his hands in surrender.

"Don't shoot!" he begged. "Don't any of you shoot."

I looked around—first at Sam, then at Todd, then at the swarm of metal tips all pointing in my direction.

Where are you, Jaxon? was all I could think.

An authoritative voice shattered the tension. "Stop this at once!" yelled Mr. Hardy.

"Lower your weapons!" Mr. Garret ordered, shoving his way through the gathering.

Hesitantly, the boys followed his command.

Oh. My. God.

No sooner had I let out a breath than Sam was at my side. He grabbed my wrist and we ran.

And we didn't look back.

Chapter Seven
Gone Fishing

Sam and I didn't stop running until we reached the graveyard. We collapsed onto the grass, panting for breath. For the first time since leaving the Academy, I realised we were alone.

"Where's Todd?" I asked between rasps.

Sam looked back to the path, almost as though he was expecting our absent brother to materialise. "Aw, Todd," he groaned. "Why didn't he follow us?"

"I thought he would," I said. "I thought he'd be right behind us."

"So did I."

I sighed and leaned back against a marble headstone. "He probably wanted to stay out of trouble."

Sam snorted. "And the rest."

I frowned at him. "What do you mean by that?"

He shrugged the remark off. "You know Todd. He likes to keep his nose clean."

"Can you blame him? We shouldn't have run. Ness is going to kill us."

Sam laughed and reclined onto the grass.

I swallowed, my throat dry all of a sudden. "Should we go back?"

"Nah. We're out now. There'd be no point in going back."

"But maybe if we—"

"No," Sam cut me off. "I'm not going back. You go if you want. Be with Todd," he added, folding his arms across his chest while he lay on the grass gazing up at the sky.

I furrowed my brow. "Why did you say it like that?"

"I didn't say anything like anything," Sam answered coolly.

"Whatever," I muttered.

"Shut up."

"You shut up!"

"On second thought," Sam snapped abruptly, "I think you *should* go back."

"Good," I said pettily. "I want to."

Sam closed his eyes against the sunlight. "Good for you."

I stood up and shook the grass from my clothes. "I'm going now," I said. " 'Bye."

" 'Bye," Sam replied curtly.

I had barely reached the path before he called me back.

"Sophie?" His tone was careful.

I glanced at him. He was sitting upright now. "Yes?" I said.

He rose to his feet and strolled towards me.

"I'm now thinking that you *shouldn't* go back to school..." Standing before me on the path, he purposefully avoided my gaze.

I made sure that he saw me rolling my eyes, however.

"Okay," he yielded. "I'm sorry. Sor-*ry*. What more do you want? Blood?"

"No. Sorry is fine. I'm sorry, too, I guess."

Sam stared down at the pebbled pathway beneath our feet. "Can I tell you something?"

"Okay," I replied guardedly. After all, I wasn't sure what would come next.

"Todd's not who we thought he was."

I almost laughed. "Oh really? What is he, then? Short like me?"

Sam's eyes shot up to meet mine. "No," he bit back. "He's perfect height. And if you're not going to take this seriously, then forget I said anything."

I made a half-hearted attempt to suppress my smile. "Go on, then. Spill. What dark secret is Todd hiding?"

Sam crossed his arms. "You won't think it's so funny when you find out." He paused. "Maybe I shouldn't tell you." Another pause. "But I have to tell you." Pause. "Or do I?"

"Just tell me."

He began walking, heading in the opposite direction from the school. I trailed behind him, waiting patiently for him to elaborate.

For a minute or two, Sam said nothing. And then, in a thoughtful voice, he asked, "Am I a bad person?"

"Of course not!" I cried. "You're my best friend." I'd never considered it before, but I supposed it was true.

Anyway, Sam seemed to appreciate the sentiment. He grinned at me.

"Aw, thanks, Soph," he said. "You're my best friend, too. Well, after Todd."

I gave him an ironic smile. "Gee, thanks."

He returned the smile. "Well, maybe if you started putting in the time on X-Box..."

"Second place is fine," is decided. "So, why do you ask?" I said, steering us back to the original conversation.

We stepped over a fallen tree branch and onto a

carpet of crisp amber leaves.

When Sam spoke again, he sounded older somehow. "I don't know. I just..." He exhaled wearily. "It's just that I always thought me and Todd told each other everything. And I mean *everything*. There's no one else in the world who would trust me enough to tell me everything."

"I tell you everything," I argued.

He gave me an incredulous look. "Who's Jaxon?"

I blushed. "Point taken."

"Anyway," Sam continued, kicking aside a mound of leaves as we walked, "that's how it had always been. And now, it's like everything's changed, and I don't even know who my own brother is anymore."

I raised an eyebrow. "Is this still about him going to the apothecary room without us?"

"No." Sam came to an abrupt halt and whirled around to face me. "It's so much bigger than that."

"How?"

Furtively, he peered into the depths of the trees. "He's not who we thought he was." There was a strange conviction to his tone. The sort of conviction that unleashed a shiver down my spine.

My stomach knotted. "Then who is he?"

Somewhere in the woodland I heard a crow caw.

Sam licked his lips. "If I tell you something, do you

promise not to tell Todd?"

My mouth went dry. "I thought you told him everything."

Sam laughed bitterly. "Not anymore." He sucked in a deep breath and blew it out in a puff of air. "Remember yesterday, when we did the, um…" he hesitated, mulling over his word choice, "spell-type thing?"

I tensed and nodded my head.

Absentmindedly, Sam kicked at a tree root. "Um, well, I think it might have worked. Or something."

I stared at him, unsure how to react.

After a long, tumbleweed silence, Sam carried on, "And here's the thing. When I started, um, what's the phrase?"

"Hearing people's thoughts?" I offered.

"Yeah. Right. That thing. Well, when I was doing *that*, I happened to overhear a pretty colossal secret that Todd's been keeping from us."

"I see." I struggled to keep my voice even. "And what was it that you… um, heard?"

Sam rubbed the back of his neck. "Todd already knew."

"Knew about what?"

"All of it." Sam swallowed hard. "He knew about the witch stuff. He knew about Ness, too. He knew that our family has… *abilities*. Wilber told him everything."

My face dropped. How was I meant to respond to that? Talk about information overload. I was surprised I didn't short circuit right there and then.

"What makes you so sure?" I asked meekly.

"Because I *heard* it," he insisted. "I even heard him try to make himself stop thinking. I heard you do that too, by the way," he added shrewdly. "And I heard Todd remembering that Wilber had specifically told him not to tell me. *Me*! And you too. But, I mean, *me*? Why not *me*?"

"Why not me?" I countered.

"Todd knew about this and he didn't tell us. But more importantly, he didn't tell *me*. How messed up is that?"

I flipped my palms skyward.

"And what does this mean?" he went on. "If it's in the family, in the genes, what does that make us? Some sort of *thing*? Like a freaky witch *thing*? Because I sure as hell don't wanna be a thing."

I racked my brain for something useful to say, but no sound passed my lips.

Sam let out a frustrated sigh. "Damn, Wilber. Even from the grave he's screwing me over."

"Hey," I protested. "It's not Wilber's fault."

"He should have told us," Sam muttered. "What are we going to do, Sophie? What are we going to do if we're *things*?" He stared at me, waiting for me to fix this.

Share some wise words, I told myself. *Calm, rational thinking. Perhaps say something profound.*

"So, what games have you got on X-Box?" was the best that I could come up with.

#

Sam and I wandered through the woodland for a long while, not knowing where we were heading but not especially caring, either. We walked in silence, immersed in our own private thoughts. After all, we had a lot to think about.

Sam had said that Todd knew about our abilities. What abilities? Was I a witch like Ness? I didn't feel like one.

And was it true? Could Todd and Wilber have really kept this from us? I didn't like the thought of it. It felt sordid.

It was kind of a relief when Sam finally broke the silence. "Look who it is!" he cheered.

I followed his gaze. It was the tree-carved bird that we'd spotted on our first day in Phoenix Holt.

"Nice beak," Sam commented.

"Let's get a closer look." I grabbed hold of his jacket sleeve and towed him through the undergrowth.

We weaved between the sycamores towards the sculpture. Up close, the bird was even more impressive than I'd imagined. Every detail was immaculate. Its smooth, hollow eyes glinted with reflecting sunlight and its feathers had been sharpened into fine points.

I traced my fingers along the bark, feeling a strange affinity with the carving. I felt as though it had been meant for my eyes only. It was mine.

"Yep," said Sam, "that thing is possessed for sure." He feigned a shudder.

"Well, I love it," I replied. "I think it's beautiful."

"So, it's true what they say," Sam teased. "Love is blind."

I scanned the area. "I wonder if there are more…"

Something amidst the foliage caught my eye. But the object of my interest wasn't another carving. There was a glimmer of red submerged beneath a scattering of fallen leaves.

"What is that?" I muttered to myself. As I approached, I wondered if I'd found roses, or perhaps poppies, but when I brushed the leaves aside, I noticed that the red flower was unlike any I'd ever seen before. The bold, scarlet petals were long and slim, and they floated on the breeze like angel's wings.

"Sam!" I called.

"What? Have you found the bodies?"

I glanced back at him. "I think this is the plant that Ness was talking about. Phoenix Tail."

Sam yawned. "Oh, wow. Tell me more."

I ignored his sarcasm. "This is the flower that only grows here in the holt," I recounted Ness's words. "Remember? The plant that sprouted from the phoenix's ashes."

"Fascinating story." Sam mimicked a snore. "And even better the second time around."

I skipped back to him.

"Hey, at least now we'll be able to find our way home," I said, recalling our first trek to the cottage. "There's the path that takes us straight to it." I pointed to a trail of trodden-down foliage.

Sam smiled wryly at me.

I frowned. "What?"

"You called it 'home'."

"Did I?"

He nodded.

"Oh." I wasn't entirely sure how I felt about my slip of the tongue. If Phoenix Holt was home, then what was Port Dalton? If I wasn't calling Port Dalton home, then what was I calling it? A memory? Or did it quite simply no longer exist for me anymore? And if that was the case, where did that leave Wilber? If I chose to detach myself from Port Dalton, how could I possibly hold onto him? No. I couldn't allow myself to forget the past. Phoenix Holt could never be home.

"Port Dalton is home," I said decidedly.

Sam laughed. "No, it isn't."

"Yes, it is. We grew up there."

"And now we live here," he reminded me.

"But Wilber doesn't."

Sam sighed. "No, he doesn't. But we do."

My expression must have fallen, because he hastily amended his comment.

"Just until I'm eighteen," he said.

We began walking towards the footpath.

"And then what?" I asked.

"And then we can make anywhere our home. We can go back to Port Dalton, if you want. We'll get jobs as fishermen, and we'll live in a huge mansion overlooking the sea. We can drink Champagne on our balcony while we drive golf balls into the tide." He draped his arm over my shoulders as he painted his picture of bliss.

I pulled a face. "Why do we have to be fishermen?"

"Because fishermen get boats."

"Can't we just get a boat anyway?"

"No."

"Why not? We've got a mansion; can't we afford a boat, too?"

"No."

"Why not?"

"Because we're not wasting money on a boat when we can get one for free."

I decided not to point out that being a fisherman didn't automatically entitle a person to a free boat. Instead, I shrugged his arm from my shoulder and said, "Okay. I'll be a fisherman."

"Good. Until then, we'll live in the land that takeaways forgot. But we'll escape soon, I promise. And do I ever make promises that I don't keep?"

I grinned. "Yes. All the time."

He gave me a good-natured shove. "No I don't! I'm not talking about fake promises like I promise not to break your stuff, or I promise not to spray you with the hose, or I promise I didn't steal your diary—"

"I knew it was you!" I exclaimed. "Where did you hide it?"

"I mean *real* promises," Sam went on, "like I promise to keep us together. Those I keep."

In spite of my exasperation, I felt a lump form in my throat. Sam's words served as a bleak reminder of just how close we'd come to being separated, and how much we'd been through to avoid that fate.

A part of me longed to return to Port Dalton and live out the rest of my days as a golf-loving, mansion-owning fisherman, and forget all about our alleged *abilities*.

However, something nagged at my subconscious.

Ness. *She* was our family now. Wasn't she?

And what about Jaxon? I wondered. *If I leave, I'll never see him again. I'll never know him.*

"Hey, Sophie," Sam's voice broke through my reverie. "I think there's something we need to do. We need answers."

I bit my lip. "Answers?" I echoed.

"Answers…" he went on cryptically. "And there's only one sure way to get them."

I had a sinking feeling that I knew where this was going.

Sam flexed his hands. "You know," he began as he inhaled deeply, "I'm in the mood for some herbal tea."

That was what I was afraid of.

#

Sam and I sat cross-legged on the floor of the apothecary room, the book laid open in front of us.

"How about this one?" Sam read from the yellowed page, "The Scorned Lover's Revenge."

I frowned. "Neither of us has been scorned."

"Speak for yourself! *I'm* a scorned lover."

I raised my eyebrows dubiously. "Since when?"

"Um, hello? Suzie Lincoln."

135

Suzie was a girl from Port Dalton who, for years, had followed Sam around like a lovesick puppy—until she met David Ashton. In a matter of minutes, Sam had become yesterday's news, which in turn had catapulted his sudden interest in her.

"You didn't even like Suzie Lincoln," I exclaimed.

"I *did*!" he yelled. "She broke my heart. Ergo, I'm a scorned lover."

"She didn't break your heart," I scoffed. "You only liked her when you couldn't have her."

"You don't know that," he argued. "Maybe I was just shy. An introvert, or whatever they're called."

"You're not introverted, Sam. Narcissistic, perhaps, but not introverted."

"Ha! Joke's on you—I don't even know what narcisseptic means. Anyway, she *did* break my heart."

"Wounded your ego, more like."

"It's the same thing."

I turned the page. "Forget it. We're not getting revenge on Suzie." I inspected the faded ink scripture in front of me. "Look at this," I said. "See No Evil. To temporarily blind your opponent, simply crush the petals of an orchid and say the words 'see no evil'."

"You're not blinding me," Sam groused. He flipped to the next page.

"Okay," he said, "this one could be good. Secrets Be

Known. To uncover the truth you seek, ingest one small drop of the brew you reap, envision the person whom you wish to reveal, and let the mind show you what is known to be real. Additional advice: do not exceed the recommended dose, and keep off tiled floors."

"Tiled floors? You made that part up," I accused.

"No, I didn't. See?" Sam underlined the passage with his finger.

Keep off tiled floors?

"Weird," I said. "So, if we drink the brew and concentrate on a person, we'll find out what we want to know about them?" I was ashamed to admit it, but the concept struck a chord with me.

"Looks that way."

"Whose secrets do you want to know?" I asked, attempting to sound blasé.

"Todd's, I suppose. What about you? If I go Todd, you could go Wilber? That way we'll definitely get to the bottom of this."

"Mmm-hmm," I said. I avoided eye contact, fearful that he might be able to tell that I was more interested in *Jaxon's* secret than Wilber's. "How do you think it'll work?"

"Not sure. Probably the same as the Hear You Me spell. We drink the brew, say a little rhyme, then…"

"Then what?" I pressed.

"I don't know. You hear stuff, I guess."

I sat forward, eager for more. "But what was it like? Did you hear voices, or was it just a feeling?"

Sam pondered over it for a moment. "It was voices. But muffled voices. It was as though you and Todd were calling to me from underwater. I could only pick up on a few words clearly; the rest were just mumbles."

"Were you scared?" I asked.

"Not really." He shrugged. "What is there to be scared of?"

"Well, it is kind of frightening when you think about it."

"So don't think about it," Sam resolved with a nonchalant shrug. "Don't think, just do." He patted me on the arm. "That's some grade-A brotherly advice for you, right there."

"*Don't think, just do*?" I repeated. "That's not very good advice."

"I didn't say it was *good* advice. I said it was *brotherly* advice. Now, I'm going to call out the ingredients and you can go get them."

"Thanks," I said, dryly. "Give me the worst job, why don't you."

"I'm sorry, princess," he shot back. "How cruel of me to suggest you actually get up off your ass and help me. Milk thistle extract. Go."

Grumbling indignantly, I rose to my feet and lumbered about the room in search of milk thistle extract. I found it, the jar filed efficiently on the shelf under 'M'.

"Got it," I called to Sam.

"Powdered orris root," he reeled off the next item.

I trotted to the 'O' section.

"Check," I reported back. I lifted the jar from its space and popped off its lid. Nursing it to my chest, I scooped out a handful of orris root.

We continued with our system until all of the ingredients were gathered in the base of the cauldron. Sam ignited the oil lamp and propped the book open on its stand.

As I watched the mixture slowly turn to mulch, Sam collected two glass pipettes from off the shelves before returning to the cauldron.

"Ready?" he asked, handing over one of the pipettes.

I examined it with a mistrustful expression.

"Just one drop," Sam reminded me. "Then all we have to do is say the verse and think about..." he cleared his throat, "them."

I nodded my head.

Sam went first, dunking his pipette into the brew and drawing the liquid into the glass tube. This time, the mixture was a cloudy orange hue that smelled like lemon peel and sandalwood.

I followed his lead, dipping my pipette into the cauldron. Billows of black smoke rose from the concoction and disappeared into the chimney pipe.

"Stand next to me," Sam directed.

Feeling like the novice that I was, I did as he asked. My palms began to feel clammy.

Sam raised his pipette and clunked it against mine. "Cheers," he said before squeezing a drop of the liquid onto his tongue.

My heart began to race. *Don't think, just do*, I told myself. And with that inner pep talk, I poised the pipette above my mouth and squeezed out one drop.

It wasn't bad. I didn't really taste it, actually, although it did leave a faint herbal aftertaste that didn't particularly bother me.

Sam gestured to the book, and we began to read.

"May the secrets which are hidden deep, be shown to me while I doth sleep."

I closed my eyes. My fingers began to tingle and my body felt weightless, as though I were no longer inside of it.

I need to focus, I thought, woozily. *Jaxon.* I played back our time together, watching it like a home movie on rewind.

It wasn't long before I became swamped by images

spinning through my mind. It was as though I was in a dream that I couldn't quite wake up from. Somewhere in my consciousness, I heard my glass pipette smash onto the floor, though I hadn't noticed it slip from my grasp or seen it fall. In fact, I couldn't actually see anything in the apothecary room. Not Sam. Not the book. Nothing. All I saw was Jaxon, preserved in the scene my mind had settled upon. He was standing in the meadow graveyard, exactly where I had bumped into him the previous day. But as the meadow grew more vivid, Jaxon started to fade.

I blinked, and when I looked again, Jaxon had disappeared completely. Instead, it was *me* who stood in the graveyard. And I wasn't alone. There were dozens of other people, all dressed in black. I saw Sam and Todd there, too, standing with their heads bowed.

At once, I realised that I was watching a memory— the memory of Wilber's funeral back in Port Dalton. I saw Sam take my hand as we stood at the graveside.

And then the funeral began to replay backwards. In a flash of vibrant colours, my entire life with Wilber sped before my eyes. I saw him. Every detail of his kindly face and weathered skin. I saw him celebrating birthdays, singing in his car, reading a book on the pier, nursing a crying baby...

And then all I saw was light—blinding light glaring

into my eyes until I cowered away from it.

I was no longer with my grandfather; instead I was alone, somewhere between my memories of him and the reality of the present.

I blearily made out the shape of the apothecary room.

Was it over?

I couldn't tell whether hours had passed or mere seconds. But I felt a degree of frustration, knowing that my thoughts had wandered away from Jaxon. I became even more dissatisfied when I realised that I was no more enlightened about Wilber, either.

Had I done the spell wrong? And why was my vision still so distorted and my body so unsteady?

I felt a hand grab mine. Distantly, I knew it was Sam, although the only thing I could truly be sure of was that I was moving. No, not moving. Falling.

I hit the floor with a smack.

Lucky it isn't tiled, I thought vaguely.

"Sam?" I tried to call out to him.

I heard his voice return to me, subdued and yet urgent at the same time. "We'll be okay," he assured me.

I felt him squeeze my hand, and then everything went dark.

Chapter Eight

Secrets Be Known

Twelve-year-old Wilber Ballester stood at the pine counter in the Phoenix Holt bakery. The smell of fresh pastries made his stomach growl. He gave it a little pat while Henry the baker slipped a loaf of bread into a paper bag.

"You tell that mother of yours that I'll be wanting payment tomorrow," Henry groused, thrusting the bag into Wilber's hands.

"I'll bring the money first thing, sir," said Wilber. He cast his eyes down to the floor, unruly tendrils of brown hair drooping over his brow.

"I'm sick and tired of you Ballesters," Henry grumbled under his breath.

Wilber walked out the door, pretending not to have

heard Henry's final comment. But he had heard it. He'd heard all the snide remarks and whispers around town.

Peasants, they'd deemed his family. And worse, Witches.

Of course, the Ballesters were good enough to call upon when somebody wanted an illness cured or an ailment healed. Yes, the neighbours would come knocking on their door at all hours of the night—less chance of being spotted at night time—begging for one of Sulinda Ballester's potions.

Sulinda, Wilber's mother, was an apothecary by trade. Of course, no one ever paid her for her service. And she'd never pushed for payment, either. She'd say, "As long as I've got my two children and my happy heart, I've got all the riches I could ever desire."

But a happy heart couldn't pay the debt collector.

Wilber sighed. Although he would never admit it aloud, he was ashamed—ashamed that they couldn't pay the baker. Or the grocer. Or the milkman. Ashamed that his father had left them. Ashamed that his mother was a witch. And ashamed that he was, too.

"Hey, Ballester!" someone shouted his name.

Wilber cringed. He glanced across the cobbled street. On the opposite side of the road, a few trees and lampposts lined the dusty pavement and a dozen or so locals strolled in and out of shops, going about their *business as usual.*

One smartly dressed boy in a flat cap stopped and waved.

I recognise him, *Wilber thought.* He's a few years above me at school.

The boy jogged across the road towards Wilber. He had a rolled-up newspaper tucked under his arm and the sleeves of his shirt were pushed back to his elbows.

"You're Wilber Ballester, aren't you?" the boy asked. His cap was lowered to shade his eyes from the glaring sunlight.

"Y-yes," Wilber stammered.

"I'm Jesse," the boy said, with a self-assured grin. He offered his hand for Wilber to shake.

Wilber timidly obliged.

"I've been meaning to thank you," Jesse told him. "You and your family... Miracle workers," he stated.

Of course, *Wilber thought, suddenly remembering where he had last seen the boy.* He called at the house the other week to collect a remedy for his mother.

"My mother's right as rain after that medicine," Jesse went on. "Sulinda said it'd take a week or two to clear, and she was spot on. This morning, my ol' ma wakes up and she's better than she's ever been! I couldn't believe my eyes. She's been sick for months, and then suddenly... poof!"

Wilber smiled bashfully.

"I'm telling you," Jesse' eyes glinted in awe, "she was sick for months. My mother, that is." He adjusted the rim of his cap. "Anyway, she's gone to the market today. She'll be getting a pound of liver to take to your family. It's her way of saying thank you. But I don't know… liver isn't much of a thank you, if you ask me."

Wilber's face lit up. "I like liver."

Jesse grinned. "I'd say that's lucky, then. And what about you, kid? The carnival's starting tonight. You going?"

Wilber blushed. "Oh, no. I can't."

"Why not?" Jesse frowned. "It's only here for three days. By Monday morning it'll be just an empty field again."

"I don't think I'll be going at all," Wilber admitted.

"Why not?"

"Everyone in town will be there."

"Exactly!" Jesse exclaimed. "You'd be off your head to miss it!"

It's alright for him, *Wilber thought.* People like him. He's popular. I wouldn't be welcome there.

"I'm not sure…" Wilber uttered aloud. "I don't think my mother wants to go. I've got a baby sister, Ness, and she'll be needing to be put to bed early—"

"So come with me," Jesse offered. "I'll be there on my

own, anyway. I could use the company. I'd go raving mad if I didn't have anyone to talk to!"

Wilber fidgeted nervously. "Um..."

"Come on," Jesse cajoled. "You'll have a blast."

"Okay," Wilber agreed reluctantly. "I'll have to ask my mother first, though."

"Sure, sure. I'll come by your house after supper."

#

"Sophie? Sophie, wake up."

I felt a firm hand grip my shoulder.

Was it morning already? No. My eyelids felt far too heavy for it to be morning.

"Sophie." There was that voice again. Who *was* that?

"Huh?" I mumbled.

"Open your eyes," the voice said.

"Ness?"

"Open your eyes," she said again. Yes, it was definitely Ness. And she sounded cross.

This time, I forced my eyelids open.

Where was I? Not in my bedroom, that was for sure.

Oh, no. Suddenly it all came back to me: I was in the apothecary room. *The spell...* A hazy memory of a dream lingered in my consciousness. I had dreamed about Wilber as a young boy. Buying... bread?

I blinked.

Ness glowered down at me. "Concentrate," she told me sternly.

I blinked a few more times, focusing on her bonnet of grey-brown curls.

There was a groggy slur from beside me. I craned my neck in time to see Sam, stirring from what looked like a deep slumber.

"Sam," Ness spoke to him now. "Open your eyes."

"No," he groaned.

"Open your eyes," Ness ordered.

Sam rolled over. "No. I'm sleeping. Crazy woman."

Ness let out an irritable sigh. "You're not sleeping. You're under a spell. Now look at me, both of you."

I did as she said. It didn't take a genius to figure out that we were in trouble. And if she told me to jump, the only thing I'd be asking was how high.

"I'm sorry," I offered meekly, sitting up and rubbing my sore head. "We didn't mean to sneak around in your room. We just—"

"No time for that now," Ness interrupted. "Come on. Up, up, up. We must get out of the cottage."

Sam and I shared a bewildered look.

"You're not kicking us out, are you?" Sam choked.

"Yes. I'm kicking *all* of us out. Now, come along. Quick, quick." Ness helped me to my feet. "I don't know how you managed to get in here in the first place," she muttered, confounded. "The door's been locked the whole time!"

Sam staggered to his feet. "What's going on?"

"Quickly," Ness said again. "I'll explain on the way."

Obediently, Sam and I headed for the duct tunnel.

Ness frowned at us. "This way, dears," she said, gesturing to the far wall.

We stared blankly at her.

A look of recognition spread over Ness's lined face. "Oh," she drew out the word with a little chuckle. "So *that's* how you did it! You've been crawling through the vent. My, my. You must have been terribly determined to get in here. You do know there's a door, don't you?"

I saw Sam's shoulders sag. "There's a door?" he groaned.

"Where?" I asked. I couldn't see a door. Only shelves and jars.

Ness toddled to the back wall and gave it a shove. Before my very eyes, all of the shelves from 'G' to 'J' swung backwards, revealing a black, iron stairwell.

"Come along," Ness beckoned to us. "Make haste."

We slipped through the exit and embarked down the metallic staircase. In single file, we descended the steps, spiralling into the darkness below.

When Ness reached the final step, she called back to

us. "There's a bit of a drop down," she warned. "I'd say it's two or three feet. Then you'll need to take a sharp left, and remember to duck on your way out. We don't want you getting any bumps to the head, now, do we?"

Needless to say, I had no idea what she was talking about. But I was beginning to learn to just to go with it.

So, after Ness hopped off the stairwell, I took my turn. I dropped down, landing beside a heap of chopped logs. Following Ness's instructions, I stepped over the logs, and ducked beneath an archway.

Oh. My. God.

That was the fireplace! I realised as I clambered out into the den. The secret stairwell was in the chimney.

Sam appeared behind me. "No way," he murmured.

Ness gave him an approving smile. "Yes, dear. Now, get a move on."

"Where are we going?" I stammered.

"Averett Academy," Ness replied.

"School?" Sam exclaimed. "No way! I'm not going back to that place."

Ness held up her index finger in a no-nonsense fashion. "No arguments, deary. We're safer at the Academy."

Safer? I froze. "Is it not safe here?"

Ness shook her head. "Not if there are Divellions on our scent." She hustled us into the hallway.

Divellions? *Wait. I know that word from somewhere...*

"Divellions," I sounded it out on my tongue. "Mr. Garret told us about them."

Ness paused at the front door. "Oh he did, did he?" she said, tutting. "Oh well, I dare say it matters now," she muttered. "I knew you'd find out sooner or later. Although I must admit, I didn't expect it to be *this* soon."

"Whoa, whoa, whoa." Sam slapped his hand to his brow. "I'm lost."

"Walk and talk," Ness advised, flinging the cottage door open and leading us into the moonlit garden.

It was dark outside. Well into the evening, I guessed. Sam and I stumbled through Ness's flower garden, unable to see the pebbled path beneath our feet.

"Tell us what's going on," Sam pleaded. "And where's Todd?"

"Todd's at school," Ness answered. "When I couldn't find you two, Todd let slip that you might be in my apothecary room. I thought it was best to send him back to the Academy. He'll be waiting for us there."

Sam came to an abrupt halt. "Todd's at school?"

"Yes," Ness confirmed.

"And you want *us* to go to school?" he said. "Now?"

"Yes. Walk and talk, dear," Ness told him. "Walk and talk."

We began bumbling forward again.

"Did you hear me? I said I didn't want to go back there," Sam repeated as we began our ascent up the wooded slope.

"I'm aware of that, dear."

"So I don't get a choice? Is that it?"

I knew Sam well enough to know how his mind operated. He was the kind of person who would thrive off a battle of wills. It was one of the things that drove our grandfather nuts. Not that Sam was unreasonable, but he was hot-headed and impossibly stubborn. I knew, without a doubt, that if I hadn't been standing right there, and if Todd wasn't currently being held prisoner at the school, Sam would have bolted. He'd have been halfway to China before Ness even had the chance to blink.

As it was, over the years I'd become quite the pro at defusing Sam's flight-risk. He was going to need answers. Convincing answers.

"Ness?" I trotted to keep in stride with her. "Why is the cottage not safe? Please, you have to tell us what's going on."

Ness sighed. "You're right. You deserve the truth…"

I felt my stomach knot.

"It was your grandfather's wish," Ness carried on indistinctly, "and I promised that I'd respect that. I didn't agree with him, mind you."

"His wish?" I echoed.

"Witchcraft," Ness clarified. "Wilber wanted nothing to do with it. And he didn't want the three of you having anything to do with it, either."

Sam stopped walking again. "You spoke to Wilber about us?"

"From time to time, yes."

In the shadows of the night, I saw Sam's body tense.

"So, you were all in on it?" he stammered. "It was all lies?"

Ness met his stare. "Not lies, dear. Well, yes, perhaps they were lies. But they were never intended to hurt you."

Sam laughed resentfully. "Oh, well, that makes it alright, then."

"Yes, I suppose it does," Ness replied. "Keep walking, dear. Walk and talk, remember?"

We shuffled on.

My mind raced. "So you *were* in contact with Wilber?"

"On occasion," Ness admitted. She linked her arm through mine, hurrying me along through the maze of towering sycamores.

"But you told us you'd lost touch with him," I stuttered. "Why?"

Sam raked his hands through his hair. "Because she

doesn't respect us enough to tell us the truth!"

Now it was Ness's turn to stop walking. "You must understand, I had to respect *Wilber's* wishes. He didn't want you finding out about your abilities."

Abilities. There was that word again. "And by *abilities* you mean..." I trailed off.

Ness shot me a compassionate smile. "Witchcraft."

"So it's true?" I asked shakily. "We really are witches?"

"Ballesters are witches, yes."

I hesitated. "All of us?"

"Yes." Ness began walking again.

"Wait!" Sam called after her. "Hold up. So, are you telling us that we had to leave the cottage because we're..."

"Witches," I finished for him.

"I suppose you could put it that way," Ness agreed. "After all, it's not a safe place for a witch to be right now."

"Divellions," I backtracked.

"Yes." Ness seemed disconcerted to hear that word coming from my mouth. "If I'd known you'd found my apothecary room, I would have warned you. Please understand, I'm not angry that you've used the book. After all, it's as much yours as it is mine. However, there are only two safe times to brew a potion, and they are dusk and dawn. Only in the hours between night and day can the potion's smoke go undetected."

I envisioned the opaque billows of black smoke rising from our brew and drifting into the chimney pipe.

"Divellions caught the scent," I guessed.

Ness chortled to herself. "I'd be very surprised if they didn't. Divellions live for power. Even the slightest trace of it would not go unnoticed."

Sam jogged at my side, his face drawn. "What are the Divellions? Cops?"

"Police?" Ness guffawed. "Of course not, Sam. A Divellion is a creature of darkness. A power hunter. If they pick up the scent of a brewing potion, they will stop at nothing to steal the power."

"So these things steal your potions?" Sam presumed.

"No. The potions are nothing. It's the people who make them that source the power."

"Us?" My stomach flipped. "They want *us*?"

"They want your power," Ness corrected. "And the only way to take your power is to…"

"Kill us?" Sam deduced.

"Which is why we'll be safer at the Academy."

Panic rose in my throat. "What makes you think school will be safer?"

"Ah. That's another thing I perhaps should have told you earlier," said Ness sheepishly. "The boys who attend

Averett Academy are—"

"Don't tell me," Sam cut her off. "Witches?"

"No. More like soldiers. *Our* soldiers."

Her words made my blood run cold. "What do you mean?"

"The boys are gifted. You may have seen it in their strength and agility. They are natural combatants, here to protect us and guard what's left of our land."

I thought back to Jaxon—how he'd lifted me clean off the ground when I'd stumbled, how he'd fired the archer's bow with such incredible precision...

"You see," Ness continued, "a long time ago, Phoenix Holt was more than just woodland and hills." She let her aged fingers skim a tree trunk as we strode past it. "It was a thriving town. Of course, the original town was a few miles south of here. It moved after the Divellions claimed the land as their own. Those who survived— myself, Wilber, Mabel Winterford—"

"Mabel?" I choked. "The school receptionist?"

"Yes. And some of your teachers, too, like Mr. Garret and Mr. Hardy. There weren't many of us left, but we made our home in the sanctuary of the woodland, and we joined together to create an army..."

As Ness talked, my head spun. Surely this was some sort of joke? Witches? Divellions? And what did that make Jaxon? Some sort of superhuman soldier? Again I pictured him with the archer's bow. The litheness and prowess of his movements...

No. This couldn't be true.

"Jaxon," I blurted out. "He's one of your soldiers?"

Ness gave me what appeared to be a rueful smile. "Yes."

"But he can't be," I gasped. "He's...human."

"We are all human, Sophie."

Sam's hands balled into fists as we paced through the woodland. "So the school houses these...*soldiers*? And it's all run by witches?"

"Not witches. *One* witch. Me. Witchcraft is unique to the Ballester family, although the others help out where they can. I suppose when the Divellions took over, the survivors evolved into one big, happy—albeit dysfunctional—family."

Sam and I glanced at one another.

He exhaled heavily. "If what you're saying is true, then we can't just wait around here to be..." he let the sentence end there. "We need to get out of here. I think I should take my sister to the train station. I'll come back for Todd."

"Don't be foolish," Ness beseeched him. "There are Divellions on your scent! Besides, there'll be no trains this time of night. We're safest at the Academy."

"We're safest in Port Dalton," he contradicted.

157

Port Dalton. My heart skipped a beat. *Home.* That was what I'd wanted all along. Wasn't it?

"We need to catch the first train out of here tomorrow," Sam decided.

Ness wavered. "If you really want to leave, I can't stop you. Though, I should tell you," she added, "I would be very sorry to see you leave."

We fell into a pensive silence.

I listened to the crunch of leaves beneath our feet as we trekked through the moonlit woodland. Would we really leave Phoenix Holt? Surely getting away from this madness was a good thing, wasn't it? But if I honestly felt that way, then why did my eyes start to sting? Could it really all end here? Would I never see Jaxon again? Or Ness, for that matter?

One thing I did know for sure was that, at that moment, I was grateful for the darkness, because it hid the tears that began to roll down my cheeks.

#

We arrived at Averett Academy in record time. The old building was unlit, and in the darkness, the surrounding wall was more oppressive than it had ever been, throwing long shadows across the lawn.

Sam stiffened as we approached.

"These soldiers," he said, making air quotations around the word 'soldiers', "you do realise that they're out to get me?"

"No." Ness shook her head adamantly. "I assure you they're not. The boys are driven by primal urges. You challenge them, and they strike back. But they will not seek you out. Not like Divellions."

I hastily wiped the tear tracks from my cheeks, anticipating the artificial light of the manor.

"Is there any way to stop the Divellions?" I asked.

"The boys are able if need be," Ness replied. "Although I'm hoping it won't come to that. If we keep out of sight, then eventually the Divellions will move on."

"Can't we stop them?" Sam pressed. "If we're witches, why can't we do something about this?"

"Our power lies in potions," Ness explained. "There are very few potions strong enough to take down a Divellion. Our best chance is with muscle. That's the boys' expertise."

Sam looked crestfallen. "I've got muscle!"

"Not the amount we'd need, dear."

"Then what have we got?" he grumbled. "Potions? Flowery, lame-ass tea?"

"That's not all," Ness disputed as we made our way towards the manor. "There is one other power a

Ballester has. We call it *the link*. Every one of us has a built-in tracking chip, if you will. An inherent link that connects us all to one other witch. It's a natural skill passed down through the ages."

"Like a navigation device?" I offered.

Ness chortled. "Yes. But a natural one." She gazed wistfully at the stars above. "Have you ever been sure about a person's whereabouts, even though it's impossible for it to be so? Every Ballester is linked. My link was Wilber, and his was me. That's why, I suppose, we could never truly lose contact. I always knew where he was, in a roundabout sort of way."

I frowned. "I think it must have skipped a generation, because I don't—"

"Sophie," said Sam.

"What?"

"No. *Sophie*," he repeated, sounding amazed. "I *always* know where you are. I can't explain it, and it's not exact, but I *always* know. That's why I wasn't worried when you went missing from school the other day. I just *knew* you were heading back to the cottage. It's something I've been able to do for as long as I can remember."

Ness chuckled. "Didn't you ever think to question it?"

"No. I just thought I was, like, really smart."

Ness smiled broadly. "That's it, then. Sophie is your

link."

I'm his link? I massaged my temples. *So, I'm a link now? And why don't I have this super psychic link power thing? I barely know how to find myself, let alone someone else.*

Ness heaved the main doors open and ushered us into the school.

We bundled into the candlelit reception area. The vast stairway was ahead of me, and the two lower-floor corridors were to either side.

I took a moment to compose myself. But there wasn't much time for respite, because Mr. Garret came charging down the staircase like a torpedo.

"What's the word?" he asked, joining us at the foot of the stairs.

Even in the weak lighting, I noticed that his complexion was sallow and one of his tufts of snowy hair was standing a little askew.

"No sign of Divellions," Ness reported. "But I'd rather be safe than sorry."

"Quite right," said Mr. Garret. He pushed his glasses up along the bridge of his nose. "I did say, didn't I, Ness, that the children should be told. It wasn't right that they didn't know. I said that, didn't I?"

"And I told you that I would not go against Wilber's wishes," Ness shot back.

Mr. Garret grew flustered. "Yes. Quite right. Of course." Evidently he struggled with confrontation.

"Though I'm not sure you were so eager to abide by those wishes, Mr. Garret," Ness remarked. "Sophie already knew about the Divellions from your lesson."

My teacher groped for a defence. "I was under the impression that it was only the witchcraft we were not to disclose."

Is everyone in on this secret? I wondered, dazed. It seemed that the only person who didn't know who I was, was me. And perhaps Sam.

As Ness and Mr. Garret talked shop, something caught my eye. It was a figure, concealed amidst the web of shadows. I hadn't noticed him before, but Jaxon was standing rigid, halfway up the staircase. He gripped the banister with one hand.

Our eyes met.

In that brief instant, I felt as though I'd shared everything with him. Somehow I knew he was able to see far beyond my eyes. He saw straight through me, decoding what I'd held inside: the panic, the remorse, the desperation...

I resisted the urge to run to him.

But I couldn't bring myself to look away. I was frozen. Only he existed to me. The rest of the world had dissolved away. Somehow he gave me comfort beyond words.

At least, until Ness placed her hand on my arm, jolting my attention back to her as if I'd been struck with a taser.

My breath caught in my throat.

"Sophie, dear," Ness said kindly, unaware of Jaxon's presence. "I'll show you to your bedchamber. And Sam," she said, motioning to him, "you, too. You'll all be sharing a room tonight. Todd's already there."

The words scarcely registered with me, but I trailed behind as Ness, Sam, and Mr. Garret walked side by side upstairs. As we passed Jaxon, Ness gave him a fleeting smile, but nobody spoke. I glanced back at him, hoping for further reassurance—but this time, I only saw dread in his eyes.

Chapter Nine
Whispers in the Night

I dragged my fold-out camp bed across the room, repositioning it as far away from Sam and Todd's beds as possible. Fortunately, the bedchamber that Ness had selected for us was large enough to allow for such a thing. It was more or less how I'd envisioned a manor house bedroom to be: spacious, with high ceilings and ornate furnishings. Above our heads hung a chandelier light fixture, although it wasn't particularly glamorous because three of the bulbs were missing and the one that remained flickered erratically, illuminating the cobwebs that spun from it.

Before our arrival, someone had offloaded the three camp beds into our room, along with a couple of ratty-looking sleeping bags and pillows, and what appeared to be a box of surplus camping equipment: a torch minus the batteries, a mini saucepan, and half a dozen tent pegs.

Yeah. Thanks.

I hadn't had a chance to explore the manor, but it was plain to see that the Academy was enormous. On the way to our designated bedroom, I was astounded by the endless chain of closed doors. Ness singled out a couple of bathrooms and a kitchenette, and suggested that we make ourselves at home. Once we were safely inside our bedroom confines, however, we opted to stay put, not exactly jazzed on the idea of socialising.

Alas, cabin fever set in faster than any of us had expected.

We tried to go to sleep, but mostly, Sam and Todd bickered amongst themselves. I imagined they were both too wired for sleep. I, on the other hand, lay on my slender camp bed, staring up at the dismal ceiling, generally in shock.

Over the past few weeks, my life had changed beyond recognition. So much so that I wasn't even sure who I was anymore. My world had turned upside down, and I knew it would never restore itself. At least, not to how it had once been. I felt like I was floating through some strange gravityless planet, longing for someone to lasso me back down to solid ground.

Who am I?

"Ow!" Todd wailed from across the room.

Oh, that's right. I was a sister. I sighed wearily.

"I didn't touch you!" Sam protested.

"You kicked me!" Todd whined.

"I didn't kick you! I nudged you."

"With your foot!"

I sighed again, louder this time. "Can't you both just go to sleep? It's late."

"I'm trying," Todd complained. "Sam keeps kicking me."

"So move your beds farther apart," I grumbled.

In the darkness of the room I heard a scuffling, followed by another yelp from Todd.

I pulled my pillow over my head, but it did little to block out the fracas.

"What's your problem?" Todd yelled.

"What's yours?" Sam retorted.

"*I* didn't do anything!"

Sam laughed, acrimoniously. "Oh, didn't you? *Didn't you?*"

"What did I do?" Todd protested.

"Go to sleep," I implored them. "Now's not the time."

To my surprise, my request was followed by a few minutes of blissful peace. I should have known not to trust it.

"How would I know what you did?" Sam said lightly, returning to the dialogue as though there'd never been a pause. "*I'm* not the one who you share your secrets with."

Oh no, I thought. *Not now.*

Todd was silent.

"Nothing to say?" Sam noted. "Bet if Wilber was here you'd talk to him. That's how it was, wasn't it?"

"I-I-," Todd stammered.

"Yeah, that's right," Sam interrupted. "The cat's out of the bag. The whale's out of the aquarium. The goose is out of the—"

"Okay, I get it!" Todd cried.

Another silence.

I found myself wondering how that sentence would have ended. I considered asking, until I saw Sam's silhouette sitting upright.

"Is it true?" he demanded. "Did you really know?"

"It's not what you think," Todd replied. He was sitting upright now, too.

"Oh, really?" Sam scoffed. "Did you, or did you not, know that we were witches?"

Todd hung his head. "Yes," he said quietly. "I knew."

For a second, I couldn't believe my ears. It was true. Todd had known all along.

"Then why the hell didn't you tell us?" Sam exploded.

167

"I'm your brother!"

"Wilber asked me not to. He made me swear."

"So?" Sam spluttered. "I'm your *brother*! And it was my right to know, anyway. This isn't just about you and Wilber."

I lay in my bed, watching the scene play out. I didn't feel betrayed like Sam did, but I was certainly confused. There had to be some sort of explanation.

"Why didn't Wilber tell us, too?" I asked.

"He didn't *tell* me," Todd clarified. "Well, not really. I kind of found out by accident."

Sam and I waited for him to continue.

"Do you remember the Orionids a couple of years ago?"

Huh? I wrinkled my nose. *The Orion-who?*

Even in the diffused light, I could see that Sam's expression mirrored my own.

"You mean, like, the cookies?" Sam asked.

Todd carried on, "No. It's a meteor shower. I stayed up late and took my telescope onto the roof to watch for it. Anyway, at about three in the morning, I heard mumbling coming from Wilber's study. I thought it was odd for him to be awake at that time of night, so I climbed down to the ledge to get a closer look. The study window was open, and I heard Wilber on the phone to someone called Ness. At first I thought maybe

168

he had a girlfriend or something—"

"Eww!" Sam and I groaned in unison.

"Right," Todd went on, "but then I heard him talking about *spells* and *witchcraft*. Anyway, I ended up listening to the whole conversation. Normally I don't like to eavesdrop, but I couldn't help it. I thought he'd lost his mind. He was rambling on about a phoenix spell, or something like that. And he kept saying the name Jesse. *Get Jesse. Give Jesse another chance*..."

Jesse, I thought, and frowned. *Where have I heard that name recently?*

"The worst part was," Todd continued, "by the time the phone call was over, Wilber was sobbing. I didn't know what to do. I mean, he was *crying*. I had to do something. So I climbed through the window and told him I'd heard everything. After that, he opened up to me. We talked all night, actually. He told me about his sister, Ness, and his mother, Sulinda. He told me about Phoenix Holt, and he told me that we, the Ballesters, were witches."

"And you didn't think to tell us?" Sam challenged, though his voice had less of an edge to it now.

"I wanted to tell you! I wanted to wake you up and tell you there and then. Both of you," Todd added. "But Wilber begged me not to. He said it was too risky. He was worried that Sam might do something reckless, and he couldn't bear to lose him. He couldn't bear to lose any of us. He made me promise that I'd forget all about it."

"And did you?" I asked.

"Of course I didn't! It was all I could think about. But as the years passed, I let it fade to the back of my mind. In a naïve way, I never thought it would come up again, until…" he trailed off.

"Until we moved here," I finished for him.

Sam let out a long breath, then flopped back onto his camp bed.

It was a while before any of us spoke again.

Sam was the first to break the hush. "I'm still mad at you for lying to me," he said to Todd.

"I know."

"And I'm also kind of mad at you for telling Ness that we'd been in her apothellcary room," he added.

"Apo*the*cary," Todd corrected. "I had to. She was worried."

"Actually, Todd, you've been double crossing me a lot lately," Sam mused. "For starters, I *know* you took my last pair of clean socks."

"I did not!"

"Oh," Sam drawled. "So they sprouted legs and *walked* onto your feet, did they?"

As the boys debated back and forth, I closed my eyes.

I didn't know what to think. I wished Wilber had told me these things himself. I wished he was there to tell me them now. But more than anything, I wished that I could wake up to find that this had all been just a bad dream.

#

As the hours passed by, I was still no closer to sleep. I'd tossed and turned, punched my pillow, counted sheep—all the classics. And yet, I was more awake than I had been three hours earlier. But what incensed me most of all was that Sam and Todd both slept soundly on their side of the room. Their ability to shut off their minds so easily baffled me beyond words.

By the time I'd reached my umpteenth pillow punch, I knew the game was up. I untangled myself from my sleeping bag and sat upright.

Having not had the chance to pack an overnight bag, I was restricted to the stiff pair of jeans and a now-creased white top that I'd been trying to sleep in. I combed my fingers through my hair, doing my best to untangle the tendrils.

I wasn't especially thirsty, but I decided that a glass of water couldn't hurt. And if I made a trip to the kitchenette at this time of night, there'd be little chance

171

of bumping into anyone en route.

Or so I'd thought.

I crept out of my bedroom and my hands flew to my mouth.

Jaxon stood in the hallway, with what I was suddenly able to recognise as the bearing and stance of a soldier. There was a small oil lamp at his feet casting a wavering and subdued orange glow.

"What are you doing out here?" I asked, quietening my voice and closing the bedroom door behind me.

We were alone in the dimly lit corridor. It was the sort of late-night meeting that many would consider 'too perfect'—a cloak-and-dagger sort of time reserved for illicit lovers and secret rendezvous, where the darkness liberates reticent hearts.

"Are you okay?" Jaxon asked. His voice was low and careful.

"I don't know," I replied honestly.

For a short while, we were silent.

"I don't know who I am," I elaborated at last.

Jaxon smiled, although his expression seemed guarded. "I know who you are, Sophie."

I gazed at the planked floor beneath my feet. "Do you know... what I am?"

He thought about it for a moment. "Yes. Do you know what I am?" he returned the question.

172

"I know that you're some kind of soldier," I replied. "Do you know that I'm a..." I struggled to spit out the awful word, "*witch*?"

"Yes."

I studied his face. It held no judgment or shock of any kind. His scar crossed the bridge of his nose and disappeared into the shadows on his jaw.

"Doesn't it bother you?" I questioned.

"No."

"I keep thinking there must be some mistake." I searched his expression for answers. "I'm not a witch."

He met my eyes but said nothing.

I leaned back against the wall. "At least, I didn't think I was. And now, I find out that there are Divellions hunting me—"

"No," said Jaxon, sharply. "No Divellion will ever come near you."

I shot him a sideways glance. "Because you'll protect me?" I guessed, sounding a little more sardonic than I'd intended.

Jaxon laughed huskily. "Yes."

I stared at him for a long moment. Something about his presence made me feel at ease, like the way I felt when I watched breaking waves shatter against the shore, or feathery clouds drift along an azure sky. Amidst all the drama that left me free-falling through the solar system, Jaxon was my anchor.

"You make me feel calm," I found myself telling him.

"Good," he said, watching me pensively. "You've no reason not to be."

"Aren't you worried about the Divellions?" I asked.

"No."

"Ness is," I told him. "So is Mr. Garret."

"Maybe," Jaxon replied, impassively.

I gave him a shrewd smile. "So how come they're worried and you're not?"

He shrugged. "Because I know what I'm capable of."

I felt my breath falter. "And what's that?"

"Whatever it takes," Jaxon said instantly.

Not knowing how to respond, I twiddled my thumbs.

We slipped into a comfortable silence, and as the seconds ticked by, my focus came to rest on the chestnut-coloured wall, which was humbly lit by Jaxon's flickering oil lantern.

"I have something I'd like to ask you," I began. I turned to him, and his eyebrows slanted upwards.

"Do you, now?"

I took a deep breath. *Here goes...*

"I saw one of your sketches yesterday."

Jaxon tilted his head towards me. "Is that so?"

"I hope you don't mind," I added.

"I don't."

"It was of a pier. And it looked so much like the place I used to live…"

"Yes," he said, "Ms. Ballester did mention that you lived there."

My eyes widened. "So, it really was Port Dalton?"

For a second he seemed sad. "Yes."

"How did you…" I hesitated. "Have you been there?"

"I have. Many times."

"When?"

With a melancholy look in his eyes, Jaxon gazed across the shadowy corridor.

"I went there every summer. It was a family tradition. Until my mother got sick and…" he let the sentence trail off, closing his eyes in remembrance.

A huge part of me wanted to push the conversation further. I wanted to find out more. But I knew that was all he could give me. His memories were too raw.

"I'm sorry," I said quietly. In the back of my mind, I recalled the gravestone I'd seen him stand beside. It made me wonder…

"Do you miss it?" Jaxon asked, startling me out of my thoughts.

"Port Dalton?"

He glanced at me and nodded.

"Yes," I told him. "I miss the life I had there."

"Aren't you happy here?"

"It's all so different," I murmured. "*I'm* different."

"How?"

"I'm a…" I hushed my voice, "witch."

"But you've always been a witch."

"I didn't know it, though," I pointed out. "And on top of that, my grandfather's gone, and I'm living with a stranger." I felt a pang of guilt for saying it, but I supposed it was true. It was not that I wasn't fond of Ness, but she wasn't my grandfather, and she was a stranger.

"She won't be a stranger forever," said Jaxon. "I'm sure every day she gets less strange."

He frowned at his choice of wording and I giggled.

"Actually," I said, "I think every day she gets *more* strange. I like her, though."

"It'll get easier," Jaxon promised me.

"Speaking from experience?"

"Yes, as it so happens." He exhaled slowly. "When I first arrived, I felt the same way you do. Confused, missing my family…"

His comment threw me. But what had I expected? That he'd just magically appeared one day from out of nowhere? I knew he'd been at the Academy for two years, but of course he'd had a life before that. He carried his own scars, literal and metaphorical.

"Are you happy here now?" I asked.

There was a long pause while Jaxon brooded over his answer. At last he broke the tension with a roguish smile.

"Right now, this second, I'm happy."

I returned the smile. "Me, too."

"There, you see?" he said, winking at me. "You're going to be just fine."

The tone of his voice struck a place in my soul that no other person could reach. I believed him when he said that I'd be fine. And I believed that it would be, in no small part, because of him.

I slid down the wall and sat on the floor.

Jaxon joined me.

"If you want to sleep," he said, "I'll make sure you're safe."

We were shoulder to shoulder now, creating a closeness that sent little waves of electricity between us, flowing through his body into mine and back again until we were fused together.

I studied him carefully. "What's it like being a solider?"

My question took him by surprise. "I don't think I can answer that."

"Why not?"

He rubbed his jaw. "Because I don't think I want you to know."

"Is it that scary?"

Jaxon laughed darkly. "No, it's not scary. *I* am."

Chapter Ten

Battle Scars

Each year the carnival would come to Phoenix Holt. Red and yellow circus tents would invade Garlands Fields, along with stalls, rides, and the sweet smells of candyfloss and hot, buttered popcorn. It was the one weekend of the year when the whole town would come together to enjoy the festivities.

Well, almost the whole town.

For Wilber, this was a brand new experience. He gazed in wonderment at the scene. The sun had set, and was replaced by blue and red ultraviolet spotlights. A gigantic arched sign stood to mark the entryway, spelling out the word 'carnival' in curvy red lettering. Hundreds of people swarmed the entryway, buying their tickets from scalpers and purchasing snacks from the refreshment stands.

"Tickets!" a stout man hollered to the milling crowd.

"Get your tickets here, folks!"

"Come on!" Jesse said to Wilber, towing him through the throngs of people. "Hey, mister!" he yelled to the man selling tickets. "How much?"

The plump gentleman tucked his thumbs into the front pocket of his apron. He leaned back on his heels, sizing up the two boys.

"One shilling," he decided.

"One shilling?" Jesse mulled it over. "For both tickets?"

"In your dreams, kid," the man replied. "It's one shilling a pop."

Jesse snorted. "Two shillings? Forget it. We'll get them somewhere else. C'mon, Wilber." He turned to walk away.

"Hey, wait!" the man stopped them. "You're not going to get a better price than that. I'm doing you a good deal here, kid." He took two tickets from his apron pouch and waved them seductively at the boys.

Jesse glared at him. "I don't think so, pal," he said, cannily. "There are a million other guys selling tickets around here. We ain't paying two shillings."

Wilber nudged Jesse. "Maybe we should," he said under his breath. After all, they were still less than the full marked price.

"No way," Jesse scoffed. "We'll pay one shilling for both, or we'll walk away."

"Ha!" the man guffawed. "See you boys later. I wish

you luck." He slipped the tickets back into his apron.

Jesse spun around, but before he could take a step, the man called him back.

"Wait a second, kid."

Wilber saw Jesse smile before turning back to face the scalper.

The man cleared his throat. "I'll tell you what. Just because I like you, I'll do you boys a deal."

Jesse, who even at fifteen years old could comfortably hold his own with a grown man, stared him straight in the eyes.

Ready for the haggle, the man produced the tickets again. "One shilling and one half—"

"One," Jesse interrupted, in an obstinate tone. "One shilling or we walk."

Well and truly beaten, the man's lips formed a tight line. "Fine," he mumbled gruffly. "One shilling. Now, give me my money and get gone."

Wilber dug into his pocket.

"I've got this," Jesse said, shoving a shilling into the man's greedy paws and snatching the tickets in exchange.

A grimace spread over the ticket seller's face.

The corner of Jesse' mouth twitched upwards.
"Pleasure doing business with you, sir."

"Get out of here!" The man shooed them away. "Damn kids."

Laughing wickedly, Jesse dashed into the crowd.

Wilber raced after him, completely in awe of his new friend.

He caught up with Jesse at the arched entry. The parched ground was dusted with sawdust, and up-tempo music boomed from one of the nearby tents.

The carnival.

At that moment, Wilber thought it was the greatest thing he'd ever seen in his entire life. The buzz of energy made him feel as high as a kite. He couldn't understand why his mother had never taken him there before. She'd had twelve years to do so.

Oh well, at least she let me come today, *he thought gratefully, remembering how they'd scraped together just enough money to cover the ticket cost and one ride.*

Two rides, now, *he amended, almost bursting with excitement. And one for Jesse, too!*

Nothing in the world could spoil that night.

Or so he'd thought.

"Ballester? Is that you?"

Wilber turned around. Oh, no. His heart sank.

"It is you!" A tall, fair-haired boy sauntered over with two other boys tailing him.

"Hello, Mick," said Wilber.

Mick gave him a heavy pat on the shoulder, causing Wilber's slim frame to hunch forward.

Jesse frowned.

"What a nice surprise seeing you here, Ballester," Mick sneered. "Isn't it, fellas?"

His two lackeys nodded sneeringly.

Mick rubbed his chin. "So, you working tonight, Ballester?"

"W-working?" Wilber stuttered.

Jesse dipped his flat cap over his eyes and muttered irritably under his breath.

"Yeah, working," Mick went on with a snide smile. "You work the carnival, right? You're the freak show, aren't you?"

His friends cackled with laughter.

Jesse scowled. "Lay off him," he warned Mick.

The older boy gave him a fleeting glance, then smirked crookedly at Wilber. "So?"

"I-I don't w-work here," Wilber stammered.

"Too bad," said Mick. "But if you're searching for a career, I'm sure the carnival would snap you right up. A filthy witch like you."

"Hey," Jesse snapped. "That's enough!" He slammed his palms into Mick's chest.

Startled, Mick staggered to regain his footing. When he noticed his hangers-on watching, he straightened his shoulders, towering over Jesse.

"You wanna take me on?" Mick hissed. He let out a

mocking laugh.

Jesse flexed his hands, more blasé than cowed. "Okay."

Wilber stood rigid, his face ashen. "Jesse," he urged, "let's just go."

"We're not leaving," Jesse told him.

Mick's lips curled up over his teeth. "The freak's right," *he spat. "It's time for you to leave." He dived past Jesse and pushed Wilber to the ground.*

Wilber landed on his hands, wincing as mud and sawdust pierced the skin.

I should never have come here, *he realised.*

He gingerly clambered to his feet, just in time to see Jesse swing his fist at Mick.

A stream of blood exploded from Mick's nose, gushing down his face like an opened faucet.

"He broke my nose!" Mick wailed.

"Holy crap!" Jesse cried. "Okay, now we can leave!"

Jesse and Wilber pelted into the carnival, weaving in and out of the stalls as fast as their legs would carry them.

#

I awoke to the sound of screaming. Deep, bloodcurdling screams of agony.

"Sam!" I cried out.

It was him. I knew it was him.

I untangled myself from my dream. As hazy as it was, I remembered Wilber. *Secrets Be Known*, the name of the spell turned over in my mind.

It took me a few seconds to work out where I was. I realised that Jaxon was gone, and I was alone on the hard corridor floor.

Another cry of pain came from the bedroom.

I scrambled to my feet. "Sam!"

Stumbling over myself to get into the room, I came face to face with a sight that terrified me to my core.

Sam, lost somewhere between dreams and consciousness, thrashed on his camp bed, projecting the most chilling cries I'd ever heard. Stooped over the bed, Jaxon pressed his forearm against Sam's chest, pinning him down.

"Stop!" Sam pleaded, lashing out at the air around him. "Tell them to stop!"

Across the room, Todd stood frozen with his back pressed up against the wall.

"What's happening?" I cried, rushing over to the camp bed.

Sam broke free of Jaxon and struck out as us blindly. "Get away from me!" he shouted. "I have to stop them!"

I grasped Sam's shoulders and shook him. "What's wrong?" I called. "Can you hear me?"

His eyes were rolled back, but I noticed a flicker of recognition at the sound of my voice.

"They're going to kill them," he choked.

"Wake up," I ordered, speaking steadily and clearly. "I think you're still under the spell. I think we both are."

Sam's hands trembled, but he lay still now. "We have to stop them. They think they can beat them—"

"Wake up," I said again. "Open your eyes."

I watched him struggle to bring his eyes to focus. Beads of sweat glistened on his brow.

I glanced helplessly at Jaxon, who stood steadfast at my side. His expression was unreadable, but I could tell from his rigid stance that he was as alarmed as I was.

Sam let out another earth-shattering howl.

With that, the bedroom door flew open and Ness hurried in. Her wispy hair was in rollers and she wore a long purple dressing gown tied at the waist.

"Stand back," she ordered.

We did as she asked.

"Do you remember the name of the spell you did?" Ness asked me, carefully lifting my brother's eyelids and inspecting his pupils.

"It was called Secrets Be Known," I told her.

Ness pressed her forefingers against the point between Sam's eyebrows. "Wake up. You're not there, you're here. Your name is Sam Ballester, and you're in

186

Phoenix Holt, living with your Aunt Ness. Your sister and brother are here with you. Can you tell me their names?"

"Sophie and Todd," he replied in a slurred voice.

"Very good, Sam," Ness told him. She took hold of his trembling hand and squeezed it gently.

"Can you feel that, Sam?" Ness asked him.

"Uh huh," he said, his eyelids lifting and dropping in constant motion.

"Who is holding your hand?" Ness persisted. "Do you know?"

"You," he said.

Ness exhaled in relief. "Good. Wake up, now, dear."

Since the thrashing had stopped, Sam looked immobilised, exhausted, and weakened.

"Is he okay?" Todd asked from across the room.

"He'll be fine," Ness assured us. "Sam? Can you tell us what you saw?"

His eyes opened slowly and he stared up at us with rueful sorrow. "They went," he murmured. "They promised Wilber they wouldn't go, but they left us with him while they went to hunt the Divellions. They think they're going to win..."

"Ah," Ness said as she perched on the edge of his camp bed. "Your parents."

When Sam spoke again, something about his tone

seemed almost delirious, as though he still wasn't entirely with us. "They've gone to fight the Divellions, but I know they won't come back for us."

Suddenly it occurred to me, he hadn't thought about Todd during the spell. *He wanted to know what happened to our parents,* I realised. *That's the secret he wanted to reveal.* I couldn't blame him. In fact, if I'd thought of it myself, I would have done the same thing.

"Okay, dear." Ness mopped his brow with the sleeve of her dressing gown. "There, there. It's okay."

"Our parents were killed by Divellions," I murmured, more for my own benefit than for anyone else's.

Ness cast her benevolent gaze at me. "I'm so sorry. So very sorry." She let out a long breath. "I'll prepare a brew to reverse Sam's spell. I think it's safe to say he doesn't need to see anymore." She hesitated. "What about you, Sophie? I can make enough of the remedy for you, too, if you so require it."

Perhaps I should have jumped at the offer. After all, I didn't want to endure what my brother had. And there was not much I could learn about Wilber that would make any difference now. But I found myself refusing Ness's offer all the same.

I watched as Sam stared woozily around the room.

"Are you sure?" Ness tried again. "Sometimes these spells have a way of baring a little *too* much of the truth."

I glanced at Jaxon. There was a pleading, almost desperate look behind his smoky eyes. I knew he thought I was making a mistake—especially after witnessing what had happened to Sam. But it didn't change anything. I was going to see the spell through, whatever it unveiled.

#

It took almost an hour for Sam to completely calm down. And for a while after that, I wondered if he was a little too subdued. But gradually he became more like himself. More human. We all did. In many ways it was a relief to finally know the truth about our parents, no matter how awful that truth may have been.

By mid-morning Sam and Todd had joined Ness in her office, waiting while she prepared the brew to counteract Sam's spell. She was certainly right about one thing: he didn't need to see anymore.

As for the rest of the school, with the threat of Divellions still at large, lessons were cancelled—at least, lessons in the traditional sense of the word. With the exception of Sam, Todd, and myself, the students were scheduled for a day of Intensive Crisis Training. I didn't really know what that meant. As near as I could figure, it was an insanely rigorous P.E. lesson. The kind of P.E. lesson that would have brought on a mysterious stomach ache if I hadn't already been excused. I breathed a sigh of relief when Mr. Garret suggested that I 'watch and observe today.'

Jaxon, on the other hand, had not been excused. But before the training began, he took me on a tour of the manor, showing me around the rooms I'd not yet seen— including his own bedroom. I couldn't hide my surprise when I caught sight of it. It was a fraction of the size of the other rooms. It was small and rectangular, with a narrow bed pushed against the wall, a wood floor, and a battered mahogany wardrobe. A solitary strip of daylight crept in through a vertical aperture in the wall—for all the good it did in that dreary confinement.

At least, it *was* dreary, until I spent some time there and began to see it in a completely different way. In fact, we ended up staying in his room until it came time to head outside. And it was nice—we talked and laughed, mostly about school stuff, like Mabel and the other boys in middle group. When it came time to leave, I made a quick dash to my own room to collect my notebook and pen before hurrying back to meet Jaxon at his chamber.

At the door, I twisted the handle and stepped inside.

I gasped.

Jaxon was at his wardrobe. His shirt had been tossed

onto his bed. He stood with his back to me, exposing olive skin from the waist up. But what I saw was a thick, jagged scar trailing along his shoulder blade and diagonally across his back until it reached his waist.

Jaxon glanced at me, then hastily shrugged into a clean shirt.

Mentally kicking myself, I covered my mouth. I knew it was futile to hope that he had not heard my shocked reaction.

Of course he had heard.

"I'm sorry," he said, quickly buttoning his shirt. "I forget, sometimes. I'm sorry you had to see that."

"No," I replied quickly. "*I'm* sorry. I didn't mean to... I should have knocked."

Jaxon licked his lips. "So it scared you."

"No," I told him, honestly. "I just... I didn't know. How did it happen?"

He gave me a doleful smile. "Battle scars."

I took a step closer. "Did it hurt?"

He exhaled. "At the time, maybe. I don't remember." He turned away from me, pretending to sort through the loose papers on his desk.

I moved towards him and gently placed my hand on his back. I could feel the groove of the scar beneath the thin shirt.

Jaxon froze.

"Am I hurting you?" I asked.

He let out a quiet breath. "No."

He turned around slowly, catching my hand in his. Our fingers linked together like missing pieces of a jigsaw puzzle.

As I found his charcoal eyes in the dim light of the room, I couldn't help but wonder, what else had the battle done to him? Where were the scars that couldn't be seen?

Chapter Eleven

Combatants

By mid-afternoon I'd resorted to sitting on a patch of grass at the back of the school, watching the groups train.

According to Ness, last night Mr. Hardy and some of the boys had executed a raid on the cottage, gathering a bag of essentials to keep us going until god only knows when. For me, they'd heaped together a couple of pairs of jeans and tops, along with my wash bag and towel. I was less than pleased at the thought of them rifling through my personal belongings, but simultaneously overjoyed by the luxury of clean clothes and toiletries.

Unfortunately, however, the troop had neglected to pack my jacket, which proved to be an issue when sitting outdoors on an overcast September afternoon.

I rolled the hem of my top around my hands, shivering intermittently. A more sensible person would have retreated indoors at that point. But I'd come to accept that my sensibleness was with my jacket— somewhere very far away.

Although I had to admit, sitting outside wasn't all bad. The views from behind the school were breath-taking. When I'd been there for archery the day before, I hadn't had the chance to truly appreciate the scenery. Even on a grim day such as this, the hills looked fresh and vibrant green, and the rolling woodland was layered with the colours of autumn.

And then, of course, there was Jaxon. I had to admit, he was fun to watch. Especially when it came to archery. It was incredible to see him operate. He would start with a dozen arrows in a holster strapped to his back, then make shot after shot after shot without even so much as a pause in between. Each arrow would hit the target tree, severing through its predecessor with impeccable precision.

At one stage, I timed him. I'd scarcely made it to ten seconds before he'd fired every single arrow from his holster. That was less than an arrow per second!

I admired how naturally the ability came to him. His movement was fluid and seemed effortless. And I knew from firsthand experience that the bows were not the easiest instruments to manoeuvre. He was, I decided, quite extraordinary.

It quickly became apparent, however, that some of the other boys didn't share in my esteem. Reuben the Magnificent, for one. Several times throughout the day, I caught him glowering at Jaxon.

But Jaxon didn't once return the stare. He didn't speak to him, either. Or to anyone, for that matter.

After the archery portion had finished, Mr. Garret collected the bows and gave the boys a five-minute break before the next training exercise.

Jaxon collected what was left of his arrows from the tree, then jogged across the clearing and crouched on the grass in front of me.

"Are you cold?" he asked.

"No," I said, attempting to sound nonchalant—a feat that was tricky to do above my chattering teeth.

Jaxon smiled, his shimmering eyes the same wintery hue as the brewing rain clouds.

"You're really good at this," I told him, gesturing to the now-abandoned glade.

He shrugged.

"No, you're *really* good," I said.

"It is what it is," he replied vaguely.

I frowned. "But, you're the best—"

"If you're cold I can get you a jacket."

I hesitated. Was he trying to change the subject?

"It's okay," I said. "I'm fine."

All of a sudden, something came hurtling towards us; it was a long wooden pole soaring through the air, on course for my head.

I braced myself for the impact.

With lightning speed, Jaxon swivelled around and caught the pole mid-air. His knuckles turned pale as he steadily gripped the centre.

We looked up to see Reuben the Magnificent staring us down from across the glade. Dark, sunken circles framed his eyes, and his matted black hair fell heavily over his brow.

I let out a shaky breath. *Jerk*, I thought.

"Break time's over," Reuben barked.

Jaxon locked eyes with him—for a second, they reminded me of animals in the wild. And for a second, I felt afraid.

A look of pure ferocity crossed Jaxon's face; it was an anger that I hadn't witnessed in him before. His grasp began to bow the pole.

"Hey," I whispered, tugging at his sleeve. "It's okay." His arm felt like steel beneath my fingers.

He tore his gaze from Reuben and turned to me. For the first time, I noticed that his pupils had engorged into two black vortexes. He was trembling, too.

"Everything alright over there?" Mr. Garret hollered, peeking out from over the rims of his spectacles.

Some distance away from us, Reuben sneered. "Everything's fine, sir."

"Good-o," Mr. Garret beamed. "Lads, pair up and we'll begin combat."

My hands slipped away from Jaxon and he made an instant beeline for Reuben. Their pairing didn't need to be confirmed aloud—it was a foregone conclusion. Though I, for one, wished it wasn't so. Especially when I caught sight of the playing-to-win look plastered all over Reuben's smug face.

It sent a whole new shiver over my skin.

Squared up to each other now, Reuben twirled his staff, smiling menacingly while Jaxon stabbed his weapon into the ground.

On Mr. Garret's command, they began.

The sparring was like nothing I'd ever seen before. It was as though I was watching two Roman gladiators combat, only much, *much* faster.

I was afraid to blink. Jaxon ducked and spun with ease, his staff thudding and clunking against Reuben's as they battled. There was not a moment's respite. Every move was swifter and more unexpected than the last.

I knotted my fingers through the blades of grass, terrified that at any second, Reuben could strike a fatal blow. They were moving faster and more purposefully

197

than any of the other boys. I kept hoping that Mr. Garret would notice and put a stop to it. But he didn't. He wandered between the pairs, observing quietly.

And then it happened.

With a forceful smack, Reuben knocked the pole out of Jaxon's hands. It hurtled into the air and landed several metres away from them. Not that Jaxon had a chance to retrieve it, anyway. No sooner had the weapon left his grip than Reuben was upon him. He pressed his staff to Jaxon's throat and drove him to the ground.

"No!" I cried, leaping to my feet. "Don't!"

The other boys paused and looked over to see what all the commotion was about.

I rushed to where Reuben had Jaxon pinned to the grass.

With all my might, I yanked at Reuben's arm. But, unaffected, he propelled me away as though I were nothing more than a pesky fly.

As I stumbled backwards, I saw Jaxon's eyes darken. He thrust the pole away from his throat, ramming it into Reuben's chin before pouncing to his feet.

"Stop!" Mr. Garret ordered. "Hold your tempers!"

Both boys shook with wild rage.

Mr. Garret positioned himself between them. "What seems to be the problem?" he asked calmly.

"*Him*," Reuben seethed. "Getting that girl to help him."

"Mr. Garret," I spluttered, "Reuben went too far. He was trying to—"

Reuben snarled at me.

"He's growling at me!" I exclaimed, pointing an accusing finger at my new rival.

Jaxon lunged at him.

"Stop!" Mr. Garret commanded, jamming his arm between them. Then, in a lulling voice he said, "Hold your tempers, gentleman. Remember what I've taught you. Deep breaths."

Jaxon's body began to quake and my heart started to race.

"Hold him!" Mr. Garret said at once.

The redheaded boy Lewis and his friend Carlton threw their arms around Jaxon, pulling him to the ground.

Reuben smirked.

"What are you doing?" I cried. "Let go of him!" I tried to rush forward, but Mr. Garret held me back.

"Nothing to worry about, Sophie Ballester," he said, trying not to sound anxious. "Perhaps it would be wise for you to head inside until it's passed."

The boys pulled Jaxon towards the trees. He glanced over his shoulder at me—although I got the feeling that he could no longer see me.

#

By the time I got into the manor, my hands were shaking and my stomach was in knots. What had happened out there? Why had they taken Jaxon away like that?

Because he's... I swallowed. *Dangerous?*

I hurried up the staircase and made a left for my bedroom. My footsteps followed me in a ghostly echo as I made my way along the wood-planked corridor.

I slipped into my room. It was empty, and our sleeping bags remained bunched and crumpled on our camp beds.

Sam and Todd must still be with Ness, I presumed.

From the window, I could see the misted hilltops and a bank of grey clouds looming in the distance.

Breathe, I told myself. The handy thing about countryside living was the calming effect of the endless greenery. And to someone who'd grown up with a not-so-spectacular window view of generic houses, the picturesque scenery was one massive advantage that Phoenix Holt had.

Actually, when I really thought about it, what had I truly left behind in Port Dalton? It wasn't as though I'd had a huge group of friends or anything. So, what else was it? The sea? Maybe. But substituting the sea for hills and woodland wasn't such a bad trade.

Wilber.

I've got news for you, I scolded myself. *Wilber isn't in Port Dalton anymore.*

All of a sudden, it was as though someone had thrown a bucket of cold water over my head.

Wilber wasn't there. And he never would be again— no matter how much I wished it to be so.

This wasn't about Phoenix Holt, or even Port Dalton, for that matter. It was about *me.* I needed to find some way to let go, or else I feared I'd waste my life clinging to a world that simply didn't exist anymore. I had to figure out a way of holding onto Wilber's memory without letting it hold onto me.

It reminded me of a picture I'd once seen in an art book of a rose suspended inside a block of ice. That was me, frozen in the preservation of Wilber's memory. The irony of it was, if I could find a way to melt the ice, there was a chance that I would flourish with the water it created.

I crawled into my camp bed and pulled the nylon sleeping bag up over my head.

Please be okay, Jaxon, I urged silently.

And that was the last thing I remembered before I

drifted to sleep.

#

*As the carnival's stalls began to close up for the night,
Wilber and Jesse sat on the dusty ground, sharing a bag of
popcorn. They leaned against a fence—the cut-off point
to Garlands Fields and as far away from the carnival as
they could be without actually leaving its perimeters.*

*After the run-in at the entrance, the boys didn't see
Mick and his gang again. Wilber considered it a lucky
escape. Even with the incident fresh in his mind, this had
been the best night of his life.*

*He and Jesse had been on a dozen rides—most of
which they'd snuck onto without paying. Wilber would
have never normally done such a thing, but with Jesse it
was like a game.*

*There was something thrilling about walking for one
night in Jesse' shoes—something that made Wilber feel
alive inside. It gave him a rush of excitement to be so
carefree and rebellious. He never wanted it to end.*

*Jesse tipped the last of the buttered popcorn into his
cupped hand and offered some to Wilber.*

*Wilber took a couple of pieces and popped them into
his mouth.*

"We should ask the candyfloss lady for a handout,"

Jesse mused. "The stalls will be packing up soon. For sure she'll give us the leftovers, right?"

Wilber groaned. "I couldn't eat another bite!" He wasn't used to gorging so indulgently. However, he was starting to notice that Jesse had an insatiable appetite for everything: fun, food, life... Wilber admired it. Idolised it, in fact.

Jesse screwed up the popcorn bag and tossed it towards a nearby metal waste bin. The balled-up bag soared neatly into the target.

"I've always got room for more," Jesse said and grinned. "Besides, we've got to live it up while we can. This is our summer holiday!"

Wilber's ochre eyes glinted. "It's the best summer holiday I've ever had."

Jesse picked up a stick and trailed it through a patch of sawdust. "If you think this is good, I know a fairground that's ten times the size of this." He drew out the word 'ten' with wide-eyed enthusiasm. "And the best part is, it's open all summer long!"

Wilber sat forward eagerly. "Can we go?"

"Sure! But not this year, though. Me and my mother go every summer. This is the first year we've missed it. We cancelled because she's been so sick. Until your mother Sulinda fixed her up with that herbal medicine. She's as fit as anything now, so I said to her, Let's go. Let's pack a bag and get out of here, old gal. *Am I wrong? I'm not wrong, Wilber. Still, she said..." Jesse put on a high pitched, nagging voice,* "Will you keep quiet, Jesse? If I've told you once, I've told you a thousand times. It's too late to go this year. I've got to pay the bills, blah, blah, blah..." *He slipped back into his normal tenor. "Could have been 'cause I called her old, though. But next summer the old gal reckons we can go for two weeks. Maybe more if I play my cards right. And you can come along, too. Bring your mother and sister, if you want."*

"I'd like that," Wilber exclaimed. *"Do I have to bring my family, though?"*

"No, you don't have to. Why? Don't they like this scene?"

"It's not that..." Wilber trailed off. He winced at what he was about to say. "It's just... I think I want to get away from them. Just for a while," he added, looking down at the dusty ground.

Jesse frowned, but his voice remained neutral. "You fight a lot, or what?"

"No. Nothing like that." Wilber paused. "I love them. It's just... sometimes I wish I could be part of a normal family."

"No such thing as a normal family," Jesse laughed. "Besides, what mother could be better than yours? The woman's a miracle worker."

"That's exactly it!" said Wilber, flustered. "We're cursed. You hear what people call me, don't you?" He lowered his voice. "Witch."

Jesse, who had been idly drawing patterns on the ground with the stick, stopped and looked Wilber in the eyes.

"Near as I can figure," he said, "you and your family are good people and you do good things. If that means you're a witch, then I sure as hell wish I was one, too."

Wilber let out a weighty sigh. "But the people—"

"I don't give a damn about the people," Jesse interrupted. "And neither should you. Your mother is a good person, Wilber, and don't you forget it." He resumed trailing the stick along the ground. "Now, are we all going on our summer holiday next July or not?" He shot Wilber a boyish grin.

Wilber smiled.

"That's more like it, kid." Jesse reached over and ruffled his hair.

Wilber shrugged him away in good humour. "So, where is this place that has a fairground all summer long?"

Jesse' eyes lit up. "It's half a day's travelling from here, but we get a sleeper cabin on the train and you're there in no time. It's right by the sea and always smells like salt water and toffee." He closed his eyes in bliss. "It's called

Port Dalton."

"Port Dalton," Wilber mused. "Sounds nice."

" 'Nice' isn't the word. When you see it, you're never gonna want to leave."

"And you promise I can go?" Wilber asked hopefully.

Jesse laughed. "Yeah. I swear."

"I wish I had a brother like you," said Wilber.

"Ah," Jesse said as he patted him on the shoulder. "You've got a sister, though. Me, I've only got my mother."

"What about your dad?"

Jesse picked up his stick again and began tracing more patterns into the ground. "He went off to war when I was a baby. He never came back. I think he was probably a really good guy."

With that, a piercing scream sliced through the carnival, followed by a ripple of cries, each one more harrowing than the last.

Wilber and Jesse leapt to their feet.

"What's h-happening?" Wilber stammered.

"I don't know," Jesse murmured. He stared into the carnival.

It was as though a tornado had just struck, instantly devastating everything in its wake. Stalls were overturned and the distant Ferris Wheel groaned and teetered unsteadily. The florescent lamps no longer lit the trodden-down grass with colourful rays, but instead began crashing to the ground one by one, shattering on the hard-packed dirt in explosions of glass.

In the pit of his stomach, Wilber knew what was coming. And he knew it was coming for him.

"I think it's a gang!" Jesse yelled. "Quick, Wil—over the fence! We'll cut through the fields!"

But Wilber didn't budge. "They're coming for me," he said grimly.

Jesse grasped his arm. "No, Wilber, they're not coming for you. They're rioting."

Wilber stared vacantly at the destruction, his body quaking in fear.

"I can't outrun them," he whimpered.

Jesse hauled him towards the fence. "Listen to me!" he shouted. "We have to get out of here. Now!"

Wilber dropped to the ground, burying his head in his knees and wrapping his arms around his legs. "No! No!" he wailed. "They're coming for me! I'm the weakest! They're on my scent!"

Jesse heaved him back upright. "You're talking crazy! No one's on your scent, buddy. I'll look after you, okay?"

And then, in the distance, Wilber saw them—the monsters he'd feared his whole life. The monsters that his mother had sworn were long extinct.

Divellions.

Three had come for him. Their skin was like leather,

red and black as though it had been singed, surrounding bulging bloodshot eyes and twisted faces with long, jagged teeth. Their ogre-like bodies were shrouded in rags, and they started towards the boys in swift, feverish movements.

Wilber clung to Jesse' arm.

"It's okay," Jesse reassured him, his voice wavering slightly. "I'm going to get you out of here, you got that?"

Wilber nodded, tears spilling freely over his cheeks.

"You think you can get over the fence?"

"No," Wilber whimpered. "It's too high."

"Okay..." Jesse thought about it for a moment. "There's a gap down there, at the bottom. Can you fit through it?"

"No," Wilber choked, "I can't!"

"Well, you're going to have to try," Jesse told him. "You're going through the fence, and I'm going to hold off these...things. Then I'll be right behind you. But don't stop running until you get home. You hear me?"

"They're too strong," Wilber protested. "I can't leave you here alone with them!"

"The hell you can't!" Jesse argued. He hauled Wilber to the fence, and with a forceful shove, he pushed him through the gap.

Wilber scrambled onto the grass on the other side of Garlands Fields.

"Jesse," he pleaded, "you can't fight them. They're too

strong."

Jesse peered at him through the gap. "Don't worry about me. I'll hold them off until it gets too dicey, then I'm gone."

"But—"

"I know what I'm doing," Jesse insisted. "I'll be fine. Like I said, I'll be out before they get a look in. Hell, if my old mother sees a scratch on me, she'll know I've been scrapping again, and she'll be so mad she'll cancel Port Dalton 'til I'm twenty-five," he joked blithely. But there was no humour in his eyes.

A low, hissing sound came from somewhere beyond the candyfloss stall.

"Jesse!" Wilber cried from the other side of the fence. "Come with me!"

Jesse didn't move. "Go!" he shouted at Wilber. "I'll be right behind you. Run!"

And so Wilber ran.

But for Jesse, trapped inside the carnival boundaries, there was no place to run.

The first Divellion came into view, emerging from the shadows like a creature from a nightmare. Jesse ducked out of its path, drawing it away from the fence.

It lunged at him, blocking him and striking his face with a clawed hand.

Jesse fell backwards, his flat cap skidding across the

ground. Blood began to spread through his sandy blonde hair. He rolled onto his stomach, shielding his head.

A second Divellion leapt out of the darkness, pouncing onto Jesse' back and pinning him to the ground. It clawed at his shirt, ravenous and thirsting for his powerful essence.

But as the monster's teeth penetrated Jesse' throat, it let out a feral roar, suddenly aware that Jesse was not, in fact, the witch they'd sought. Indeed, he was not a witch at all.

However, for Jesse, the realisation came too late.

Chapter Twelve
Heroes' Welcome

I awoke in a cold sweat, trembling helplessly.

"Jesse," I whispered.

I staggered to my feet, momentarily confused as to where I was.

My bedchamber, I realised. *The Academy.*

In a daze, I left the bedroom, racing along the hall and tripping over myself to get downstairs.

Outside, the sun had just begun its descent, and as I burst through the main doors, I felt the first drops of rain splash onto my bare arms.

It didn't matter. There was somewhere I needed to be.

As I fled past the school boundaries, I caught a glimpse of the boys, still training in the clearing. But I barely gave them a second glance.

Leaving them in the distance, I raced along the winding footpath, always pushing myself to move faster, even though each footfall skidded on the slippery mud.

I ran all the way to the meadow graveyard where the path reached its end.

This was where I'd seen Jaxon. This was the image that had settled in my mind when I'd done the Secrets Be Known spell. He'd been mourning at a graveside, laying down wildflowers.

Now I saw those very flowers, wilted and shrivelled against the headstone and drowning in the waterlogged grass as raindrops hammered down on them.

Shuddering from head to toe, I approached the grave and dropped to my knees.

I let out a quiet sob.

It was as I'd expected.

The name on the gravestone read, *Jesse Jaxon*, and beneath it, *Died a Hero*.

I felt a sharp twist in my heart. The tears began to spill from my eyes and I cried until I couldn't see. Cried until I collapsed against Jaxon's gravestone, clinging to the cold, wet granite.

Jaxon was Jesse. He'd died that day at the carnival. And I'd watched it happen.

Through my sobs, I heard the crunch of footsteps behind me. I knew instantly who it was.

"Why didn't you tell me?" I murmured.

I didn't look up. I didn't need to.

Jaxon's hand grazed my back, and for a long while we were both silent. The sound of the pattering raindrops fell alongside my tears.

"I think that's wrong," Jaxon said at last, sitting on the boggy grass beside me and hiking his thumb towards the gravestone. "I wasn't a hero."

"Are you...?" I looked up at him now, suddenly seeing the same boy I'd watched in my dreams, only he was older now and marked with deep-set scars. "Are you dead?" I choked.

"I was," he said. Rain dripped from his hair, darkening the hue before rolling over the bridge of his nose.

"But..." I swallowed. "How are you back?"

Jaxon pushed the wet hair from his brow. "Do you know what a phoenix is?" he asked warily.

"A bird," I whispered, scared of what may follow.

"It can be."

My heart started to pound faster. "What else can it be?"

He smiled ruefully at me, answering my question with his cool grey eyes.

"You?" I said hoarsely.

He held up his palms.

213

I drew in a quick breath. "How?"

"The elders," he said. "Ness, Hardy, Garret, they needed an army…"

"Ness did this?" I stammered.

"She brought me back," Jaxon replied. He idly picked at the wet grass. "There's a spell," he said, "a very rare spell. One that almost borderlines on dark magic." He paused again. "Have you heard of the flower in the holt—the one that's said to have blossomed from phoenix ashes?"

"Phoenix tail," I answered in a haze.

"They say it's the only plant strong enough to reawaken the…" he hesitated. "To reawaken those who have been lost," he worded tactfully. "The catch is, they return… *different*. As a phoenix. Stronger. Faster. Less… human. The elders raised us. All of us. Everyone who died as a hero was given, as they called it, a second chance. To come back as a monster," he added with a grimace.

"You're not a monster," I murmured. "You're…"

My mind returned to the image of the phoenix etched into Ness's fireplace, and to the flawlessly carved tree. And now to Jaxon. They all shared one thing in common: they had me spellbound.

"You're a phoenix," I stuttered. "That's how you're so strong. That's how you are able to shoot the arrows…"

Jaxon stared at his hands. "When I came back, my aptitudes were heightened. I mean, I was always a pretty good shot, but now..."

"And your eyes," I said. "Today when you got angry, your eyes changed. *You* changed."

Jaxon cringed in shame. "I hate it," he said quietly. "I can't control myself sometimes. I'm an animal."

I flinched.

His jaw clenched and he stared down at his hands.

"I thought about telling you," he reflected in a distant voice. "Earlier, I mean. But I couldn't find the words. How could I have told you that I've been alive for nearly a century, most of which I was actually dead? How would you have reacted if I'd told you I wasn't human? That I could have hit those targets blindfolded? That I can bend steel with my hands—"

"You can do *what*?" I spluttered.

"Oh, right. You didn't know about that part yet." Jaxon gave me a careful smile. "I lived and died many years ago. I was at peace for a long time. And then I was back, picking up where I'd left off—only the world as I knew it had changed. *I* had changed."

I gazed over at him until my eyes landed on the spot above his rain-soaked shirt collar—the fatal bite mark that now scarred his skin.

My breath came out in a rush.

"The thought that you would see me for what I truly was..." he trailed off. "I wanted more time. You're the first person who's made me feel... I don't know." He leaned against the headstone and looked up at the murky sky. "I kept thinking, just one more day. One more hour. One more minute..."

"How did you know I was here?" I asked softly.

He returned his focus to me. "Because it was bound to happen sooner or later, wasn't it? When I saw you run from the Academy, I just knew my time was up. You'd found out my secret."

It was only then that I realised that the Secrets Be Known spell had worked after all. I'd thought my visions were of Wilber, but actually I'd been watching Jesse all along. I'd wanted to find out Jaxon's secret, and here it was.

"It doesn't change anything," I breathed. "You're still you."

"I—" Jaxon began, then paused. He stared intently into the fringing woodland. A sheet of rain swept through the trees.

Jaxon rose to his feet.

"What's wrong?" I asked.

"Divellions," he said stiffly. "A Divellion is near."

I scrambled up, shivering in my drenched clothes.

Jaxon met my eyes. "Go back to the Academy," he

told me in a low voice.

"No!" I cried. "I won't let this happen again. This is how you..." I couldn't bring myself to finish the sentence.

Jaxon exhaled in a taut breath, causing raindrops to spray from his lips. "This isn't the same as last time. I'm *different*," he reminded me. "Now, please, go back to the school."

"Come with me," I begged.

He clenched his teeth. "Please," he said, jerking his head away from me. "You need to leave!"

My stomach flipped. "No. I can't leave you."

He scowled. "Go," he repeated. "Get away from me!"

All of a sudden, the Jaxon I knew was gone. His pupils had swollen, and the smoky eyes I knew so well had turned black. When he looked at me, I saw only fury. I *felt* only fury.

"Go!" he shouted.

And, this time, I did.

#

I burst into the Academy and dashed along the corridor towards Ness's office.

When I reached her door, I flung it open without knocking.

"Ness!" I cried.

She sprung up from behind her mahogany desk. "Good grief!" she gasped. "You're soaked through."

"Divellion," I panted, gesturing vaguely to the cherry red walls. "Jaxon's still out there! He's at the graveyard."

Ness rushed over to me, her glasses hanging from a chain around her neck. "Divellions? How many?"

"One, I think."

"Are you hurt?"

"No," I rasped. "I didn't see it, but Jaxon told me it was near. He's still out there. We have to help him!"

Ness frowned. "Jaxon told you?"

I nodded my head frantically.

"What did he say, exactly?" Ness asked.

My heart was racing at what felt like one million beats per second. "He said a Divellion was near, and then told me to leave."

To my astonishment, Ness smiled curiously. "My, oh my."

I furrowed my brow, baffled as to why she wasn't jumping into action.

"Jaxon said that, did he?" Ness mused, looking pleased rather than troubled. "And tell me, Sophie, does he speak to you often?"

"What? Uh... yes. Quite often."

"Really? Well, isn't that something." She returned to

218

the desk chair, chuckling quietly to herself.

"Ness," I pleaded, "Jaxon is in danger!"

"Take a seat, dear," she advised, gesturing to the visitor chair opposite her.

I stumbled forward and collapsed into the seat. All the running was taking its toll on me.

Tomorrow, I decided, *no running.*

Ness pressed a button on the intercom.

Mabel's voice came through fuzzily above the static. "That you, Ness?"

"Yes, Mabel, me again. Do we have any clean towels handy? Sophie's had a bit of a soaking." She lowered her voice and mouthed to me, "Cup of tea?"

I shook my head no. A cup of tea was the last thing on my mind.

"Come on," Ness urged in her hushed voice. "A nice cup of tea."

I grimaced. "No."

Ness returned to Mabel. "And perhaps a cup of tea for Sophie. With sugar. She's had a shock."

I rolled my eyes.

"Ah," Mabel agreed. "Nothing better for shock than a cup of tea with sugar."

I huffed loudly.

"Thank you, Mabel," Ness chirped. "Oh, and I have wonderful news: Jaxon spoke to Sophie."

Mabel let out a long hoot. "I told you!" she cheered. "Didn't I say he's got a voice in there, somewhere?"

"Yes. I must admit, I'm relieved."

I stared blankly at Ness.

She glanced at me, evidently catching on that it was time to say goodbye to Mabel.

"Right," Ness said, after the intercom line went dead. "Jaxon spoke to you, did he?" She folded her hands on the dark wooden desk.

I threw up my arms in sheer frustration. "Yes. But aren't there more important things we should be—"

"Excellent! Truly excellent. You do realise that he's never spoken to any of us?"

Huh.

"Actually, no," I said petulantly. "I did not realise that."

"Oh, yes. We were worried that he *couldn't* speak."

I fidgeted in my seat. "I was, too, at first."

Ness leaned across the desk eagerly. "How did you find out?"

"Um... I asked him."

"Genius!" Ness declared. "I can't wait to tell Mr. Hardy! Does Mr. Garret know?"

I thought about it for a moment. It hadn't occurred to me until then, that I'd never heard Jaxon speak to anyone other than me. Nor had he ever spoken to me

220

when other people were within earshot.

"I don't know," I answered at last. "I don't think so. Anyway, what are we going to do about the Divellion?"

Ness smiled warmly at me. "Jaxon knows what he's doing. I'm not worried."

I rapped my knuckles on the desktop, desperate to get through to her. "Divellions killed him!"

For the first time that evening, Ness looked genuinely shocked. "You know?"

"Yes! I saw it."

"Ah," she said, pursing her thin lips. "The Secrets Be Known spell. You wished to see Jaxon."

I blushed.

"Yes," I mumbled.

"I see," she said, knowingly.

"And now the same thing is happening again."

Ness stared at me, steadily. "May I ask, are your feelings for Jaxon platonic?"

My cheeks reddened further. "Not entirely," I admitted.

Ness lowered her eyelashes. "I'm sorry, Sophie," she said, her tone abruptly sombre, "but I cannot allow that."

I almost laughed. "You cannot allow what? For me to have feelings for Jaxon?"

"Absolutely not," she said brusquely. "Those feelings

must stop this instant."

I stared at her in disbelief. "No."

Ness began fussing with a stack of paperwork. "I'm sorry, Sophie. I'm going to have to put my foot down."

"Hold on a second. You're the one who pushed us together in the first place!" I exclaimed. "You forced him to be my mentor."

"The poor boy was mute! I thought, by the greatest stretch of the imagination, that perhaps one day you could be friends—that you could be some form of company to one another. But *this*? I never would have assigned him to you if I'd suspected something as unspeakable as *this*."

"Unspeakable?" I crossed my arms. "Okay, now you're seriously overreacting."

"Sophie," Ness implored, clasping her hands together, "you have no idea what you're getting yourself into. Please understand, I only want what's best for you. Jaxon is fine to sit beside in lessons and help you with your school work, but you are not, under any circumstances, allowed to be alone with him."

"You're being unfair," I protested. "Besides, don't I get to choose who I spend time with?"

"You must listen," she begged. "In the future, you'll thank me. I care deeply for Jaxon, but he is volatile. More so than the others. When Jaxon turns... he *really* turns."

"You brought him back," I stated. "*You* made him a phoenix."

My comment must have stung, because Ness winced at the words.

"Yes," she admitted quietly. "I truly believed that I was giving him a second chance. One that he rightly deserved. But there is always a price. The laws of nature are not to be toyed with, and I will forever carry the burden of what I turned that poor boy into."

A lump formed in my throat. I didn't want to hear this.

"I'm sorry, Sophie," Ness said tightly. "It's my responsibility to protect you, and I will not debate the issue further."

"How can you be so…" I took a shaky breath. "Will you do one thing for me, at least? I'm not leaving this office until I know he's safe. Just get him back. Please?"

"Okay," Ness yielded. "That I will do." She rose from her seat. "I must confer with Mr. Hardy. He will arrange for reinforcements to be sent to Jaxon's aid."

"Thank you," I said stoically.

Ness gently squeezed my shoulder, then strode towards the office door.

"Aunt Ness?" I called.

She glanced back at me.

"Don't you trust him at all?"

She sighed. "I trust him to protect us." As she spoke, her hand enveloped the brass door handle. "I trust him to protect the holt."

"But you don't trust him to protect me?"

"I trust him to protect you, but whether I trust him *around* you is a different matter entirely." She met my eyes in earnest. "There is no doubt in my mind that Jesse Jaxon is a hero," she said. "But sometimes even heroes have their flaws."

#

Ness Ballester, Rip Hardy, and Allan Garret stood side by side in the Phoenix Holt graveyard. The sky was oppressive and churned black with a brewing storm. No sun broke through the clouds that morning, and no birds sang.

"Jesse Jaxon," Mr. Hardy read from the headstone. "Are you sure he's the one?" The broad man towered above Ness's petite, aged frame.

Ness nodded her head once. "He's the one. Last night I made contact with Wilber. I informed him of our plans to raise an army. He told me that if I was going ahead with the Phoenix spell, I was to give this boy a second chance. After all, he died saving my brother's life."

"What about the others?" Mr. Hardy asked. "We'll need more than one."

Ness sighed desolately. "Children of the war? Those lost in combat? We can be sure they'll have the soldier instinct, at least. They'll certainly be heroes, too," she added.

Mr. Garret joined the conversation. "I know the name of a young boy who had great soldier instincts. He was a friend of my father's. His name was Daniel Reuben. He died at fifteen too, I believe."

"And Victor Thompson," Mr. Hardy offered. "He died in combat during the Second World War, aged sixteen."

"We shall require at least fifty," said Ness. "And all young. The spell only works on those who were taken young."

Mr. Garret stared down at the grass that blanketed the grave. "Well, for now, we start with Jesse Jaxon."

"Yes," Ness said softly. She produced a glass vial from her satchel; the liquid inside it was blood red. "Stand back," she instructed the two men.

They did as she asked.

Ness straightened her shoulders, holding herself with the stance of a noblewoman.

"My darling boy," she whispered to the still grave. "You gave your life to save my brother, and now I will repay the favour." She unscrewed the cork from the vial

225

and sprinkled a few drops of the liquid onto the earth. She began murmuring in a slow, practised voice, "Hero lost in battles roar, return to me yourself and more, become the warrior you were destined to be, and awake as a phoenix, strong, fast, and free."

A rumble of thunder sounded overhead. Beneath their feet, the ground began to judder and crack.

Mr. Hardy stepped forward, extending his rough hand to the splitting ground.

A new hand burst through the soil and took the older man's grasp with a clap that rivalled the lightening above.

Mr. Hardy smiled triumphantly. "Welcome home, Jaxon."

Chapter Thirteen

Existence

I awoke to the sensation of being lifted. I knew at once I was in Jaxon's arms. I recognised the scent of his skin and the curve of his shoulders as I linked my arms around his neck.

He was carrying me somewhere.

In a stolen moment, I buried my face into his chest, listening to the steady rhythm of his heartbeat. His clothes were damp from the rainstorm.

I opened my eyes to see a flash of red, followed by the familiar lamp-lit corridor with its auburn wood walls and slate floor.

"I fell asleep," I said blearily, more to myself than to Jaxon.

"You're awake," he realised with a start. "Sorry, I

thought you were under a spell." Carefully he placed me onto the cold, hard floor.

I found my footing and stood facing him, blinking through my woozy state.

"Ness's office," I mumbled, slowly returning to the present. "I fell asleep in Ness's office."

Jaxon nodded.

"I was waiting for you," I told him, a little more lucidly now.

"I know."

That's right, I thought. I'd refused to leave Ness's office until Jaxon had returned. Falling asleep hadn't exactly been part of my big noble plan, though.

I studied him thoughtfully. Yellowed bruising coloured his jaw.

"What happened?" I asked.

"There was one," he confirmed. "Tracked and eliminated."

I frowned. "A Divellion? You eliminated a Divellion?" 'Eliminated' sounded like a strange word choice, but I rolled with it.

"Yes."

We began walking again, heading towards the staircase at the other end of the corridor.

"Is it over?" I asked, naïvely hopeful.

"Too soon to say."

"I hope it's over," I whispered.

Jaxon's hand brushed against mine and he caught my gaze. His eyes were restored to their usual smoky hue. There was a gentleness to them now. A carefulness.

"You have no reason to be afraid of them," he said. "They will never get to you. That will never happen."

I couldn't help but trust the conviction in his tone.

"I'm sorry you saw me like that," Jaxon murmured in a pensive state as we began ascending the wide staircase. "I wish you hadn't."

I remembered Ness's harrowing words, warning me away from Jaxon, saying that he was volatile and I shouldn't be alone with him.

Well, I was alone with him now.

"Do you know?" I broached delicately. "When you change, I mean. Do you know that it's happening?" I trailed my fingers along the elegant banister, waiting on tenterhooks for his response.

He sighed. "In a way, yes. But it's so consuming that I don't even care. In fact, I don't want it to stop."

I bit my lip. "But if you did want to stop, could you?"

He sighed again. "No. Probably not."

"I think you could," I argued.

Jaxon laughed bleakly.

"I'm not afraid of you," I told him. "I trust you."

We reached the top of the staircase and came to a

229

standstill in the upper hallway. Oil lamps hung from the dark walls, casting crooked shadows all around us.

"Ms. Ballester doesn't want me to be the mentor thing anymore," said Jaxon, running a hand through his damp hair.

I smiled to myself. We were *way* past the mentor thing.

"And I think she has a point," he added.

I frowned at him in the low lamp light. "You think who has a point?" Surely he couldn't be talking about Ness.

"Ms. Ballester," he replied. "I think she's right. I don't think we should be spending so much time together."

His words struck so hard they almost knocked me over.

"Why not?" I blurted out.

"I don't think it's a good idea for us to get too close," Jaxon went on. "I think today has proven that on more than one occasion."

"When?" I stammered.

"What happened in the graveyard, when I turned on you. And earlier, with Reuben—"

"The Reuben thing? That was *his* fault. He was provoking you."

"And look at how I reacted. I have no control, and it's only getting worse. It's worse when I'm around you."

"When you're around *me*?" I blinked at him in disbelief. "So you're saying that you don't want to be around me anymore?"

"Yes," he said.

It would have been kinder if he'd torn out my heart and stomped on it.

"I just..." He hung his head. "I just *can't* be around you anymore. I don't want this."

This time I couldn't respond. It was the final blow that left me empty.

"Let me walk you to your bedroom," Jaxon offered, as though that meagre act might somehow alleviate the devastation that gripped me.

"I think that counts as being around me," I murmured. And with that, I turned on my heel and walked away. I knew Jaxon wouldn't follow me, and I fought every urge not to look back at him.

How could he? There was nothing in the world that could have stopped me from wanting to be around him. Even after all the hurtful things he'd said, I still found myself pining for him.

Why didn't he want to be around me? What had I done wrong?

A solitary tear escaped from my eye and rolled down my cheek, leaving its track like my very own battle scar. How could this have happened? He was no longer just a crush—I felt connected to him now. And I'd thought he felt connected to me, too.

I reached my room and noiselessly slipped inside. Sam and Todd slept soundly in their beds. Fully clothed, I crawled into my camp bed and pulled the sleeping bag over my head.

More tears poured from my eyes. I couldn't hold them back anymore, and they seeped into my pillow like the blood-spill of my broken heart.

I couldn't breathe. I didn't want to.

How could I have read this so wrong? Would he simply stroll off to his bedroom and sleep restfully, knowing that he'd 'done the right thing'?

The right thing for who? I demanded silently. *For him? For Ness and all the other elders? Certainly not for me.*

There was a knock on the bedroom door.

I stayed buried inside my sleeping bag.

The door creaked open and I heard Jaxon's voice, low and almost inaudible.

"Sophie?" he said.

"Go away, Jaxon," I hissed back.

"I was hoping we could talk."

"I thought you didn't want to talk to me," I replied frostily.

I heard no footsteps, but when Jaxon spoke again, his

voice was nearer. "I've been silent for a long time," he whispered. "I'm out of practice. I think I might have said the wrong thing."

I sat up and found his eyes in the darkness of the bedchamber.

"That's no excuse," I snapped. "You may have been silent, but you still had a brain."

"Were you crying?" Jaxon murmured, evidently noticing my tear-stained face.

I fumbled to wipe my puffy eyes. "What does it matter to you?"

He let out a tragic sigh.

"Well?" I prompted. "What is it that you came here to tell me?"

"I don't think telling you is going to work," he muttered under his breath. "Like I said, I'm out of practise. I think I'd rather show you. Do you feel like taking a walk?"

#

I stepped out into the cold night air. The rain had stopped, and the breeze wrapped around me like a cloak of silk.

"Where are we going?" I asked, knotting my hands together for warmth.

"I want to show you who I am." Jaxon led me around the building, heading for the glade.

I trotted, trying to keep in stride with him.

"I know who you are," I said.

"Humour me."

We paced across the empty clearing. Trees lined the enclosure. We passed them, heading for the huge circling wall.

In the dark of the night, the stone barrier loomed high above me like a tidal wave.

I ran my fingers along the uneven stone. "Is this what you wanted to—"

The words caught in my throat. Without warning, Jaxon's hands were around my waist as he lifted me into the air.

"Hold onto the top," he instructed.

I did as he said, clinging to the top of the cold stone wall, then scrambling to sit upright on its ledge.

Jaxon cleared the wall and pounced down onto the grass on the other side.

"Jump!" he called up to me. "I'll catch you."

I swung my legs over the wall and let myself slip from the edge.

In the split second that I was free falling, I thought of all the injuries a person could sustain by dropping from such a height. Broken bones being the most obvious.

Yeesh.

But I landed unbroken in his awaiting arms.

As for Jaxon, his body didn't even jolt with the impact. He simply dipped me and stood me on the spongy ground.

"Good catch," I said, dusting myself off.

"Good fall," he replied.

I glanced at my surroundings. I'd never been on that side of the wall before. It was dark, but I noticed a few trees marking the beginning of the woodland, and in the distance the peaked hilltops crept towards the stars.

Jaxon took my hand. "This way," he said, leading me into the trees.

We walked in silence for a while, our hands fused together. I wondered where he could possibly be taking me. What was it that I would learn about him in the woods that I couldn't learn at the Academy?

And then, I saw it.

Jaxon's world.

Trees—dozens of them, all striped of their leaves and carved into shapes. Some were spiralled like helter-skelters, while others were sculpted into animals and flowers. It was like stepping into an exhibition.

"You did this?" I asked, breathlessly.

Jaxon dropped my hand and strolled over to a tree that had been crafted into a waterfall. He ran his knuckles along the serrated bark.

"When I came back here," he said tenderly, "I found it hard to speak. Hard to... *be*. The only way I could feel anything was," he gestured around, "by doing this. Creating the things I loved, to make me feel alive again."

I wove in and out of the carved trees in awe. Each and every one of them told a story. They were *him*.

"The phoenix in the holt," I remembered. "Did you carve it?"

Jaxon nodded. "Doing this was the only thing that kept me sane," he admitted with a little laugh. "In the early days, I couldn't understand why I was what I was—why they'd brought me back and made me into a monster." He grimaced. "I was so angry at what I'd become. One day, I came out here, trying to escape, and I found myself drawing on the bark. I focused everything I had into this. . ." He began walking away from me.

I followed, unquestioningly.

"Is that why you draw?" I asked, thinking back to his sketch of Port Dalton.

"Yes. I suppose it's something I did in my previous life, and for a long time at the Academy, I needed it. But I did it to the point where I took no enjoyment from it anymore. I was trapped, afraid that if I stopped drawing and carving, I would lose myself."

"What changed?"

Jaxon gave an enigmatic smile. "This was the last thing I did," he said, resting his hand against a tree. The trunk was sculpted into two parts: one broad section with a second strip of bark running through it, winding like ivy. The sections were apart and yet always intertwined. "I started it a while back," Jaxon told me, "some time before I met you. Although, when I look at it now, I feel as though it was done for you. It was as though somehow I knew you were coming for me. That you already existed, and that you'd appear one day out of nowhere and bring me back to life." He paused. "Then, the day I met you, I knew I was done. I could stop."

I gazed up at the interlacing tree. "It's beautiful," I said quietly.

"A part of me was missing for so long. And then somehow you came along and gave it back to me." He snapped his fingers. "Just like that."

I looked into his eyes. "Why me?" I whispered. "What made you speak to me, and not to them, after two years?"

"I don't know," he answered diffidently. "I just... *wanted* to."

"And now you don't want to anymore?"

"No," he murmured. "Now I want to too much. I'm

scared I'll slip up. I'm scared I'll hurt you."

I shivered at his comment.

"So, you've seen one side of me," he said, exhaling slowly. "You've seen who I am, and I've told you everything. But you need to see the rest." He strode through the woodland, honing in on a large oak tree.

"Stand back," he said.

I stood a short distance away, watching as Jaxon took a quick swing at the trunk, as though he were casually swatting a fly. The bark exploded into a cloud of dust and woodchip. I covered my eyes, and when I dared to look back, the tree trunk boasted a dent the size of a beach ball. Jaxon had dented it, with nothing more than the flick of a wrist.

Jaxon dusted off his hands, having not even broken a sweat.

"That's the other me," he said. "That's the me you should be afraid of."

I swallowed. "I'm not afraid."

"I know," he replied. "And that's what *I'm* afraid of."

Chapter Fourteen

Out of Sight

A week went by with no further Divellion sightings. However, Ness insisted that we stay at Averett Academy until we could be absolutely sure that the threat had passed. She urged us to stay inside the manor at all times, constantly reminding us that if Divellions were on our scent, they'd be looking for any opportunity to isolate the weakest.

One guess who they all thought the weakest was.

Me.

On top of everything else, Ness did her utmost to keep me away from Jaxon. The woman was relentless, and she went to any lengths possible—including scheduling my lessons in her office. Just me, Ness, and an ancient algebra book.

Although, it wasn't as if Jaxon fought particularly hard against it. On the rare occasion we did bump into each other, he was careful around me. Never getting too close. Never letting *me* get too close.

I hated him for it.

And I liked him for it, all at the same time.

As for Sam and Todd, they were as fed up with the Academy as I was—but for very different reasons.

It was on a particularly cold Wednesday morning that Sam came storming into our bedroom, slamming the heavy door behind him.

"I'm leaving," he stated.

I sighed. "You say that every day."

Sam pounded his fist against the dark wall, rattling the glass casing on a wall-mounted oil lamp. "But I mean it this time," he swore. "I'm sick of this place. I'm sick of all the jumped-up planks thinking they own the world. Calling themselves phoenixes, like we're meant to bow down before them." He rolled his hand in circles and mimed an elaborate bow.

Todd turned down the page of the book he'd been reading and placed it on the camp bed where he was sitting. "We can't leave. Not until Ness says so."

Sam scowled at him. "I don't give a damn what *Ness says*. I'm out."

"Don't go, Sam," I implored him. "It can't be much longer."

He snorted. "If we wait around for Ness, then we'll never get out of this dump. She's happy here with her boyfriend."

I frowned. "Her boyfriend?"

He waved his hand impatiently. "You know, that guy she's always knocking about with. Whatshisname. Tufty hair."

Tufty hair? I mused. *Surely he doesn't mean...*

"Mr. Garret?" I said. "He's not Ness's boyfriend."
Perish the thought!

"Well, he might as well be," Sam scoffed. "They're both in on it. Keeping us here in lock-down, all so they can shack up together. Selfish is what it is."

I rolled my eyes.

Sam shrugged. "Anyway, I'm outta here."

"Where will you go?" I asked.

"Back to the cottage, where my clothes are. I've had it with recycling the same two T-shirts on a loop."

Todd laced his fingers together. "But when they find out you've gone, they'll just bring you back again."

Sam groaned. "Todd, I don't care. I just want to get out of here now. Right now. Come, don't come, whatever."

Uh oh. I had a feeling that I was going to say

something that I might later regret.

"If you go, we all go." Yep. There they were. Regrettable words in all their glory.

Camaraderie in the air, Todd rose to his feet. "Come on, then," he said wearily.

Sam smiled at us, and I half expected him to say something sarcastic.

Instead, he simply nodded and said, "Thank you."

#

I had to admit that even with the bite in the air, it felt good to be outside. I'd spent far too long cooped up at the Academy. And, for the first time since moving to Phoenix Holt, the route to the cottage began to look familiar. At last, my homing instinct was kicking in.

Home. I'd done it again—called the cottage 'home'. *I guess that's the funny thing about time,* I thought. It had the wonderful ability heal all wounds. And it had somehow blurred the lines I'd set between Port Dalton and Phoenix Holt in such a way that I hadn't even noticed it happening. Just a short while ago, I had refused to allow Phoenix Holt to be anything other than a stop gap—a temporary hiatus until I could escape. And now, as I trudged through the woodland towards the cottage, I was gripped by the strong sensation of *heading home.*

As I reflected over the changes that had come to pass, I let the fresh air flow in and out of my lungs—the taste of freedom.

Just ahead of me Sam took off, pelting down the wooded slope towards the cottage.

Todd raced after him.

I felt a rush of gratitude when I caught sight of the little stone cottage. Yes, it was finally home. *We* were finally home.

"Door's open!" I heard Sam declare. He was already inside the cottage by the time I'd reached level ground.

I hurried inside after my brothers. We'd made it to sanctuary.

Todd and I collapsed onto the sofa. I sank into the cushions, relishing the marshmallow softness.

The sound of clattering came from the kitchen, followed by Sam's whoops of delight. He began singing to himself, loudly and out of tune.

"Put the eggs in the pan, shooba-da-wap-wap... Todd, get in here!" he hollered between verses.

When Todd didn't respond immediately, Sam bellowed again, "Todd, get in here! Da-da-da-da-da wap-wap-whooo..."

Todd heaved himself off the sofa and loped to the kitchen.

Alone, I spread out across the cushions. I gazed into the fireplace, where the phoenix's wings spanned across the chimney wall, guarding the entrance to the secret stairwell.

In front of the fireplace, the rug was patterned with strips of sunlight dancing in through the criss-crossed window pane. I traced the shaft of light back to the little window. On its ledge stood an arrangement of colourful candles and framed photographs.

I'd never really paid much attention to the photos on the windowsill—not up close, anyhow. But at that moment, my curiosity got the better of me. I rose to my feet and ambled to the sill.

I picked up the first frame; it was pink and faded from years of sunlight. Three people smiled back at me. I spotted my grandfather at once. He was as I remembered him, but much younger—in his late twenties perhaps. He stood with a curly haired girl who couldn't have been much older than me, and a middle-aged woman with dark hair and a kindly face.

Ness and Sulinda, I guessed. Seeing Ness in her youth gave me a whole new insight into the family resemblance between us.

I smiled down at the photograph for a while before replacing it and moving on to the next one.

The second frame was purple, and oval in shape. A

man stared back at me from behind the framed glass. For a second, I was taken aback. The man in the picture was Sam. Not Todd, but *Sam*, mirrored in the way he stood and the look in his golden eyes. And yet the man was older, captured in a different lifetime.

"Sam!" I called.

"What?" his voice came back to me.

"Could you come in here for a second?"

I heard the pound of feet before Sam materialised in the den. In his clutches he held a bulky wooden crossbow.

"Check this out!" he exclaimed.

I ducked instinctively. "Aim it at the floor! *At the floor*!"

"It is aimed at the floor," he said, idly swinging the contraption from left to right.

I edged out of its line of fire. "Look at this," I beckoned to him.

He sauntered across the room and took the oval frame from my hands.

"Oh," he said, his voice softening.

"It's you," I laughed. "Isn't it?"

He smiled, quite beautifully, and I was suddenly able to see a glimpse of the man that he would one day become.

"That's not me," he said pensively. "It's our dad."

It was a good thing I hadn't been holding the photo, because I probably would have dropped it.

"Dad?" I said.

"Dad," he replied.

I liked the way the word sounded.

"Dad," I said again.

"Dad," Sam replied.

#

It was well into the afternoon before our time at the cottage was interrupted. At the time, Sam was settled in the den, attempting to decipher the crossbow. Todd and I were seated at the kitchen table, picking at the last of our lunch.

"Ough!" I heard Sam wail from the other room.

I jumped, startled.

We'll never find a hospital, I thought, assuming the worst. *If he's shot himself, I'll have to stitch him up with a needle and thread. He's not going to like it, though.*

"Todd," I said, "get the frozen peas, and rip up some sheets—"

"That smell," Sam gagged. "That is foul! What *is* it?"

I let out a sigh of relief.

"What *is* that?" Sam carped.

I couldn't smell anything, apart from the vague scent

of lavender lingering in the air.

"Ugh," Sam groaned. "It's getting worse."

It must be something in the den, I presumed.

"Bleuch!" Sam kept on. "It's so bad. My eyes are watering."

"It's probably you," I yelled back.

He appeared in the den archway, crossbow tucked beneath his arm and a look of revulsion on his face.

"It's *not* me," he griped.

I was about to disagree when the front door burst open. And *burst* is precisely what it did. As in, it flew right off its hinges, crashing at the foot of the staircase.

I shrank back, shielding my eyes from the airborne splinters.

Then came a sound that made my blood run cold. A hiss—the kind I'd only heard once before. In a dream.

Divellions.

Two of them.

I scrambled up from my seat.

The *things* slunk into our hallway. Their skin was leathery and red, and looked burned. Sharp, rotten teeth hung from their jaws, dripping with saliva.

One of the Divellions cricked its neck towards me. Its top lip curled back and it let out a wild hiss.

There was a brief instant when time stood still. I met Sam's eyes from across the hall.

247

"Run," he mouthed.

I couldn't.

But it was too late for running, anyway. The Divellions had crossed the threshold and were inside the cottage.

Todd and I backed into the kitchen, clambering for pots and pans—anything we could use as a weapon.

Across the hall, I saw Sam fumbling to lock the crossbow into place. His hands quaked, and the arrow slipped from his grasp and fell to the floor with a clatter.

I looked around for anything—*anything*—I could use to protect myself.

A toaster… A flower pot… A spatula…

Wait. The flower pot.

I dived for the windowsill and yanked a handful of purple orchids out of their pot. Soil and water dripped from there stems.

Please be right, I willed. My memory was hazy, but I recalled something I'd come across before, when I'd been skimming through the spell book with Sam. Weren't orchids the flower used to temporarily blind an opponent?

How does that spell go again? I racked my brain, envisioning the yellowed pages of the book and the faded text.

I can do this, I told myself.

I crushed the petals in my hand. "See no evil," I whispered before throwing the flower mulch at the beasts.

To my amazement and relief, the Divellions hesitated. They were still hissing, but disorientated now.

Had it worked? Had I really blinded them?

I didn't dare take a breath.

And then I heard Sam reel off a few choice words, followed by that detrimental statement, "I'm blind!"

Uh oh.

Todd let out a strangled howl. "My eyes! I can't see anything!" He tried to run and collided head first into the fridge.

I could hear Sam crashing about in the den. "Argh! I'm blind! I'm blind!"

Oops.

"It's only temporary!" I told them hastily. "Sorry."

The Divellions stooped to the floor, inhaling the scent around them.

"You blinded me?" Sam yelled. "Of all the times to blind me!"

"I didn't mean to! I was trying to blind the… things. It worked, by the way."

"Oh, ya think?" Sam cried.

Todd flapped his arms, bumping into cabinets and

chairs.

I grabbed hold of him and shoved him under the kitchen table. He nursed the toaster he held in his embrace.

"Stay there," I instructed.

"Where am I?" he yelped.

"You're under the kitchen table. With the toaster."

One of the Divellions rose to its full height, staring directly at me through its sightless red eyes.

I staggered backwards, inadvertently boxing myself against the sink unit. I couldn't escape. I was trapped.

So this is it, I thought hopelessly. *This is how it all ends for me. Squashed against a pile of dirty dishes.*

I glanced at Todd and the toaster, cowering under the table. And then Sam, spinning in circles beneath the den's archway. One Divellion crawled across the hallway floor, hissing and spitting, while the other steadily made its way towards me.

I had no way out. No defence. Just me, and a room full of blind things.

Any last words?

"Sam, tell me where you hid my diary."

"Why?" he wailed. "Am I going to die?"

"No, *I* am!"

With that, a metal-tipped arrow shot past my face, pinging against the sink.

"For crying out loud, Sam!" I exclaimed.

"Did I get it?" he asked.

"No, but you almost got *me*!"

"Okay, okay. No need to shout. I'm blind, not deaf. And we all know who we have to thank for that," he muttered under his breath.

"I said I was sorry!"

"Yeah, well, sorry doesn't bring my sight back."

"It's only temporary," I huffed. "Not like, oh, I don't know, *death*."

The Divellion cocked its head, its mouth frothing in anticipation. I noticed its eyes were edged with green markings, almost snake-like. It slithered closer until it was near enough for me to smell the foul stench of its breath.

I recoiled until I was practically *in* the sink.

Another arrow skimmed past my head, ruffling my hair as it went.

"For god's sake, Sam!" I screeched. "Stop shooting at me!"

"I can't help it! I'm blind!"

"What's happening?" Todd yowled from under the table. "Who's attacking who?"

"Everyone's attacking *me*," I reported back.

Todd placed the toaster on the floor. "Don't worry, Sophie. I'm coming. I'll save you." He began clambering through the table legs.

Oh, jeeze.

"Todd, stay where you are," I ordered.

Another arrow whizzed past my head.

"Did I get it?" Sam called.

"No!" I screamed. "Stop shooting that thing!"

The green-eyed Divellion let out a feral snarl.

This is it, I thought desolately. *Goodbye cruel world.*

As I submitted to the idea of my untimely demise, one thing I hadn't accounted for was a hero. For a moment, I thought he was an illusion. Kind of like a mirage of water when a person's dying of thirst.

But no, it was real. Jaxon was there.

Startled by the intruder, the green-eyed Divellion backed away from me.

My first instinct was to get to Jaxon. I ducked past the creature and made for the hallway.

"Run!" I shouted to whoever would listen.

Nobody listened.

In the hallway, the second Divellion was lurking. Jaxon grabbed it from behind and, to my utter disbelief, snapped its neck with his bare hands.

The beast slumped to the floor, lifeless.

I cried out in shock.

"What happened?" Sam shouted. "What happened?" He tripped over his own feet and fell backward into the fireplace. "Whaa!"

I was lost for words. I stared at Jaxon, dumbfounded. He had killed a Divellion... with his hands.

His raven black eyes darted around the cottage.

"Jaxon," I murmured.

He looked straight through me, as though I were made of glass—and considering how close to shattering I was right then, I may as well have been.

In a sudden flurry, the green-eyed Divellion bounded past me, almost knocking me down as it sped out the front door.

Jaxon's focus shot to the kitchen.

I followed his gaze, only to be greeted with the sight of Todd lying motionless on the floor.

The world seemed to freeze for a second. "Todd?"

Todd groaned and rolled onto his side. "I'm okay," he mumbled.

Before I'd had the chance to catch my breath, the booming voice of Mr. Hardy came from outside.

"Jaxon, fall back!" the older man commanded.

"No!" I cried. "Don't leave!"

He stared down at me through his tormented black eyes.

"I—" he swallowed. His voice was different somehow, dark and rough.

It seemed implausible, but I could literally *feel* him

trying to resist Mr. Hardy's order. Jaxon was fighting to stay with me; I felt it.

"Jaxon, fall back!" Mr. Hardy's authoritative voice came again.

Jaxon flinched, but he stayed cemented to the spot.

His hand touched my arm, protectively. "Are you okay?" he asked.

"I think so," I answered. "Are you?"

He nodded.

I looked up into his eyes, they were still black and vacant, but I wasn't afraid. I knew him.

"I can see shapes!" Sam cheered from the den.

And then they came—loud, intrusive voices rupturing the cottage. Mr. Hardy and his soldiers.

"Secure the area!" Mr. Hardy roared. "And take him down."

Before I knew it, Jaxon was wrenched away from me.

"No!" I cried, grasping the air where he had just been.

Jaxon was dragged out of the cottage by three stocky boys—one of whom was Reuben the Magnificent. Jaxon struggled to break free, but the boys restrained his arms and covered his mouth.

"He's turned," one of the boys yelled to Mr. Hardy. "He would have killed the girl."

"No!" I shouted. "You're wrong!"

254

All around me, commotion drowned out my pleas. Todd stood helplessly in the kitchen, and Sam in the den. They looked through bleary eyes, watching the scene unfold with quiet remorse.

"Get him out of here," Mr. Hardy ordered.

"No!" I propelled myself forward, racing outside after Jaxon.

Within seconds, two of Mr. Hardy's boys had pulled me back.

"Hey," Sam yelled, at my side in a heartbeat. "Don't touch her!" He yanked me away from the boys, throwing his arms around me like a shield.

"Jaxon!" I screamed into the falling dusk.

But the only thing that returned to me was the echo of my own voice.

"They've taken Jaxon," I cried to Sam and Todd. "I have to help him!"

My brothers swapped an anxious grimace. Together they herded me into the den, away from the others.

"Calm down," Sam said "I'm sure he's fine. They'll be taking him to the Academy, that's all."

Todd rubbed his neck fretfully. "Are you hurt, Sophie?"

I shook my head. "No."

"Are you okay, Sam?" Todd asked. "You're not hurt, are you?"

"Only my ass," Sam grumbled. "You know me, always falling around *blind*."

"Okay, good," said Todd. "Guys, I have to tell you something." He slipped his hand from his neck, and a trickle of blood leaked down his throat. "I think I've been bitten."

Chapter Fifteen

The Fallout

Ness and Mr. Garret arrived shortly after Todd's revelation. The fact that he had been bitten and was still alive baffled the elders beyond words. The truth was, they'd never had a case like that before. Usually when a Divellion struck, it would feed until the transition was complete. The victim would die, and their essence would transfer into the Divellion. No one had ever escaped mid-feed before, but thanks to Jaxon's impeccably timed arrival, Todd's life had been spared.

After we'd told Ness everything we knew, she took Todd upstairs to clean his wound while Mr. Hardy reattached the front door to its hinges.

I waited patiently for Todd to return, hoping for an opportunity to catch some alone time with Ness. I had to speak to her, and I'd have rather it be done in private.

I found Ness upstairs in her bedroom. The door was ajar; I could see her perched on the edge of her bed, staring into space.

I knocked.

She jumped in surprise, then smiled warmly at me.

"Come in, dear," she said.

I stepped inside the room. It was small, and decorated in light floral patterns. Her dressing table was cluttered with dozens of near-empty perfume bottles, and everything smelled like peppermint.

I took a seat on the bed.

"I'm sorry," I said, looking at my feet.

"Oh," Ness chuckled heartily, "don't be." She scooped her arm around me. "No apologies here."

"We shouldn't have left the Academy," I admitted. A bit late for hindsight, though.

"Well, my love," Ness said kindly, "perhaps I shouldn't have kept you there against your will. Perhaps there are a lot of things I shouldn't have made you do. If anyone's made mistakes here, it's me."

I gazed at her. "That's not true. You've been wonderful to us. You took us in when we had no one."

Ness squeezed me tighter. "We're a family. We Ballesters have to stick together now, don't we?"

"They took Jaxon away," I blurted out. "But he was only trying to help us. I swear to you, Ness, he wouldn't

258

have hurt me. You have to believe me."

"I do believe you, Sophie," she assured me.

A wave of relief crossed over me. "Will you explain it to Mr. Hardy?"

"Yes," she said.

And yet, why was I not convinced?

"You know, Sophie," Ness went on, dropping her hands into her lap, "I didn't keep you away from Jaxon to be cruel. You do understand that, don't you?"

I remained silent.

"I don't think Jaxon is…" she searched for the correct wording, "*bad*. Nor do I dislike him. In fact, I care very much for him."

"So do I," I said.

"However, there will be times when Mr. Hardy will see fit to restrain Jaxon, or to *take him away*, as you put it. And as hard as it is for you to watch, you must accept that Mr. Hardy knows what he's doing. He is taking the necessary precautions to keep you safe. To keep Jaxon safe."

Necessary precautions? I almost laughed. "But Jaxon didn't do anything. He didn't need precautions!"

"I understand, dear. And it's natural for you to feel that way. You are so fond of him that you cannot see the—"

"No," I interrupted her. "Ness, I'm not delusional. I

see it all: the good *and* the bad. And I'm telling you, he was fine."

"Mr. Hardy informs me that Jaxon disobeyed a direct command. He also said that when they arrived at the cottage, Jaxon had turned."

"Maybe, but he wasn't a danger to *me*. And he only disobeyed Mr. Hardy because I begged him to stay with me."

"I believe you. But we simply cannot take any chances."

"Can you at least tell me where they've taken him?" I asked.

Ness flattened out an imaginary crease on the floral bedspread. "Jaxon will be at the Academy. No harm will have come to him."

I let out a breath.

"Some day," Ness went on, "I'm sure you'll understand. I can't bear to see you so distressed. But it's my job to do whatever it takes to protect you. So, for the time being, I'll just have to let you hate me for it."

I met her eyes. "I don't hate you," I told her. It astounded me that she could even think such a thing. "I just hate your rules."

Ness chortled. "Well, would you look at that?" she breathed. "I'm setting rules, and you're rebelling. Just like a real family."

I smiled. "You think I'm rebelling? Try telling Sam to wash a dish."

Ness returned the smile, her eyes crinkling at the corners. "Families, eh? Never a dull moment."

#

At twilight we began our journey back to the Academy, escorted by Mr. Hardy and several of the phoenix soldiers. The misted light of the dipping sun filtered through the sycamores, throwing colourful patterns across the ground.

Ness and Mr. Garret led the way, fervently discussing Todd's bite and how it was such a marvel. A lucky escape, they kept calling it.

Todd walked a few paces behind them, and Sam lingered at my side.

"He'll be there, won't he?" I muttered, half to myself. "Jaxon will be at the Academy, won't he?" I looked at Sam now as we trudged through the woodland.

He glanced at me. "Of course," he said. "Ness said so, didn't she?"

"Yes. But they won't have… done anything to him, will they?" A knot of guilt formed in my stomach. After all, it was my fault he'd disobeyed Mr. Hardy.

"No way. He's one of them."

I didn't like that. As far as I was concerned, Jaxon was *not* one of them.

"You don't agree with them, do you?" I asked. "About him being dangerous, I mean."

Sam didn't respond.

"You're on my side, aren't you, Sam?" I pressed.

"Yes," he said. "I'm on your side."

He still hadn't answered my question.

"What about Jaxon?" I tried again.

"I don't know. What do you want me to say?"

"The truth."

Sam heaved a weary sigh. "Okay. They seem to think he's dangerous, so... I don't want you around him."

My face fell.

Sam shrugged. "You asked for the truth."

"Yes, but I was kind of expecting you to lie."

"Wait," he added, "I'm not done yet. I was also telling the truth when I said I was on your side. And, that said, I don't want you to be sad, like you are right now. So, in light of everything, I'm decidedly on the fence."

I laughed quietly. "Hold on. *You're* abstaining from an opinion? I never thought I'd see the day."

"I didn't abstain. That *was* my opinion. I'm on the fence. I can't fully agree with it because, when all's said and done, he is still a phoenix." He mimed a gag. "But I can't completely disagree either, because, well, he makes you happy. And he's your…" Sam hesitated, "*friend*. Your friend who is a boy. Not to be confused with a boyfriend, because you're far too young for that."

I grinned. "You had girlfriends when you were my age."

"Yes. And that is precisely why you're not allowed a boyfriend."

I linked my arm through his. "Thanks for being on the fence. You're a good brother."

He beamed. "I am, aren't I? Much better than that Todd, anyway," he joked.

We neared the Academy boundary wall. My heart rate began to pick up.

"I've got to go," I said to Sam. I broke away from him, running towards the school.

At the manor, I threw open the main doors and raced up the staircase. The building felt dark and lonely, and the rasps of my breath sounded deafening in the hush.

I paced quickly along the upstairs corridor to Jaxon's room. When I reached his door, I collapsed against it, banging on the solid oak.

"Jaxon?" I called into the dense wood.

No response came.

I twisted the handle and pushed the door ajar.

The room was empty, lit only by a strip of moonlight creeping in through the narrow window.

My mouth went dry. Where was he?

#

"What's wrong?" Sam asked as I burst into our bedroom, slamming the door behind me.

"He's gone," I told them, throwing up my arms. "Jaxon's gone." I dropped onto my camp bed. "I knew it! They've taken him somewhere. God only knows what they've done with him." I raked my hands through my hair. "They wouldn't listen to me. They think he's dangerous."

Sam strolled across the room and joined me on my bed. "And you're one hundred percent sure that he isn't?"

"Yes," I replied irritably. "How many times do I have to tell you?"

"Just twice," said Sam.

"Maybe he's gone for a walk or something," Todd offered from his bed across the room.

It seemed highly unlikely, but I nodded all the same.

"Just one question," Sam ventured. "How come everyone in this place thinks this Jaxon's dangerous except you?"

"Because they don't know him," I answered.

"And you do?" he shot back. "Remember, love is

264

blind, and all that. That's what Todd's banking on, anyway," he teased, laughing wickedly.

"You do realise you're identical," I pointed out.

Sam glanced at Todd. "Yeah. I guess we do look kind of similar. Shame about his dull personality, though." He chuckled. "Hey, Todd, what's it like to have such a good looking, charismatic brother?"

Todd scowled. "Shut up, Sam."

Huh? It wasn't like Todd to get riled up so easily.

"Must be great," Sam said dreamily. "I've got this brother, but man, he's such a bore..."

"Shut up, Sam," Todd hissed through clenched teeth.

"Sorry, what was that, buddy? Must have dozed off for a second there." Sam erupted into puckish laugher.

"Shut up," Todd growled.

Sam pretended to snore. "Whoa. Sorry, bro. Just keeps happening."

Todd leaped up from his camp bed. "Shut up!" he bellowed.

This time, even Sam was taken aback. He let out a low whistle. "Whoa. I think someone went a little overboard on the crazy flakes this morning."

"Shut up!" Todd roared. "Just *shut up*." He knotted his fingers through his dark copper hair. "I'm sick of the sound of your voice."

Sam's jaw dropped. "Okay. No need to take it out on

my voice. Psycho," he added under his breath.

Todd picked up a pillow and lobbed it at Sam. "You're not even sorry, are you?"

Sam caught the pillow and tossed it aside. "Um, no. Why would I be?"

"Ha!" Todd spluttered. "Classic Sam. You're so self-involved that you don't even know what you did, do you?"

Sam looked at me in confusion.

I held up my hands impassively. It seemed safer to keep my head down for this one.

"Please," Sam drawled, "enlighten me."

"Today," Todd spat. "The Divellions. It was all your fault."

Sam rolled his eyes. "Oh, you caught me. It was an inside job. Me and the Divellions," he crossed his first two fingers, "we're like that."

Todd stalked across the room towards Sam, towering over him where he sat. "*You* made us go back to the cottage, even though we told you it wasn't safe. Everything that happened was *your* fault!"

My eyes widened. "Todd, don't say that! It wasn't Sam's fault."

"Yes it was!" Todd yelled.

"Okay," Sam said calmly. "For some reason I'm getting the impression that you're a little upset—"

"I told you to shut up!" Todd interrupted.

Sam rose to his feet, sizing up to Todd. "Oh, you *told me*, did you?"

"Oh no, please don't fight," I begged them.

"You don't get to *tell* me to do anything," Sam said tautly.

"That'd be right," Todd sniffed. "You don't like to be told what to do. You prefer to do the *telling*."

"Yeah, me and all the other billions of people in the world."

"Well, I'm not following your orders anymore," Todd spat. He tugged on the collar of his T-shirt, exposing two purple marks. "*This* is your fault. I was bitten because of you."

For several seconds Sam was lost for words.

"Todd didn't mean that," I jumped in.

"Yes I did!" Todd exclaimed. "I meant every word of it."

"If I could have stopped it..." Sam stammered. "I would have done anything—"

"It was *your fault*!" Todd looked Sam square in the eyes. "*You* did it! *You* made me the weak one!"

It suddenly dawned on me—the Divellions hadn't been tracking me, like we'd initially thought. They'd been after Todd. That's why they'd hesitated before attacking me, and that's why they'd zeroed in on him instead.

But surely I was weaker than Todd, wasn't I? I cast my mind back to the worksheet Mr. Garret had assigned on my first day of school. One of the questions stood out above the rest: Which of the sins will a Divellion prey on?

Envy.

I gasped. "Todd, are you jealous of Sam?"

"He has everything!" Todd shouted. "And he always makes sure that I have *nothing*!"

Sam frowned. "Are you for real? We have the same. Anything I've got, you've got too."

"No!" Todd barked. "You *have* to be the popular one. You *have* to be the better looking one—"

"Don't blame nature," Sam interjected.

"You *have* to be bigger than me," Todd went on. "You can't stand it if anyone speaks to me first."

"Guys," I cut in, "I hate to tell you this, but most people can't even tell you apart."

"And what about you, Mr. Perfect?" Sam scoffed. "You, with all your secrets and lies. All this time, knowing that we were witches and never telling us. Was that just so you could be Wilber's favourite? You can get off your perfect high-horse pedestal because—"

Todd raised his voice and interrupted, "You're not happy unless I'm in the background. You make sure I am always less than you." He took an agitated step forward and shoved Sam forcefully. "You made me weak."

"No, Todd," Sam spat, shoving him back. "*You* made you weak."

Todd staggered backwards. He lifted his hand, and for a second I thought all hell was about to break loose. But Todd simply touched the bite marks on his neck.

"I'm dizzy," he murmured.

And he collapsed.

Chapter Sixteen
Beneath the Surface

Todd lay on his camp bed, motionless and serene. Two swollen puncture wounds stained his throat.

Sam and I watched with bated breath while Ness and Mr. Garret peered over Todd.

Mr. Garret straightened his glasses. "He's been infected," he deduced at last.

I stared at the two elders. "Infected? With what?"

Ness looked drawn. "The Divellion's venom," she muttered grimly. "I'm afraid it may be too late."

"Too late for what?" Sam demanded.

The elders swapped a helpless grimace.

Mr. Garret cleared his throat. "Your brother was bitten by a Divellion. When a Divellion bites, a venom is excreted from the fangs. The venom acts as a sort of magnet, drawing the essence from the victim and pulling it into the attacker. In this instance," he glanced at Todd's motionless form, "the attack was interrupted, so only a minute amount of poison was leaked. Here at the Academy, we've never come across a case like this before, so we had no way of knowing what the consequences would be. We were hoping that Todd would be strong enough to repel the venom. However, it seems that the poison has worked its way into the bloodstream and the transition is beginning. Slowly."

"Transition?" I whispered.

"The exchange," Ness said quietly. "The Divellion will draw Todd's essence. As Mr. Garret explained, usually the Divellion emits enough venom to make the transition immediate, but in Todd's case, it will take time for him to fully—"

"Stop!" Sam yelled. "How can you speak about him like that? Like he's some sort of lab rat?"

"What can we do?" I asked frantically. "We can still save him, right?"

Both Mr. Garret and Ness looked to the floor.

"Tell us what we have to do and we'll do it," Sam appealed.

Mr. Garret cast his gaze at us. "There is only one way to stop the transition, and that is to vanquish the Divellion whose poison infects him."

Sam clapped his hands together. "So we'll do that, then. Get your little army together and let's go."

Ness and Mr. Garret shared another rueful look.

"What?" I asked. "What are we waiting for? If all we need to do is vanquish the Divellion…"

"I'm afraid it's not that simple, dear," Ness murmured.

"Why?" I pressed. "Jaxon did it. I know it's possible." I shivered at the memory of Jaxon snapping the Divellion's neck with his bare hands.

Mr. Garret shook his head solemnly. "There is only a small window of time. We would have to vanquish it before the essence transfers. Besides, we'd have no way of knowing which Divellion is the—"

"It had green markings around its eyes!" I exclaimed.

Ness sighed. "It would be like searching for a needle in a haystack."

"So?" Sam spluttered. "People find needles in haystacks all the time."

Mr. Garret bowed his head. "I wish there was something we could do—"

"There *is* something we can do!" Sam exclaimed. "You said it yourselves, vanquish the Divellion. Sophie saw it—it had a green marking around its eye. There's your needle. What more do you want?"

Dismally, Mr. Garret carried on, "Divellions inhabit the original town south of the holt. There are *hundreds* of them. Perhaps even thousands. The boys are able to

272

take on two, maybe three at a time. But we are no match for the sheer numbers—"

"Well, we'll have to try," Sam argued. "We don't have to take on thousands. It's only one Divellion. We find it, then we're done."

Ness let out a broken breath. "I wish it could be so. Please believe me when I say that."

"It *is* so!" Sam protested.

Mr. Garret took off his glasses and mopped his brow with the back of his hand. "No doubt the Divellion will be in hiding. There is even a chance that it'll be guarded. To dare venture into their territory would cost us many lives. And the chances of finding the infector are slim— that is, if it's possible at all."

"But this is my brother's *life* you're talking about," Sam choked. "Isn't Todd worth the risk?"

The elders cast their eyes to the floor.

"Look at me!" Sam shouted. "You can't just leave him here to die!"

"Please," I stepped in, "we have to do something. I saw the Divellion," I reminded them. "I'm sure I'd be able to recognise it."

"Absolutely not," Ness said bluntly. "You two cannot go. It would be suicide. As for the phoenix soldiers…" She turned to Mr. Garret.

He shook his head no.

"Don't do that!" Sam cried. "You can't just say *no* like that—not when there's still a chance!"

Ness held up her hands. "Enough. It's not doing any good getting worked up like this."

Sam shot me a cantankerous look.

"We must confer with Mr. Hardy," Ness decided. "We must settle unanimously upon the best course of action. I assure you, if it is within our capabilities to save Todd, then we will do so."

"It *is* within your capabilities," Sam said darkly. "And we *will* do so."

#

After the two elders had left, Sam and I sat alone at Todd's bedside, watching him fade in and out of consciousness. Each time his eyelashes so much as fluttered, Sam would hastily apologise for all the things he'd said during their argument.

"Do you think he heard?" Sam would ask me every time.

"Yes," I would always reply.

The minutes ticked by with still no word from Ness. The wait was torture. Waiting to hear if there was any hope for our brother. There *had* to be hope.

"Todd was right," Sam muttered. "This is all my

fault."

"Of course it's not your fault," I whispered, my voice choked.

"If I hadn't picked on him so much, then maybe the Divellions wouldn't have seen him as weak..."

"It's not your fault," I repeated.

"If I hadn't insisted we go back to the cottage..."

"It's no one's fault."

"I should have let him hit me," Sam decided. He lifted Todd's limp hand and let it slip back down again. "I should have let him win a few times. But Sophie, the thing is, I really don't like losing, you know?"

I nodded my head, compassionately.

"I should have let him hit me, though," Sam said again. "That would have been alright."

"I'll hit you if you want," I offered.

"No," he sighed. "It wouldn't be the same."

I patted him on the shoulder. "It'll be okay. Don't we always get through tough times? We always find a way."

Sam groaned in frustration. "You know, none of this would have happened if... I'm just so angry at him," he said, dropping his head into his hands. "I *hate* him for doing this to us."

"Who? The Divellion?"

"No. *Him*."

"Todd?"

"No," Sam griped, irritated that I hadn't figured it out yet. "Wilber."

I'd come to notice that Sam rarely spoke about Wilber, and when he did there was an edge to his voice. It was as though he carried a deep resentment for our grandfather. I'd presumed it was because they'd clashed so much in life, and now those things could quite simply never be resolved.

"Stop it," I beseeched him. "Wilber loved us. You have to stop blaming him for everything that goes wrong in your life."

"Exactly!" Sam exclaimed. "He loved me. Even after all the stupid things I did." He buried his face in his hands. "He kept giving me chances, and all I ever did was mess up."

"That's not true," I comforted him. It was totally true.

"How could he do this to me?" Sam murmured.

I frowned. "Do what, Sam?"

"Leave me."

I blinked at him. "Sam, he died," I said softly.

"How could he do that to us? How could he do that to *me*?" Sam vigorously rubbed at his eyes, turning away from me in the hope that I wouldn't see his tears.

My own eyes began to sting. This wasn't a side of Sam I was used to. Nor was it one I knew how to respond to.

Sam exhaled heavily before he spoke again. "A few months before he died, Wilber called me out of school and took me to the Port Dalton Stadium—"

"I don't remember that," I gasped. For one thing, it certainly wasn't the norm for Sam and Wilber to arrange outings together. Usually they couldn't be in the same room for more than ten minutes before the arguments started—not to mention the unlikelihood of Wilber scheduling a day out during school hours. "Did Todd go, too?" I asked.

"No. Just me. It wasn't planned or anything. It was just a run of the mill, boring Tuesday, and then I got a message from the secretary saying that my grandfather was waiting for me in the school office. Naturally I was thinking, *Oh man, I'm in for it. What's he found out about now?*"

I giggled.

Sam smiled. "I saw him sitting in the office with old Mrs. Timmons. He signed me out of school and told Timmons that I had a doctor's appointment. Seriously, Sophie, by then I was shaking, thinking, *What the hell did I do?* I figured it must have been bad, 'cause he didn't look at me once. Not *once* until we were outside by the car."

"Then what happened?" I asked, wide eyed.

"He told me to get in the driver's seat and head for

277

the football stadium."

"Wilber let you drive?" I spluttered in disbelief.

"Yep. And he didn't say a thing when I hit the lamppost. Or when I rammed into the back of that Volvo."

"Did you drive all the way to the stadium?" The Port Dalton Stadium was the most noteworthy thing our city had to offer. Unfortunately, it was at least a half hour's drive from our modest little borough.

"Yeah. The whole way," Sam replied. "When we got there it was completely deserted. Huge as well, with the pitch below and a ring of empty bleachers. Wilber bought us chips from a vendor and we ate them up in the stands." Sam gazed wistfully into the distance. "I would probably say that it was one of the best days of my life. For the first time in years, I spoke to Wilber and he actually listened."

I placed my hand on his shoulder.

"And then, later," Sam carried on, "he told me that if anything ever happened to him, I was to look after you and Todd."

I smiled gently at him. "What did you say?"

"I told him he didn't need to ask," Sam said and laughed. "I'll always look after you and Todd. You're the only people in the whole world who I love more than I love myself," he grinned sheepishly. "But that doesn't necessarily make me the right person for the job. How could he trust me with something so important? He knew what a screw-up I was. And now look—I've failed him again."

I'd never heard Sam speak this way before. I'd become used to the volatile relationship he'd shared with Wilber. It was a relationship that was, on the surface, constantly in conflict. Sam had fought Wilber at every corner and blamed him for every dip in the road. But what I had overlooked was something they shared beneath the surface: profound moments and trust beyond compare.

Like always, just when I thought I knew everything there was to know about my brother Sam, he found a way to surprise me.

"You haven't failed anyone, Sam." I sighed. "I don't know, maybe it's us who didn't appreciate you enough. I know you tried to keep it from me, but I saw how hard you fought to keep us together after Wilber..." I trailed off. "And you did it, just like you promised you would. You kept us together. We got through that, and we'll get through this."

"But look," he wailed as he gestured to Todd. "Look what I did to my brother."

"You didn't do anything," I argued. "This isn't your fault. There was nothing you could have done."

Sam rubbed at his jaw. "Yeah," he said quietly. "There was nothing I could have done."

"That's right."

Sam looked down at Todd for a while, then shook out his stiff arms. "I'm going to get some coffee. You want?"

"Sure," I nodded.

He rose to his feet and lumbered out of the room.

A few seconds later the door creaked open again and Sam returned.

"Actually, Sophie," he said, "do you mind making the coffee? I think I should stay with Todd."

I frowned. "Okay," I said slowly.

That was odd.

I wandered out of the room, leaving Sam alone with Todd. Perhaps that was what Sam needed right now. Besides, I was glad to have something to do—even if it was only coffee duty.

I stepped into the dark corridor, my shoes clicking against the wood-planked floor.

I'd scarcely walked a few steps before someone grabbed me from behind.

My heart leapt into my throat.

"Don't be scared. It's me," a voice whispered into my ear.

For a brief moment in time, all my fear and anxiety

melted away and was replaced by unparalleled joy.

"Jaxon," I whispered. I spun on my heel and threw my arms around his neck. So that explained why Sam had sent me on the coffee run.

Jaxon returned the embrace, then swiftly steered me into a nearby room.

Out of sight, he closed the door behind us and switched on a lamp. A weak orange glow lit a circle in the mahogany room. The ceiling disappeared into the shadows, and the few items of furniture did little to fill the barren space.

"Where were you?" I managed, finding his hands in the darkness.

"There's a room downstairs," he explained. "They reserve it for instances when we get out of control. It's solitary confinement."

"They locked you away?" I asked incredulously.

"I had to see you," he said, skirting over my question.

"I had to see you, too," I murmured. "I was so worried. I tried to stop them, and then nobody would tell me where you were..."

"I'm okay," he assured me, winding his finger through mine.

"How did you get out?"

Jaxon smiled strangely. "Reuben, of all people. He snuck me out."

"Reuben!" I exclaimed. He was the last person I'd expected to help Jaxon.

"Probably an agenda in there somewhere," Jaxon added. "But right now, I don't care. I had to get to you. I had to make sure you were alright. I had to make sure you knew that I wouldn't have hurt you."

"I know that," I told him. "And I'm fine. But Todd's been bitten."

"I know. I heard them talking."

"Ness and Mr. Garret? What did they say? Are they going to help him?"

Jaxon fell silent.

"They're not," I guessed, grimly.

"I don't know," he admitted. "They were discussing it. Hardy's not sure. The old town, the south side... it's swarming with Divellions."

I was met with a hazy memory of the town I'd seen in my dreams. "Bakeries and cobbled streets," I said to myself.

Jaxon laughed softly. "Yeah, in my day it was like that," he agreed. "At least, that's how I remembered it. When they brought me back two years ago, Hardy took me to the outskirts, just to get a glimpse of what it had become. It was bedlam. The Divellions had turned it into a wasteland teeming with their kind. Hundreds upon hundreds of them, living in squalor, feeding off each other." He winced. "It was my home. My mother used to take me fishing in a lake that is now filled with rotting carcasses."

"I'm sorry," I whispered.

"I want to save your brother," Jaxon stated. "But we need a strategy. Not to mention that, if none of us makes it back alive, then the Academy will be unprotected. *You* will be unprotected."

The colour drained from my face.

He squeezed my hand. "Don't worry. We'll come up with a plan."

"What will the elders do when they realise you escaped?"

"Well, hopefully it won't come to that. I'll return to the confinement room," he told me. "I'll wait to be formally released."

My heart sank. "But you didn't do anything."

"I could have," he said, apparently more tolerant with rules than I was. "They're taking precautions, and rightly so."

I sighed quietly.

"It won't be much longer. If they decide to attack the south side, then they'll have to release me. They'll need me."

I need you, I felt like screaming. "Is there no way you could stay at the Academy while the others go?"

Jaxon laughed as though I'd made a joke.

And then he caught me by surprise, drawing me closer to him until I was against his beating heart.

There in the darkness of the chamber, I tilted my face to his and kissed him. The second our lips touched, a surge of electricity shot through me like I'd been struck by lightning. From that moment on, I changed. I became a part of him, and he of me. And it was sealed with a kiss.

"I have to go," Jaxon murmured at last.

I swallowed a lump in my throat. I couldn't bring myself to speak.

Jaxon slipped his hand around mine and led me out into the hallway, heading towards my bedroom.

"I'll come back to you as soon as I can," he promised, tightening his grip around my fingers.

I nodded. My heart tugged when I heard him say 'goodbye'.

As he left, I stepped into my bedroom.

"No," I whispered.

Something was missing.

"No!" I cried.

Oh, god. Where was he?

"Sam!" I screamed.

My bedroom door flung open.

"What's wrong?" Jaxon called to me.

"He's gone!"

There was a scrap of notebook paper laid across Sam's camp bed.

I snatched it up and read the scrawled words.

Sophie,

I hope you found what you were looking for.

I've gone to hunt down the Dervalion.

I had to do something.

Please don't worry about me, and DON'T tell Ness.

I'll be back soon.

Luv, Sam.

Chapter Seventeen

Up in Arms

"Sam!" I cried in despair. What had he done?

Jaxon took the note from me and read it silently.

"I need to go after him," I said, making for the door.

Jaxon caught my arm. "No. You can't."

"I have to!"

His grip tightened. "No."

I tried to squirm free, but he refused to let go.

"Please," I begged him. "I have to go!"

"You can't go out there. It's not safe."

Twisting my wrist, I broke away from him and dived for the door.

My fingers had scarcely grazed the handle before Jaxon locked his arms around me and swooped me away from my escape route.

"No!" I screamed. "Let me go! Please!" Tears blinded

my vision. "I have to go after him. The Divellions will kill him!"

I could feel Jaxon's rasping breath against my throat.

"Please," I said, trying to claw my way out of his clutches. "Let me go!" I wriggled and kicked in an attempt to free myself, but his arms were like an iron vice.

"Stop," he soothed me. "I will let you go, but you have to listen to me first." He contemplated for a second, then spoke again. "I might be able to track Sam. On the condition that *you* stay here."

I stopped struggling. "But what if—"

"No, Sophie," said Jaxon. "There is no bargaining. I'll go, on the condition that you stay."

I figured it was wise not to start another sentence with the word 'but', so I opted for, "*However*, I can help. Let me come." Translation: I didn't like the thought of Sam and Jaxon out there alone.

"No," Jaxon said tautly. "Stay here."

I slumped in his arms. "Well, should we at least tell Ness and the others? I don't want you to go out there alone."

"If we tell them, then I won't be going at all. No one would. Now, do not, under any circumstances, leave this room. Do not tell anyone I've gone. Do not follow me. Do *nothing*. Agreed?"

I exhaled in a broken breath.

"Do you trust me?" he asked.

I nodded my head.

"Then believe me when I say that I will bring your brother home safely." He kissed my temple before releasing me from his grasp.

I crumbled to the floor, watching as the bedroom door swung shut behind him.

Now I was the only one left.

#

Breathless, I rapped frantically on the door to Ness's office.

"Who's there?" I heard her muffled voice reply.

"Me," I called back.

"Oh. Come in," she granted.

I opened the door, surprised to find the little cherry-coloured office crammed with half the school. Mabel sat in a rocking chair sipping tea from a china cup, while Mr. Garret and Mr. Hardy stood together with a dozen or so boys hovering around them. Ness was seated at her desk, wearing her bifocals and looking utterly exhausted.

"I have to talk to you," I blurted out. Granted, I hadn't planned on doing this with an audience, but there was no stopping me now. "Sam's gone," I cried.

I felt the room collectively deflate.

Ness took off her glasses and tossed them aside. "Sam," she muttered. "How could he be so stupid?"

Although my reaction had been pretty much the same, I had an intrinsic loyalty trigger that made me want to defend my idiot.

"He was desperate," I said. "He couldn't sit around watching Todd..."

Ness sighed. "I understand."

"That's not all," I added. "Jaxon's gone after him."

Ness hesitated. "But how did he...?"

In the corner of the room, Reuben stiffened.

"I let him out," I lied. "I'm sorry, but I found him and I needed his help."

"Oh, Sophie," Ness groaned. "What were you thinking?"

I folded my arms. "I was thinking that my brother is dying, my other brother is missing, and my only friend around here is locked in a cage for the outrageous crime of trying to protect me!"

Ness frowned. "A cage?"

Reuben the Magnificent cleared his throat. "I think she meant 'room'."

"Oh, right. Yeah, *room*," I revised. "But a metaphorical cage."

Ness's expression relaxed a fraction. "Well, if luck is on our side, Jaxon will find Sam before he gets too far."

"Does this make a difference to your decision?" I asked, looking pleadingly at Mr. Hardy and Mr. Garret. "Now that Jaxon and Sam are both out there, can you help?"

Mr. Garret shifted nervously from left to right. He wouldn't meet my gaze.

Mr. Hardy, however, stared at me through hard, russet eyes. "It is... undecided."

"Undecided?" I repeated. "You've been in here for hours!" What had they been doing? Drinking tea and talking about the weather?

"We cannot go ahead with anything until we are all in agreement," Mr. Hardy answered.

I didn't need to ask who was against the notion. The look on Mr. Hardy's face was cold enough to chill the sun.

"Please," I appealed to him. "If there's a chance to save Todd..."

"We cannot take any measures before all the elders are in agreement," he reiterated.

"But, can't you *try* to agree on it?"

Evidently taking pity on me, Mabel rose to her feet.

"I'm with you on this, lovey," she said to me, her lined face puckered in solidarity.

"Thank you," I told her.

She took a swig of tea and sat back down in her rocking chair.

"Please, Mr. Hardy," I tried again. "They're my brothers."

"We do nothing unless it is agreed on by all of us," he repeated for the third time.

I felt my cheeks flush with rage. "How can you be so heartless?" I cried.

He stared into my eyes but said nothing.

"You're evil!" I exclaimed.

"Sophie Ballester," Mr. Garret intervened, twiddling his thumbs nervously, "I must be truthful with you. It's not Mr. Hardy who opposes the action—it is me." He clasped his hands together repentantly. "You must understand, I wish there was a way... But I cannot, in happy heart, send my boys to certain death."

"But..." I trailed off. He was right. I knew he was right. That didn't mean I'd give up, though. "What have you been training the boys for, if not for situations exactly like this?"

"No. Not situations like this," Mr. Garret corrected. "The boys protect the Academy and the holt. They are by no means capable of attacking the south side."

I looked to Ness now, pleading with her to do something.

And then, the office door flung open and Jaxon stormed in.

My heart skipped a beat.

He glanced fleetingly at me before striding across the room, uninterested in anything other than a carved oak cupboard at the back of the office.

"What happened?" I asked.

He didn't respond.

As the rest of the room looked on in awe, Jaxon snapped the padlock from the cupboard doors and opened them to reveal shelves of weaponry.

Oblivious to the rest of us, he selected a large wooden archer's bow and slung it over his shoulder, then made for the door.

"You're going back out there?" I choked.

Pausing in the doorway, he stared intently at me. There was a look of determination in his stone-grey eyes—one that was combined with the profound understanding that he may not return.

"No," I murmured. "I'm coming with you."

His eyes narrowed and he glowered at me.

"Jaxon," Mr. Hardy said sternly. "Nobody leaves unless I say so."

"You won't have the faintest idea where to search for Sam," Ness warned. "He may not even be heading south. He could be anywhere!" Her focus shot to me. "Sophie," she breathed, "the link. Sam said you were his link, that he could find you anywhere. Perhaps he is yours?"

A note of panic rose in my throat. "I've never been able to do that," I reminded her.

"You must try," Ness insisted. "It may be our only hope of finding Sam."

Oh, great, I thought. *So no pressure or anything.*

I closed my eyes, vainly trying to pinpoint my brother's location. The room fell silent; only the tick of the grandfather clock continued to strike.

Okay, think, I ordered myself. *Where's my brother? Todd's upstairs, and Sam is... tick, tock, tick, tock, tick, tock...*

"Anything?" Ness asked, after a bated hush.

"No," I sighed. "I don't know."

"Then he is not your link," Ness told me. "If he was, the connection would be instinctive. Effortless."

Jaxon adjusted the wooden bow on his shoulder and turned for the door.

"No!" Mr. Hardy ordered briskly. "No solider leaves without authorisation."

The other boys looked on in curious excitement. Apparently mutiny wasn't all that common at Averett Academy.

"Requesting authorisation," Jaxon said calmly.

Every single person in the room—apart from me—

gasped in sheer disbelief.

And then I remembered...

"He spoke!" someone exclaimed.

The room erupted into mumblings, and Mabel spat out a mouthful of tea.

Mr. Hardy, though taken aback, resumed the conversation. "Authorisation denied," he said stiffly.

Jaxon made for the door, regardless.

"Wait!" I called to him. "I'm coming with you." I scrambled to get to the cupboard. If I was going out there, I was going to need a weapon...

I heard the sound of a bowstring being drawn back, and the next thing I knew, my arm was pinned to the cupboard door. A slim arrow pierced the sleeve of my top, missing my skin by a whisker.

With one arm fixed to the cupboard, I spun around to see Jaxon lowering his bow.

My mouth fell open. "You shot me!"

"I shot your sleeve," he corrected coolly.

The rest of the room gasped.

"He spoke again!" someone cried.

"Oh," I said, placing my one free hand on my hip. "So, you're shocked that he spoke, but you're not shocked that he just *shot* me?" The cupboard door rattled as I tried to free myself. "I can't believe you shot me!"

"I had to," Jaxon told me, in a velvety tone. "And I

think you'll find that I shot your *sleeve*."

The gaspers gasped for a third time.

"Yes, wonderful. He speaks. It's a miracle," I said huffily. "Now, can someone please help me out here?" I rattled the cupboard door again, well and truly stuck.

Nobody moved. I thought for a moment that Mabel might have been considering it, but she made no action.

"Jaxon," Mr. Hardy barked, "do *not* leave without authorisation."

"Apologies," Jaxon said politely before crossing the threshold.

"Jaxon!" I yelled.

"Yes?" he replied, innocently.

I scowled at him. "Get your arrow out of my arm—"

"Sleeve," he corrected.

"You're so annoying! Let me down, this instant!" I rattled the cupboard and stamped my feet all at once.

"It's for your own good," he said.

"Jaxon!" Mr. Hardy and I shouted in unison.

And I was sure I saw him smile to himself before he disappeared from our sight.

Chapter Eighteen
Magnificent

By the time I'd been freed from the cupboard, Jaxon was long gone. And Sam, well... he could have been anywhere.

I returned to my room and took my post at Todd's bedside. I watched him sleep while I drifted in and out of a disturbed sleep myself. I awoke on four occasions in a cold sweat, blinking in the haunting darkness.

I was relieved when the first break of dawn lit the room with a dusty pink glow. At least now I could wake up and escape the merciless nightmares.

As for Todd, the first blush of daylight softly lit his peaceful face. His complexion was sallow, and the bite marks on his throat were inflamed—purple and bruised.

"Come on, Todd," I whispered. "Fight this. Don't give in to it."

It sickened me to think that somewhere out there, a Divellion was slowly draining the life from Todd. And somewhere else out there, Sam and Jaxon were perhaps facing those very same monsters.

Why weren't they back yet? They'd been gone all night.

My chest tightened. *What if they don't come back?* I thought suddenly.

No. Stop it, I scolded myself. *They* will *come back*.

There was a light tap on my bedroom door.

"Come in," I called, willing it to be Jaxon or Sam, but knowing that a knock made it more likely to be Ness.

The door creaked open and a broad figure stepped inside. To my surprise, it wasn't any of my three contenders. In fact, it was probably the *last* person I'd expected to see.

Reuben. Mr. Magnificent, in the flesh.

"What are you doing here?" I asked, unable to hide the bewilderment in my tone.

He ventured further into the room, briefly glancing at Todd before staring down his nose at me. Dark, matted hair fell wildly above his full eyebrows.

"I am aware that we did not get off on the best foot…" he began.

I stared up at him, dumbfounded.

"We were never properly introduced," he continued, offering me his rough hand. "My name is Daniel Reuben."

"I know your name, Reuben," I said, my tone clipped.

Reuben laughed sinuously. "You're understandably wary of me. I've not shown myself in the greatest of lights, now, have I?" His coffee-coloured eyes bore into me like lasers.

I kept silent.

When Reuben realised that I had no intention of taking his hand, he withdrew it. "I thought," he went on, idly, "in light of your current circumstances, perhaps you could use a friend."

"Thanks," I replied, still a little terse.

Reuben perched himself on Sam's camp bed, bowing the structure with his husky build.

"For what it's worth," he added, "I agree with you."

"About what?" I asked, my voice flat.

"I say we fight. Hunt down the beast that did this." He gestured loosely to Todd. "Do what we phoenixes were brought back to do."

Oh. This was an unlikely alliance, to say the least.

"Thank you," I replied, swallowing my pride. "Is

there any word on the decision yet?"

Reuben flashed me a gentle smile. "Sorry. Nothing has been confirmed."

"We're running out of time. Is there any hint of which way it'll go?" I pressed. I noticed that I was sounding increasingly urgent with each word. Especially now that I had three people at stake.

Reuben shook his head solemnly. "I'm afraid it's not looking good."

I closed my eyes. That was what I'd been afraid of.

Reuben edged nearer to me until his hand was on my shoulder. His touch felt uncomfortable to me; I didn't like it at all. I shrank away from him.

"You know," he said, taking the hint and dropping his hand to his lap, "it riles me, if I am to be frank. Why are we waiting for permission? It's us, the phoenix soldiers, who possess the strength to fight the Divellions. And yet, our actions are under the control of the elders."

I licked my lips nervously.

"Jaxon didn't wait for permission," Reuben pointed out thoughtfully. "Why must we? Especially when there is one witch more than willing to help..."

"Who?" I asked.

Reuben dazzled me with another enticing smile. "You."

"Oh, but I'm not a real witch," I explained. "I'm just a

normal person."

His eyebrows knotted together. "Aren't you a witch?"

"Well, yes. Sort of. In the technical sense of the word."

"A witch is a witch," he simplified. "Witches brew potions, yes?"

"I- I guess so."

Reuben sat forward fervently. "Then tell me, witch, what are we waiting for?"

"Um... I don't know." I really *didn't* know. What were we waiting for? Why did the elders have to be involved, anyway?

"Just say the word," Reuben coaxed, his dark eyes glinting in anticipation.

"Why are you so keen to rush into danger?" I asked guardedly.

"All I've done for years is train. Day in and day out. Now is the time to act, and yet they choose to slink away into the shadows, fearing creatures that are *beneath* us," he spat.

I nodded my head in a jittery kind of way. "You think it's possible?" Not even Jaxon thought we'd have a chance.

"Indeed, it is."

I pressed my lips together. "How?"

Reuben's mouth crooked into a catlike smile.

"There's a spell," he informed me. "One that brews a potion powerful enough to take down a Divellion, while simultaneously preserving the essence. Once the Divellion is eliminated, the preserved essence will gradually return to the Ballester boy." Again he waved his hand in Todd's general direction.

"So, you need me to make the potion?"

"Yes. Then I shall track the beast that infects your brother and force it to ingest the brew. Ms. Ballester keeps the recipe in her book—"

"If it's so foolproof, why hasn't Ness thought of it?" I challenged.

Reuben cleared his throat rather awkwardly. "It is…" he peered furtively at the door. "It is considered dark magic," he admitted in a low voice. "The brew will create the most potent poison known to witchcraft. The elders would not consent to it. And they would disregard the approach of a Divellion ingesting a potion. They prefer the kill-on-sight method. It's safer."

"I don't know how to do dark magic," I told him. "I don't even know how to do *regular* magic."

"It's our only option. Either accept my assistance, or tell me to leave."

"Maybe if we explained the idea to Ness, she'd help us." I realised I was clutching at straws. "If she knows we're going to do it with or without her, maybe she'll be more inclined to—"

"No," Reuben shook his head. "They will never allow it. And if they suspect, they'll stop us by any means possible." He looked profoundly into my eyes. "Your only task is to prepare the poison. I will see to the rest."

His words made me shiver. My gut told me to run to Ness, but Reuben was offering me a chance to save my brother. How could I say no? I was beginning to learn that where the Academy was involved, I didn't have the luxury of compromise.

I decided to lay my cards on the table.

"Reuben," I said, "anything I can do to help my brother, I will do. But how can I be sure I can trust you?"

"I'm a phoenix solider," he answered ingenuously. "I serve you. My lady, you lead us into a new era—one that is not dictated by redundant elders. It's time for a new reign. *Your* reign."

Say what now? I didn't want a reign.

"Hold on just a second," I said as I held up my hands. "I'm not reigning anything. No one's getting overthrown here, okay, buddy? All I want to do it save my brother." I paused. "Brothers," I corrected myself. "And Jaxon."

For a second, I was sure I saw Reuben flinch at the mention of Jaxon's name. However, he quickly composed himself.

"As you wish," he said rigidly.

"So, we're going to do this?"

"I am at your service." He bowed his head. "Do you know the whereabouts of the Ballester spell book?"

"Affirmative," I answered.

Reuben didn't seem amused by my attempt at solider-speak, so I swiftly amended my reply. "Yeah. Ness keeps the book in her apothecary room."

"We leave immediately," Reuben decided. "Dawn is upon us, which means that if we are to brew the potion undetected, we must act at once. I will escort you to the cottage, where you will prepare the poison..."

As Reuben reeled off the plan, I gazed wistfully at Todd.

I'll fix this, I avowed to him silently. *Even if it's the last thing I do.*

#

Walking to the cottage with Reuben was like being hounded through the woodland by a ghost. He ushered me through the trees, trailing behind me illusively. And his presence, though necessary, was unsettling.

All around us, the awakening holt was alive with the hum of unseen activity. The last of the green leaves had bronzed and fallen from their branches, blanketing the ground with a golden carpet. Harvest mice scurried about their business, while blue jays sang their tuneful melodies, unconcerned by the urgency of our steps.

It was a time of quiet reflection, where nocturnal beings retired and a new day began—a blank canvas awaiting its story. Everything was magical and quiet. At least it was, until Reuben decided to disturb the peace in more than one sense of the word.

"What is it that interests you about Jaxon?" he asked abruptly.

"Everything," I replied, flustered by the remark. "What kind of question is that?"

We fell into a rigid silence. I looked down at the morning shadows that streaked our path as we marched on.

"Why do you think so highly of him?" Reuben demanded after a brief pause.

"I don't know." I folded my arms across my chest as we walked. "I like him. Isn't that reason enough?"

"But *why* do you like him?" Reuben nagged at me.

"Because he makes me happy," I answered at last. "When I'm with him, I feel calm, and safe, and important. And whenever I think about him, I can't help but smile…" Alert! I was sharing a little too much.

"Jaxon is unpredictable," Reuben stated. "He's arrogant, too. I'm confident that if you'd met me first—"

I gasped. "Reuben!"

He slowed his pace somewhat, leaning closer to me as we walked. "I'm right, though, aren't I? If you'd met me first, your interests would lie with me?"

"No!" I exclaimed. "It doesn't work like that! Feelings aren't based on who you met first."

"Then perhaps you'll reconsider your choice? You will consider a courtship with me?"

Courtship? I wondered what decade Reuben was from. Certainly not this one.

"No," I said sternly. "No courtshipping."

"Why *him*?" Reuben scowled.

"Because it *is* him," I said. "It's always been him. It will never be anyone other than him."

For a second Reuben was quiet, then he chuckled. "Poor girl," he said.

I frowned.

But Reuben didn't elaborate; he simply walked on, chuckling under his breath.

The sound made the hairs on the back of my neck bristle. What had he meant?

We didn't speak again until we reached the cottage.

Overheard, the sun was rising. I trotted down the wooded slope and let myself in through the picket gate. Crossing the gravel, I made for the front door and gave a little nudge. It swung open into the unlit hallway. The cottage was eerily still.

"Hello?" I called.

There was no response. Well, what had I expected? A Divellion to say 'hello' back?

"It's empty," Reuben confirmed, pushing past me and waltzing into the hallway. "The spell?"

"This way," I said, leading him into the den.

It was my first time using the secret stairwell to get *up* to the apothecary room. And as I ducked into the fireplace, my stomach fluttered with nerves.

I heaved myself up onto the metallic steps, aided by a very unnecessary helping hand from Reuben. I hastily swatted him away.

Rather anxiously, I began the ascent along the spiralling iron steps, followed closely by my new ally. I had to give the staircase credit—it sure beat crawling through an air vent.

At the top of the steps, we reached a door. I pushed my body against it until it groaned and eased open, unveiling the domed apothecary room.

It felt like a lifetime had passed since I'd last been in that room. Enough had transpired, I supposed, that it practically *had* been a lifetime.

But everything was exactly as we'd left it: spotless jars stacked neatly on their shelves, and a rainbow of light sneaking in through gaps in the roof.

"The spell," Reuben said, hustling me towards the

music stand where the leather-bound book was on display. "Find the spell."

I stood before the worn volume. "Do you know what it's called?" I asked as I flipped through the musty pages.

"No."

"Then how do you expect me to find it?"

Reuben glared at me. "You're a witch. You'll know it when you see it."

"Good plan," I said dryly. "There's no way that could go wrong."

I continued skimming titles, passing the See No Evil spell, which had effectively blinded my brothers, and the Secrets Be Known spell, which had answered more questions than I'd even thought to ask.

"Reuben, do you like being a phoenix?" I asked while turning pages.

"Yes."

I glanced at him. He was not at all like Jaxon. His general manner was harsh and domineering. Something about the intensity of his eyes made me instantly wary.

"Doesn't it bother you?" I asked. "Having all this strength and no control?"

"The strength is my birthright," he answered. "And it is only Jaxon who lacks control. Do not confuse me with him."

I flinched at his tone.

"Well?" Reuben pressed, gesturing to the book. "Did you find it?"

I returned my attention to the pages. *How will I ever find a spell that I don't know the name of?* I flipped to the next page. *This is impossible!*

"Wait…" I paused. Something held my focus on the current page—something beyond my conscious mind. "That's it." I tapped the yellowed paper. "That's the one. Black Venom."

Reuben leaned over my shoulder, his hot breath brushing against my ear.

"The poison sipped from devil's cup…" he read aloud. "Make it."

I scanned the text, memorising the ingredients. *Oleander, ground ivy root, creolin, black rose petals….*

No doubt about it, the spell was dark. I read the text. The brew would create a lethal potion that would vanquish a Divellion whilst keeping the essence in tact.

"What are you waiting for?" Reuben sniped at me.

"Nothing," I said. "Nothing."

I set to work gathering the ingredients while Reuben watched me restlessly. He stalked around the room, his dark eyes scrutinising my every movement, burning me under his spotlight.

I ferried the ingredients to the awaiting cauldron.

"I wouldn't touch that if I were you," Reuben

remarked casually as I approached a jar labelled Belladonna Seed.

"Why not?" I asked.

"It's toxic."

I peered into the jar at the tiny black pearls.

"I'll use tongs," I decided.

Once the components were gathered at the base of the cauldron, I ignited the burner beneath it. As the amber flames rippled over the pot's underside, the mixture crackled and fizzed.

I backed away. "Is it supposed to do that?"

Reuben scarcely registered my voice. He was far too engrossed in the vision of the bubbling mulch churning in the depths of the cauldron.

The brew merged into a plum-coloured liquid as thick as crude oil. And the smell was potent, so bitter that it made me retch.

"Is it ready?" Reuben asked, practically chomping at the bit.

I peeked into the cauldron, wincing as I caught of waft of the aroma. Opaque purple liquid stewed in the base.

"I think so," I said to Reuben. "Could you hand me a pipette, please? And a vial to contain it?"

Reuben slunk to the shelves, returning seconds later with a glass pipette and vial.

I went through the motions of drawing out the liquid and filling the tiny vial. I fixed the corkscrew top on extra tight before slipping it into my jeans pocket.

Step one was complete. Now all I had to do was find the Divellion who'd infected Todd, feed it poison, escape, and rescue Sam and Jaxon.

Simple.

Gulp.

Chapter Nineteen
Sleight of Hand

Reuben and I strode through the woodland. The sun had risen now, but was quickly overshadowed by a dull bank of cloud that was floating along in a constant stream of grey.

We'd disposed of the remnants of the poison, and I'd crammed a last-minute handful of orchid petals into a spare vial just in case I needed to blind anyone again.

As we approached the graveyard, I caught sight of Jaxon's headstone. It made my heart swell, as though it was him I was seeing, rather than a slab of stone with his name on it. A plaque in his honour, I liked to think. Because, after all, Jesse Jaxon was not dead.

The thought made me stop in my tracks. At least, I *hoped* he wasn't dead. I wished it was Jaxon at my side

instead of Reuben. I wished I could be with him—
wherever he was.

"What's the matter?" Reuben asked irritably. "Why
have you stopped?"

It was the first time we'd spoken since leaving the
cottage, and his voice sounded strange to my ears.

"It's nothing," I said, casting one last look to Jaxon's
grave.

"We need to keep moving," Reuben ordered. "The
south side is far, and at your pace…" he trailed off,
glaring at me reproachfully.

I began walking again. "What's our plan, exactly? We
burst into Divellion territory and hope for the best?"

"In a nutshell, yes," my sullen accomplice replied.

"Sounds good." I trotted to keep in stride with him.
"So we—" I stopped dead again.

Reuben glanced over his shoulder at me. "What is it
this time?" he grumbled.

My eyes travelled to the stone mausoleum at the far
end of the graveyard.

"Todd," I murmured.

"What about him?" Reuben snapped.

"He's in the mausoleum," I stated. It may have
sounded ridiculous, but I was sure of it. I *knew* Todd
was in the mausoleum.

I paused. But… he was also in his bedroom. I knew

that, too.

"The link!" I cried suddenly.

Reuben's dark eyes flickered with a trace of interest. Clearly the term 'link' was not entirely unfamiliar to him.

"Your link is the bitten Ballester?" he pried.

"I'm not sure…" I glanced across the meadow at the dismal building. Two sinister-looking gargoyles were perched on the roof, warding off intruders. "I've never felt this before… At least, I don't think I have." I cast my mind back, reflecting over years gone by. "I *always* know where Todd is," I muttered to myself in realisation. I'd been so busy trying to make my link with Sam that I hadn't even considered that it might be Todd.

But then, why would I sense him in two places at once?

I voiced my concerns to Reuben. "He's in the mausoleum, I'm sure of it. But he's also in our bedroom. This is so confusing." I massaged my temples.

Reuben's brooding gaze shot to the mausoleum. "You're sensing your brother's essence. It's split between him and the Divellion. Todd is in the bedchamber, and the Divellion that infects him is in the…"

He didn't need to finish that sentence. We looked at one another, our expressions grim.

However, alongside my feeling of foreboding was a wave of relief—the relief of knowing that the very monster we sought was within our grasp, and alone. Or, at least, not surrounded by hundreds of others.

"Should we get help?" I asked Reuben.

He baulked, affronted by the suggestion. "I am the all-powerful phoenix, Daniel Reuben. I need no help. Come." He began pacing across the graveyard.

I picked up my pace to keep up with the All-Powerful-Phoenix-Daniel-Reuben. Ha.

We crossed the graveyard, heading for the mausoleum. Its structure was built from black stone, which in time had weathered and crumbled in places. Overgrown weeds and moss grew around the base, proving just how forsaken it had become.

High above, the warped faces of the two grey gargoyles bared their teeth at me. Their stone tongues hung eagerly from their snouts.

"Should I go in, too?" I asked, my voice quavering slightly.

"Yes."

"O-okay," I stuttered. "The plan?"

A plan certainly would've come in handy about now.

"*I* make the plan," Reuben growled.

"Okay. Can't I be in on it? I'm here too, remember?"

"Give me the vial."

It wasn't a question.

I stared down at his expectant hand. "Maybe I should keep hold of the vial. Seeing as though I don't have any weapons, or super strength—"

"Give it to me!" he barked; his pace was swift as we strode forward. "You'll never get close enough to make it drink the poison. We've no time for silly games."

Shaking, I dug through my jeans pocket and slipped the vial into Reuben's outstretched hand. With his eyes fixed on the mausoleum and his steps unbroken, he slid the vial into his trouser pocket.

We closed in on the building. Its dense iron door was framed with sturdy nuts and bolts. They glinted in contrast to the dull stone walls.

I looked heavenward, searching for calm. I shivered at the sight of the gargoyles' black eyes, leering down at me with their mocking gaze.

Reuben reached the door first. He gripped the iron handle and yanked on it, forcing the heavy door open.

A strip of misted light lit the dank opening, then disappeared into the abyss of the crypt.

Reuben let out a deep, throaty snarl.

I heard a response from inside the cavern. An unmistakable hissing sound. One which I'd become far too familiar with.

My first instinct was to run. But I didn't. I tiptoed

into the mausoleum after Reuben.

All at once, the spongy grass was replaced by a cold stone floor. The inside of the building was empty and damp, and the click of our footsteps echoed off the ceiling. At the back of the room, I could just about make out the shape of a tomb, and hunched beside it was a crouched form.

It's just one, I realised with relief. Reuben could handle one. He didn't seem afraid in the slightest, which in turn boosted my own confidence.

And even though the darkness concealed its face, the overwhelming sense of Todd made me certain that this Divellion was indeed the one.

I slipped my hand into my pocket and felt for the second vial. It was there.

Maybe I should give it to Reuben, I decided.

But in the brief instant that my head was bowed, I felt a rough shove against my back. I stumbled forward and dropped to my hands and knees.

Reuben had pushed me!

Without a word, he ducked out into the meadow, forcing the door shut behind him.

The slam of the door reverberated throughout the hollow building, and the fracture of light disappeared like an extinguished candle.

I clambered to my feet and staggered blindly for the

door, just in time to hear the deadbolt pull across.

I bashed my fists against the cold iron.

"Reuben!" I cried. "Let me out!"

"Sorry," his voice came back to me from the other side. "Nothing personal."

"Reuben!' I screamed, banging on the door until my knuckles burned.

"Like I said, nothing personal." There was a sickening tone to his voice. "I hadn't intended for you to die—it's just a bonus, really. It's Jaxon who deserves to suffer, and this seems like a good way to start. Actually, I hadn't anticipated it being this easy." He laughed blithely. "You walked into a room with a Divellion and you handed over the poison! And the best part is, no one will suspect it was anything other than the foolish actions of a stupid little witch!"

I clenched my teeth, trying to block out the hissing from the corner of the crypt.

"Reuben, please!" I begged. "Open the door!"

"I'm afraid that will not be possible. I can't have you causing trouble. This way, your death will look like an accident. The reckless, fatal actions of a girl who thought she could take on a Divellion. It's perfect! Oh how I'll revel in the look on Jaxon's face when I tell him *I'm* the one who killed you! Right before I watch him slowly die from the poison *you* made!" He cackled

317

maniacally.

"Don't you dare hurt Jaxon!" I shouted, frantically pulling at the immovable door handle. "Jaxon, Jaxon, *Jaxon*," Reuben spat. "Do you know how satisfying it'll be to rid the world of him?" There was a clanging thud where Reuben had punched the door. "Everything I do, everything I accomplish, *Jaxon* is always one step ahead of me. Well, not anymore. Now *I'm* going to rule, and Jaxon will be forgotten."

I realised the only sound worse than a Divellion's hiss was the vile screech of Reuben's victory.

"How do you know Ness won't bring him back?" I yelled.

Reuben chuckled lightly. "You really are stupid, aren't you? Do you honestly think I wouldn't have thought of that myself? Don't you think I would have thought of *everything*? I destroyed all the phoenix tail. There are no more plants left in the holt. Or in the world, for that matter. And thanks to you, angel, I had a thorough search in Ms. Ballester's apothecary room to be certain none was preserved."

"You're twisted! You're jealous and pathetic—"

"I am a *god*!" Reuben roared. "You have no idea how powerful I am. My only sorrow is that I will not see the look on your face when I force *your* poison down Jaxon's throat."

I reached into my pocket and felt for the remaining vial. I supposed a blinding spell wouldn't be much use in the pitch black mausoleum.

It was a good thing I gave it to Reuben.

A tiny flicker of triumph crossed over me. *I'm only sorry I won't see* your *face when you realise you've got a vial full of orchids*, I told my opponent silently.

As for me... Well, I had the poison. But that was all I had. No sight, no strength, no backup. Take it all away and what was left?

Me.

Chapter Twenty
Food for Thought

I threw my shoulder into the solid iron door. It was no use—the door was jammed shut.

For a while, the Divellion had lingered at the back of the mausoleum. It had cowered from the scent of the phoenix. But, as Reuben's scent diluted, all that remained was mine

A witch.

An essence to steal.

I wondered what power smelled like. Hopefully nothing like the rank stench of Divellion, which had begun polluting my lungs the instant the mausoleum door had slammed shut.

As I succumbed to the realisation that I wasn't getting out of there anytime soon, I braced myself for the Divellion's inevitable attack. I figured I should at least try to formulate a plan.

Any plan.

However, I quickly learned that it was difficult to construct rational thoughts when facing certain death. All I could think about were the things that I had not yet done. And they weren't particularly profound things, either. Nothing momentous like climbing Mount Everest or saving the rainforest.

It was more like, *I wish I'd had a chance to wear my peach dress.* And, *I wish I'd tried peanut butter.* And, most regrettably of all, *I wish I'd said goodbye to Jaxon.* I also wished I'd told Sam that he needed to wash his best shirts on a delicate spin cycle. Oh, well; hopefully Ness would tell him.

Focus, I reminded myself. *Come up with a plan. Think, think, think... I wish I could have one last portion of fish and chips. Mmm, from Chip Palace in Port Dalton. That would have been nice... What was the owner's name again? Alex? Andrew?*

I slapped myself on the arm. *Stop thinking about food*, I scolded myself. *Think of a plan! Okay, I've got the poison. All I need to do is get the Divellion to swallow it... Andre! That was his name. Now, back to the plan...*

Okay. Recap. I had the poison. I had the Divellion. I had me.

And the plan...

Could I throw *the poison at it? No, that wouldn't work. What about sneaking up on it? No, there's more chance of* it *sneaking up on* me...

I heard a scuffling from the other end of the crypt. It sounded like knives being sharpened. Or maybe clawed feet scratching along the stone floor.

I stared, wide eyed, into the blinding darkness. Was it coming for me? My heart began to pound faster.

I flattened against the door, willing myself to disappear.

The scraping sound grew closer.

Oh no, oh no, oh no, oh no...

Why hadn't I spent more time on the plan? Curses, Andre!

And then I felt, for the second time in a matter of days, the hot, rancid breath of a Divellion brush against my cheek and wind through my hair.

I couldn't move. I had no escape. It was over.

With a trembling hand, I fished the vial of poison from my pocket and unscrewed the cork.

Oh no, oh no, oh no, I thought as I fumbled in the darkness for the grossness which was 'Divellion mouth'.

Just as I was wondering how close I actually was to

its dripping fangs, it struck me aside. Still clutching the vial upright, I staggered for my footing. My shoulder smarted from where its claw had swiped at me.

Before I could regain myself, the Divellion was upon me, seizing me from behind. With a grim understanding of what was happening, I felt sharp teeth pierce the skin on my throat.

Frantically I tried to force the poison into its mouth, but its jaws were impenetrable as it fed off me.

I began to lose consciousness, and I felt the life slipping away from me. But in my last breath, I knew I was going to do what I'd set out to do. I was going to save Todd.

I raised the vial to my mouth, and I drank.

If the beast wanted me, it was going to have to take the tainted version.

That's one way of getting a Divellion to drink poison, I mused.

A sudden flash of light stung my eyes.

I blinked, and through my fuzzy vision I saw what could only be construed as heaven—Sam and Jaxon storming into the mausoleum. Sam's link had found me. Or maybe it was Jaxon who had traced me here. I supposed I may never know.

In less than a second, the Divellion was torn away from me. It lay at Jaxon's feet, its neck broken and purple poison frothing around its mouth.

I met Jaxon's eye in rapture. He was there. And right at that moment, he looked like nothing less than an angel.

I wanted to speak, but no words passed my lips.

The last thing I remembered was my legs buckling beneath me, and Jaxon catching me in his arms.

And then, nothing.

Chapter Twenty-One
Every Door Has a Silver Doorknob

I awoke in a room. And not an especially nice room, either. It was bland, with four white walls and one white chair—a chair that I appeared to be sitting on. Directly in front of me were two doors, both white with silver doorknobs.

A voice came from behind me. "Of all people, I don't know why you chose me," came the heavy Russian accent.

I spun around in my chair. *I know that voice*, I thought.

"You!" I exclaimed, staring at the ice-blue eyes that peered out at me from behind a red headdress. "Pandora! What are you doing here?"

It was the fortune teller whom I'd met on the train during my journey to Phoenix Holt.

"Don't ask me," she replied. "I'm a figment of your imagination. Usually people choose a family member, or a friend... You chose me."

I gripped my seat. "Am I dead?"

"That's up to you," she said cryptically.

"Then I pick no, not dead."

Pandora pulled a chair alongside mine and lowered her weary frame onto it. We sat together, facing the doors.

"No offence," I said to her, "but why would I imagine you? I didn't even like you. Again, no offence," I added.

"Perhaps you thought I was wise."

I wrinkled my nose. "I don't think so—"

"I *am* wise!" she snapped, wagging her long, crooked finger at me. "Very wise indeed."

I folded my arms. "If you're in my imagination, shouldn't you agree with everything I say?"

"Noh," she said in her broad accent.

"Okay." I rolled my eyes. "Can you tell me why I'm here? And how I can leave?"

Pandora flattened the creases in her skirt. A hem of gold coins skimmed the white tiled floor.

"Do you remember what I told you on the train?" she asked. "What the cards foresaw for you, young brass-eyed Ballester?"

I cast my mind back. After everything that had gone on, the train journey seemed like a million years ago.

"Some of it," I answered. "You said I'd been through changes."

"Great changes," she drawled.

"Um, yeah. And then there was the bird. I had to free a bird?"

"Noh," she barked. "Destiny. Your actions were destined to free another. And free yourself, also."

"Was Jaxon the bird?"

"There was no bird," she sniped irritably. "The bird is symbolic."

"So, did the prediction come true?"

"Did it?" she returned the question.

"I don't know. Did it?" I gazed curiously at her.

"Did it?"

Oh no, not this again.

"You tell me," I said, rewording for variation's sake.

"I only know what you know. After all, I exist only in your mind."

"Oh, right. Okay."

Pandora waited impatiently for me to reach my epiphany. When the breakthrough never came, she stepped in.

"Yes," she said in a husky tone. "Your actions freed

Jesse Jaxon from his self-imposed purgatory. And by allowing yourself to care about him—and indeed, love him—not only did you free his heart, but you freed your own as well."

"Wow," I breathed. "I learned all that?"

"Apparently."

"What else have I learned?"

"You came to understand that, although you would forever love your grandfather, you could go on to live a happy and fulfilled life."

"Yeah, until I died, like, a week later," I remarked dryly.

"And the third card?" my imaginary fortune teller pressed.

I envisioned the card with the illustration of a man drinking from a chalice and a beautiful angel standing behind him.

"The sacrifice," I murmured.

"Correct," she applauded me, with what appeared to be a touch of sarcasm.

"You said I would sacrifice myself to save someone I loved." Of course, I hadn't expected that *love* to be my brother Todd, but... "It came true!"

Pandora placed her hand on my shoulder. "You did a brave thing. A stupid thing, but a brave thing nonetheless. And you fulfilled your destiny."

"But I'm not ready to have fulfilled my destiny yet. I'm only fifteen!" I protested. "Didn't you say it would be my choice?"

"Yes. Ultimately the decision will be yours."

"So, I'm not dead?" I asked hopefully.

"Not yet."

"What about the Divellion? And Todd?"

"Shortly before the Divellion attacked you, the transition to draw a Ballester essence was complete. Todd Ballester died."

"No!" I cried.

"However," Pandora went on without missing a beat, "the Divellion that possessed Todd Ballester's essence was killed instantly by the phoenix Jesse Jaxon. In a strange twist of fate, the poison that the Divellion drank from your blood preserved Todd's essence—meaning that it is gradually being restored to its rightful owner." She tapped her amber shoe on the floor and the tiles instantly dissolved into a rippling pool of water.

I tucked my legs up onto my seat.

"Look down," Pandora told me.

I peered into the glassy water below me. Beneath its surface I could see my bedroom at the Academy. Todd lay on his camp bed, his eyes fluttering open and his limbs reawakening from a deep slumber.

"Todd!" I called. "You're alive!"

"He cannot hear you," said my companion. "Just watch."

"Is he going to be okay?"

"He will recover."

"He's alone," I realised. I wanted to dive into the water to get to him, but I couldn't seem to move from my chair. "Where's Sam? Sam should be with him."

"Sam is with Ness," Pandora explained. She tapped her toe on the water's surface, and Todd and the bedchamber disappeared. A new scene unfolded below my chair: Ness, Sam, and Mr. Garret, frantically dashing about the apothecary room.

"Hurry!" Sam was yelling. "This is taking too long!"

"Please, Sam," Ness implored him. "The antidote must be made accurately."

"Sam!" I called.

"He can't hear you," Pandora pointed out.

"We're running out of time!" Sam shouted. "She's going to die!" He pressed the heels of his hands to his eyes.

"What's going on?" I asked Pandora.

"They are trying to make an antidote for the poison." Her voice was softer now. "You see, your essence is preserved, but your body is fading."

"How long have I got?"

"It's hard to say. The way you are being sustained

has never been attempted before. In fact, they were not even aware that it was possible, until now." She chuckled.

"How?" I murmured. "How am I alive?"

Pandora tapped her shoe on the water. The apothecary scene melted away, and what took its place was a picture much more recent to me.

It was me, lying on the floor in the dark mausoleum. Jaxon was bowed over me, his lips so close to my own that, for a second, I thought he was kissing me. And I would have believed that to be true if it wasn't for the fact that he was perfectly still, holding himself over me with his arms locked on either side of me.

"Jaxon!" I cried.

"He can't hear you," Pandora reminded me.

"Yes, I know that," I groused.

"Then why do you continue to call to them?" she muttered under her breath.

I glared at her. "I wish I'd imagined Andre from Chip Palace instead of you."

"Andre is not as wise as Pandora," Pandora said.

"Andre is not as annoying as Pandora," I retorted. "Andre would have let me call down to the people."

"Andre would not have the wisdom of a thousand lifetimes—"

I groaned loudly. "Okay, I get it. You're wise. Now

could you please explain to me what Jaxon's doing?"

"He is giving you his breath—another power of the phoenix that the elders were unaware of. So long as Jaxon breathes life into you, you will survive through him."

"So, I'm going to live?"

"Jaxon's breath cannot be a permanent means of survival," she advised.

"But they're making the antidote to the poison. That'll bring me back, won't it?"

"Whether your body responds to the antidote or not is up to you."

I stared down at the scene below. Jaxon was breathing steadily into my parted lips. It was almost inaudible, but I heard him gently speaking to me.

"I'll do this forever if I need to," he told me. "It's no trouble. Really, it isn't."

My eyes were closed and my skin was pale.

"I don't mind doing it at all," Jaxon went on. "But I know you're in there, somewhere. And I know you can hear me. I need you to fight. Come back."

"Jaxon!" I called to him again.

Pandora muttered something incoherent.

I ignored her.

"Jaxon!" I tried again.

To my surprise, Jaxon paused and glanced up. It was

only for a second, but I swore he looked right at me.

"He can hear me," I gasped.

"No, he cannot," Pandora argued.

"Jaxon!" I yelled. "I'm here!"

But Jaxon didn't look up again. He stayed motionless, breathing his life into me.

"Come on," he whispered. "You can do this."

"Jaxon!" My heart ached. "I want to wake up," I told Pandora. "How do I go back?"

Pandora stared at the two doors ahead of us.

"One door leads back," she explained. "One leads... somewhere else."

"Which one's which?"

"There's something you must see first," she went on. Her amber shoe tapped the water once again. The scene that materialised below was quite different from the others.

It was Port Dalton.

I was around eleven years old, walking along the pier with Wilber. We carried ice cream cones and, even though the sun was shining, the pier was empty. Frothing waves danced around the sides of the mint green jetty and a seagull cawed overhead.

Wilber and I strolled along the planked boardwalk all the way to the end. As my grandfather pointed out the sailboats bobbing on the horizon, I gazed up at him with unfathomable love and admiration.

Then, a young boy came pelting down the pier, almost diving on top of us as he swiped the ice cream cone from my hand.

My brother, Sam.

Ambling behind him was Todd, who shuffled towards us with his shoulders hunched and his hands stuffed into his jeans pockets.

Ah, the gawky years, I remembered fondly. Oddly enough, Sam was the only one of us to skip straight over those awkward years. He went from cute kid to good-looking boy in an overnight phenomenon.

Sam leap-frogged onto Wilber's back.

"Heck, Sam!" Wilber laughed in his jolly, Wilber way. "You'll break an old man's back!"

Sam ruffled our grandfather's thinning white hair. "Don't give me that," he teased. "You're as tough as old boots, and you know it!"

My eyes welled as I looked down upon the scene. It was perfect. It was *us*. Our little family.

Pandora tapped her foot and it all vanished.

A tear rolled down my cheek. "No," I choked, "I want to see more." I stared emptily into the rippling blue. Wilber was gone.

"One more," Pandora told me. The amber shoe made its final command, and I was met with an image that was completely unfamiliar to me.

A man and a woman, cooing over a baby. Two identical, copper-haired toddlers played on the floor at their feet.

"My parents," I breathed. "She's beautiful. My mother is beautiful."

"Look at the baby," Pandora said. "That's you—"

"Shh!" I hushed her. "I want to hear their voices!" I listened to the indistinct mumble of dulcet tones.

My parents!

I couldn't take my eyes off them. My mother had long, flowing blonde hair and light eyes. My father was a mirror image of Sam, but older and more subdued. I loved them. From the moment I saw them, I loved them.

"Can I go to them?" I asked Pandora. They were so close. Close enough to touch, and yet try as I might, I couldn't move.

I stared at the scene, memorising every inch of it.

And then, it was tiles again.

"No," I sobbed. "That's not enough. I have to see more!"

"Time is immeasurable. A second can be as valuable as a decade. It is how you use the time that determines its worth. And now, your time here is up."

I stared again at the two white doors. "Which door?" I asked, choked.

"You choose," Pandora replied.

"But, which door is which?"

"Now that I cannot answer."

My eyebrows shot up. "What? Then how will I know if I'm choosing the right door?"

"Only you can know the answer to that," Pandora told me.

"But I don't! I *don't* know! They look exactly the same! What if I go through the wrong one?"

"Your mind does not get to decide—your heart does. Pick a door. I am sure your heart will follow its true desires."

"But what if my heart picks the wrong one?"

When no response came, I turned to Pandora, but beside me stood an empty chair. My fortune teller was gone.

I was alone. And I had a door to go through.

In my fifteen years, I'd come to discover that the best way to make difficult decisions was to do it with my eyes closed. So that was precisely what I did. I shut my eyes and walked forward, blindly feeling for one of the silver doorknobs.

My hand landed on cool metal.

I'd picked a door. Where it would lead me, I honestly had no idea.

Chapter Twenty-Two

Behind Door Number One...

"She's responding!" a woman declared. "The antidote is working!"

Antidote? My eyes were too heavy to open. *Was that Ness?*

"Can you hear us, Sophie?" the woman asked.

Yes, it was definitely Ness.

"I picked the right door," I mumbled.

Sam's voice came next. "She's talking crazy. Someone slap her."

"I came back," I murmured. "Sam, wash your best shirts on a delicate cycle."

He exhaled in relief. "Sure, sure!" my brother exclaimed. "Whatever that means," he added.

I blinked into focus and saw Jaxon's eyes in line with my own. I drew in the final breath he gave me before he pulled away.

"I came back," I murmured, deliriously happy. "My heart brought me back."

Epilogue

October came and went, and November brought with it colder days and darker mornings.

It was on one of these cold winter dawns that Jaxon and I decided to take a stroll through the holt. The trees were bare now, and their branches stretched out like long, spindly arms. The fallen leaves laid out a carpet for us as we walked through the awakening woodland.

"I wonder what happened to him," I mused, mostly to myself.

"Who?" Jaxon asked. A chilled breeze whipped his hair to the side, spreading the strands in a fan across his brow.

I held my gaze to his. "Rueben," I answered quietly.

Jaxon shrugged. "I don't know," he replied. "He could be anywhere by now."

It had taken a long time for Jaxon to be able to hear

Reuben's name without wincing in rage, and even longer to speak about him.

When Reuben's attempts on our lives had failed, he'd fled the holt. No one had seen him since, and I was beginning to wonder if we ever would. I hoped not. But I often contemplated how a phoenix would survive in the real world. The rest of his kind were here. Of course, Reuben the Magnificent was no longer part of that fold.

"He won't be back," Jaxon said after a brief pause. "You don't have to be afraid."

"I'm not afraid," I told him. And I wasn't. Not anymore.

Absentmindedly I touched the bite mark on my neck. It had healed, but the scar remained. I wore it with honour.

We came to a fallen tree that had been uprooted from the previous night's storm. I stepped onto the trunk, walking along the curved bark like a tightrope.

Jaxon took my hand and walked alongside me.

"I'm sorry I wasn't there," he murmured.

It was a phrase I'd heard pass his lips often.

"You saved me," I reminded him. "You breathed life into me. *Your* life."

He smiled.

I reached the end of the tree trunk and hopped down. Jaxon's hand remained loosely around mine as we walked towards the Academy boundaries. Fingers woven, we fit together perfectly. We, I decided, belonged together.

"Look," Jaxon whispered as we crossed into the stone-walled enclosure. "We're being watched," he smirked.

There, in the window of her office, Ness peered out at us.

I waved and she quickly looked away, pretending, rather unconvincingly, to have been looking at something else.

I laughed. "Well," I reasoned, "at least she's letting us spend time together now."

Jaxon grinned. "She had to give in eventually."

I stopped on the path and turned to face him.

I loved him—hopelessly, desperately, indisputably, and eternally.

And as sun rose over the holt, I welcomed the colours of the new day. At that moment, I knew that whatever the future had in store for me, I would meet with open arms and an unconquerable heart. Just like the dawning of the new day, my life began now.

Here's an extract from

The Witches of the Glass Castle,

available from bookstores now.

Prologue

ADDO VIS VIRES

Mia gasped for unpolluted air, but the opaque purple smoke poured into her mouth and spilled down her throat, filling her lungs and suffocating her. As she scrambled up the rickety step ladder, flames licked at her legs like the venomous tongue of a serpent.

'Dino!' she cried, choking on the thick fumes. She clung to the wooden step ladder, her slate-grey eyes scanning her surroundings. But she could see nothing beyond the flames and smoke that engulfed the stone-walled basement.

Mia covered her mouth and nose with the sleeve of her knit cardigan. Her eyes smarted in the toxic air, but she forced them open.

'Dino!' she called out again, her voice hoarse.

And then her brother ruptured the flames, diving for the step ladder and pushing her up to the hatch door.

In a scuffle they burst into the hallway, coughing and sputtering. The hatch door slammed shut, enclosing the blazing basement. Mia staggered to her feet, but her legs buckled and gave way. As she fell forward her palms hit the wood floor with a smack.

Dino lay several feet away, clutching his head with both hands and writhing in pain.

Mia crawled to him, reaching out to him.

'Get away from me!' he spat. His coffee-brown eyes were fierce.

Mia shrank back, afraid of him for the first time in her life. Although he was only a year older than her, his barbed voice suddenly seemed to propel him to decades her senior. Even his face no longer seemed like the face of a seventeen-year-old boy, but more like that of a grown man.

Dino let out a tortured cry.

Dazed and frightened, Mia called out for help even though she knew nobody was home. She and Dino lived with their mother and their aunt, but neither of the two women had been home when the power had cut out. Mia and Dino had gone down into the basement to investigate and that was when the explosion had happened.

But to Mia's surprise, she heard the sound of footsteps descending the staircase. For a second she wondered if she was imagining it, but then a familiar form appeared in the hallway.

'Aunt Madeline!' Mia cried in relief. 'There's a fire in the basement. Dino's hurt!'

Madeline crouched over her nephew as he seethed in pain. He gripped his head, his chocolate-brown hair darkened from sweat.

Mia pushed her own hair back from her face, freeing strands that had been stuck to her tear-stained cheeks. The brunette shade was identical to her brother's.

'He'll be OK,' Madeline confirmed, calmly. She placed her hand on Dino's brow, her fingers cluttered with colourful rings. After giving him a cursory glance, she rose to her feet.

'Cassie!' she called for her sister, though with no real urgency.

Mia, still huddled on the hallway floor, watched as her mother appeared on the scene. Standing beside each other, Cassandra and Madeline were like mirror images. Both were beautiful, with wild red hair and bright-blue eyes. Only from their dress sense was it apparent that

Cassandra was a little more conservative than her free-spirited sister. At that moment, both women wore the same blasé expression on their faces.

Dino let out another tormented howl. 'Get away from me! All of you!'

'What's happening to him?' Mia cried. She reached out to him again, but he swiped her hand away.

'He's going to be fine,' Cassandra said in her usual motherly tone. 'Maddie, darling, perhaps you should take Dino upstairs while I talk to Mia,' she suggested – although it was more of an order than a request.

Madeline nodded her head and hauled Dino to his feet, guiding him through the hallway. He stooped and stumbled into the wall with a thump.

'Oops!' Madeline chuckled light-heartedly. She aligned him back on course to the staircase.

With her aunt and brother gone, Mia returned her focus to her mother. 'There's a fire in the basement,' she blurted out. The words seemed to jumble in her mouth as she spoke.

'Don't worry,' Cassandra told her. 'It'll burn itself out.'

Mia paused. 'No. It's a...' she stuttered, trying to explain herself, '...it's a huge fire. There was an explosion. I lit a candle and it...it just blew up. The entire basement is on fire.' She waited for the severity of

350

the situation to sink in for her mother. But it didn't happen.

'Yes,' Cassandra said smoothly. 'I understand. Did you read it aloud? The writing on the wall, I mean.'

Mia's head whirled. There had been writing etched into the stone wall: ADDO VIS VIRES. And she had read it aloud.

'Did you, Mia?' Cassandra pushed.

'Yes,' she admitted, confused as to whether or not she should be feeling accountable for something disastrous. After all, what repercussions could there possibly be for reading out some nonsense words?

'Oh, good,' Cassandra breathed. She helped her daughter upright and carefully steered her into the living room. 'I had a feeling it might happen today.'

With her legs still trembling, Mia collapsed on to the beige couch.

'Oh, no!' Cassandra sucked in her breath. At last her reaction seemed appropriate. 'Mia,' she went on, 'there's a hole in your cardigan!' She picked at the torn fibres on Mia's shoulder.

Mia stared at her, aghast.

Mistaking her expression, Cassandra added, 'Never mind. I'll sew it for you. It'll be as good as new.' She tugged at the loose threads on the cherry-red cardigan.

Mia gawped at her now. She couldn't understand why her mother was so concerned about the cardigan when there were clearly much greater issues at hand. For one thing, their house was on fire!

"*Mum!*"

With a reluctant sigh, Cassandra took a seat on the couch. She stroked her daughter's hair. 'You are fine. Dino is fine. Everything is happening just as it should.'

'But the basement?' Mia whispered. Her usual peach complexion was now ashen.

'Let me explain this to you as best I can. You were destined to go to the basement today. Actually,' she corrected herself, 'today, tomorrow, yesterday – I suppose it doesn't matter. The only thing that matters is that the writing was on the wall. And it was, wasn't it? You saw the words?'

Mia nodded shakily.

'You read the phrase out loud?'

'What does it mean?' Mia asked. She didn't dare speak the words aloud again; all of a sudden they felt like a lot more than just words.

Cassandra took off her own cardigan and draped it over Mia's shoulders. 'Loosely translated, it means, "To give power. It's Latin, I believe.'

'What sort of power?' Mia murmured. Her heart was pounding so wildly that she felt as though it might burst out of her chest at any moment.

'The power which was already yours. Your birthright. Myself, Aunt Maddie, Dino, you, we're all entitled to it. And now is your time to take it.'

All of a sudden Mia felt short of breath. 'Take what?'

'Power, my love,' Cassandra said each word meticulously. 'You're sixteen now. You're old enough to use it. I suppose you could think of today as a sort of rite of passage.'

Mia dropped her hands to her lap. She noticed that they were trembling. She was scared. Scared by the explosion, scared for her brother, and even scared of her own mother.

'Mia,' Cassandra said, smiling gently, 'you're a witch.'

Books by the same author:

How I Found You (2012)

Evanescent (2013)

The Witches of the Glass Castle (2014)

Look out for the sequel to *The Witches of the Glass Castle*,

coming December 16th, 2014!

For more information visit: www.gabriellalepore.com

Or follow on Twitter @GabriellaBooks #PhoenixHolt

Thanks for reading!